WHEN the doors of the isolated, mysterious sanitarium closed behind her, Peggy's only concern was to be cured of the illness that had blighted her childhood and now threatened her happiness as a woman.

But she feared the cure could be worse than the curse, a trial by agony not even a Phenwick woman could survive. . . .

PEGGY, THE CONCERNED

Saga of the Phenwick Women, #31

THE SAGA OF THE PHENWICK WOMEN

#31
Katheryn Kimbrough's
Saga of the Phenwick Women

PEGGY, THE CONCERNED

FAWCETT POPULAR LIBRARY • NEW YORK

Saga of the Phenwick Women #31: PEGGY, THE CONCERNED

Published by Fawcett Popular Library, a unit of CBS Publications, the Consumer Publishing Division of CBS Inc.

ISBN: 0-445-04563-9

Printed in the United States of America

First Fawcett Popular Library printing: May 1980

10   9   8   7   6   5   4   3   2   1

DEDICATED TO
WILLIAM COLLIN FRANZ

Book XXXI—*PEGGY, THE CONCERNED*
CAST OF CHARACTERS

PAUL PHENWICK	Head of the San Francisco side of the Phenwick family.
LOTTIE PHENWICK	His wife.
John Adam Phenwick	
Luke Phenwick	His twin sons.
Carol & Joyce Phenwick	Respectively the wives of John Adam & Luke.
HAYDEN PHENWICK	His third son.
PEGGY PHENWICK	The elder of his two daughters.
LOLA PHENWICK	His younger daughter.
H. Caswell Stocker	Wealthy businessman and associate of Paul.
AMANDA STOCKER	His socialite wife.
William Stocker	His son.
DAMIEN BRUSCO	A man of adventure, a gigolo.
ANDRE CEILLO	Like Brusco, he is an opportunist.
DR. KRISTOFER WERNER	A German doctor who runs a sanitarium.
HELGA KRANKENSCHWESTER	A kind and considerate attendant.
Agnes Van Cleff	A patient at the sanitarium.
BARON MAX KRAMER	A member of impoverished German nobility.
Eric Schmidt	A dress designer and creator.
JORGE CATALON	A man of Spanish aristocracy, a playboy.
PADRE JUAN PEDRO	A humble and devout priest.
Violette and Gilda	Entertainers.
MILLIJOY PHENWICK	The grand dame of the Phenwick family.

Tommy & Evelyn Phenwick	Her son and daughter-in-law.
LANNY PHENWICK	Her granddaughter.
Victor Samson	Her butler and longtime servant.
DONALD PHENWICK	The personable, crippled member of the famous clan.
KATHERINE PHENWICK	A Phenwick woman who is psychic and clairvoyant.
PHILIP PHENWICK	Her husband.
	and
COLLIN WILLIAMS	An entity Peggy first meets on the train from San Francisco to Boston.

Reader's Note: For complete genealogy of Phenwick family, see volume 30 of the Phenwick Saga: KATHERINE, THE RETURNED.

Prologue

One's concept of beauty varies from another's, although there are certain universal ideals. A woman in love always appears more beautiful than one who is not. And various eras have defined beauty in different ways. At the turn of the century, the plump, hourglass figure was in vogue. A slender woman was considered not nearly as attractive as one with fleshy pulchritude.

Yet, in spite of the standards of abundantly formed women, those who were proportioned beyond the accepted criteria were looked on with disfavor. Also, certain ethnic groups had their own preferences as to what was considered beautiful.

All of the Phenwick women were not born physically beautiful, although there seemed to have been a genetic strain that endowed them with certain qualities of loveliness. I mention this at the beginning because the heroine of this tale, although she was born into the Phenwick family, was considered an ill-proportioned ugly duckling, as it were. Perhaps her story is all the more exciting because of the obstacles she had to overcome. Nature creates its own mysteries.

Of the three living sons of Peter Phenwick, Paul was the renegade, the adventurer. When just a teenager, he left home and, without benefit of family financial support, he set out to make his own fortune in San Francisco. His eldest, twin sons, John Adam and Luke, had married.

Luke and Joyce had settled in Denver, Colorado, while John Adam and Carol went to San Francisco.

Paul's next son, Hayden Mark, was extremely intelligent, a creative artist and a man-about-town. His aesthetic qualities set him apart from the rest of his family, certainly from his siblings.

Paul's two youngest children were girls. Lola, the baby, had inherited the fabled Phenwick loveliness. She was pert and cute from infancy. The world was hers, and she seemed to know it, which at times gave her a disagreeable disposition.

The elder of the two daughters was less fortunate than Lola. She was a chubby baby, and that chubbiness did not leave her as she grew into her teens. Peggy was beyond being pleasingly plump, and the more she felt self-pity for her condition, the larger she became. It seemed people unkindly compared her with Lola, and those lacking tact made statements about her appearance which sent her into moods of depression.

Is it any wonder that Peggy was concerned?

Chapter One

1892

The limp was obvious. He could no longer walk without a cane. His posture was thrown slightly off balance, which called attention to his movement. Furthermore, the patch over his eye, where that member had been lost during a childhood mishap, gave him an even more mysterious appearance. Despite his handicaps, however, he was an extremely handsome man, as so many of the Phenwick males were. Donald Phenwick was distinguished looking with a remarkable personality that cast an aura of excitement around him.

At twenty-one, Donald was gregarious and family conscious. That was in an era before his father Stuart made his earthly transition, and the young man was free to travel. Due to his concern for family unity and a desire to see that distant ties continued, he had taken the train from Boston, Massachusetts to San Francisco, California to visit the family of Paul Phenwick, who was his great-uncle.

The train had terminated in Oakland, and Donald ferried across the Bay. He had not announced his arrival, thus the Phenwicks of San Francisco were not expecting him. The sort of person who liked to appear without warning, he checked into the St. Francis Hotel and spent his first day in the city purchasing gifts for the relatives.

The Phenwick home in San Francisco was a large manse on Nob Hill, from which the family had a magnificent view of the bay. The crystal clear, bright air around the building on that day in spring created a glistening attitude to the brick structure. Donald had hired a carriage to deliver him to the elegant house. As he was paying his fare, he noticed a tall, long-legged man striding up the hill toward him. He had a lithe body and delicate gestures, which somehow managed not to look out of place with his aggressive stride.

"Is it Hayden?" Donald asked as the young man approached him. "Hayden Phenwick?"

"I am. Where do I know you from?" Hayden returned. His voice had a lilt to it, and he enunciated with precise speech.

"We are distantly related. I am Donald Phenwick from Boston."

"Ah, Cousin Donald! I should have recognized you." With that the tall young man of twenty-three embraced Donald warmly. "Here, let me give you a hand with your things. I didn't know you were expected in San Francisco."

"I'm not. A perversity of my nature causes me to arrive at various places unannounced," Donald replied. "Call it a quirk, if you like. Frankly, it's me."

"I like that," Hayden said with a laugh. He took several neatly and attractively wrapped packages from his cousin. "Your timing is a bit off, Donald. I'm afraid you'll only find the butterball and the brat at home just now. This is Mother's club afternoon, and, of course, Father is still at his office. I know, I just left him there. But do come in." He looked curiously at the packages. "I must say you have a remarkable way of carrying your belongings."

"These aren't belongings, they're gifts," Donald

corrected with a flow of laughter. "I've taken a room at the St. Francis. Not only have I come to visit, I'm here to be a tourist as well."

"I see."

Hayden led the way to the front door of the large, imposing structure with the stained oak trim around it. The lawn and shrubbery were well manicured, and pink azaleas blossomed in profusion along the walk. Donald was amply impressed, recalling that the snow had just begun to melt in Boston when he left.

"You mentioned the brat and—?"

"The butterball." Hayden chortled. "I was alluding to my two sisters, Peggy and Lola."

"Isn't that an unkind reference to them?"

"Well, dear cousin, Lola has always been a perfect brat for as long as I can remember, a condition she refuses to outgrow," Hayden explained as he rang the bell to have the butler open the door for him. "And Peggy—well, she is terribly overweight and seems to be perpetually on the increase."

Even before he saw his cousin, Donald felt compassion for Peggy. Not wishing to alienate Hayden, he said no more about the matter and was relieved when the door was opened to them.

Fourteen-year-old Lola came bouncing down the stairs. Her lovely sky-blue, ankle-length dress twirled as she moved. Long blond finger-curls bounced at the sides of her face. Flashing blue eyes cast an impish look before she recognized her brother and stopped on the third step from the bottom. "Oh, it's the grand lady of the manor! I thought you were someone else."

"Really, Brat!" Hayden scowled. "How dare you call me that?"

"Why shouldn't I? That's the way you act."

Donald cleared his throat.

"Who's your friend . . . *this* time?" Lola asked with snide implications.

"I am your Cousin Donald from Boston."

"Oh." Lola bounced the rest of the way down the steps and went to where Donald was standing. "I suppose I should have recognized you because of your—I mean—I recall hearing that you had lost an eye."

"Yes, when I caught a stone thrown by my sister Polly," Donald said, unruffled by the reference to his misfortune. "We were both children at the time. And I brought it on myself for teasing Polly. I suppose that is why it displeases me when I hear other siblings teasing one another."

"I'm sorry, Donald," Lola apologized. "I shouldn't have said what I did." She glanced at Hayden. "Maybe I should apologize to you, too."

Donald took a small package from those he was carrying. "This is for you, Lola." He found another wrapped box and handed it to Hayden. "And for you, Hayden."

"You shouldn't have brought gifts," Hayden replied, embarrassed by the situation.

"Nonsense. It's one of my eccentricities," Donald stated. "I like doing things like this. It is more blessed to give than to receive . . . but one must learn to be a gracious receiver as well as a giver."

"Thank you, Donald." Hayden wanted to wrap his arm about his cousin's shoulder. But he glanced at his sister and decided against it.

"Oh, how pretty!" exclaimed Lola as she unwrapped a gold chain with a locket attached to it. "It's so lovely."

Hayden fumbled with paper. When he held up a thin

watch on a gold chain, tears came to his eyes, which he quickly brushed away. "I'm speechless, Donald." He turned to his sister. "Get Butter—I mean—ask Peggy to come down and meet our cousin, if you please, Lola."

Lola was busy fastening the chain about her pretty neck at the large hallway mirror. She caught Hayden's eye reflected in the glass. She had an impulse to say something else, instead she quietly agreed to fetch her sister.

"I shall always wear this, Donald," Hayden commented as he examined the watch. "I feel inadequate to accept it, however." His arm went about Donald's shoulder and he hugged him. "What a marvelous idea, bringing gifts. It has a way of breaking down barriers very quickly, hasn't it?"

"I trust there are no barriers between us, Hayden." Donald hobbled to the mirror to set the other packages down on the long table before it. He examined his reflection, then glanced back at Hayden. "Would you mind if I asked you to permit me to meet Peggy alone?"

"Meet her alone? Whatever for?"

"Because that is my way, Hayden. If you don't mind."

"Certainly. I'll go freshen up a bit, then we can have tea in the drawing room." Hayden smiled, looked at his watch again and gracefully moved from the room.

Three years previous to that time, Donald had met Hayden at Greenfield, Maine when his brother Luke had married Joyce Calder. Neither Peggy nor Lola had made the trip cross-country with their parents. Even then Hayden was unquestioningly handsome and precocious appearing. He had made several sketches of the actual ceremony and had drawn likenesses of many of the relatives.

The first Donald saw of Peggy was through the looking

glass. She was more than just pudgy. Her face was round, and her eyes were almost swollen shut. With effort, she took the steps one at a time. The plain black dress she wore was a bit too tight, and she seemed uncomfortable in it. Short, thick fingers clung to the banister to give her support. Reddish blond hair was wrapped in a bun at the back of her head. Heavy eyebrows gave a gloomy attitude to her eyes until she smiled.

"Are you Cousin Donald Phenwick?" Peggy asked. Her words had an aspirant sound, but her voice was basically pleasing and melodious.

"I am." Donald turned to greet her. He held out his arms, went to her and kissed her on the cheek. "I'm pleased to meet you, Cousin Peggy."

"You've come all the way from Boston? What a long and exhausting trip that must have been," Peggy said, trying to be polite.

"I enjoyed it. The scenery was most interesting. It's quite a spectacle coming through the Rocky Mountains. That alone was worth the entire trip. However they managed to lay railroad tracks where they did, I'll never begin to guess." He handed Peggy a package. "This is for you, Peggy."

"A gift? What is the occasion?"

"My arrival from Boston. Isn't that sufficient?" Donald laughed merrily. "Well, open it."

"I rarely receive gifts—other than from my parents," Peggy said, feeling awkward about the situation. She had difficulty getting the ribbon untied. "Will you do it for me? I'm clumsy about such things."

"Certainly." Donald unwrapped the box and opened it for her.

"A cameo brooch! Oh, my goodness! I've always

wanted one." Peggy held it up to examine. "Oh, I love it! I—well, I can wear it to church. Will you pin it at my neck, Cousin Donald?"

"I would be pleased to do so," Donald replied, somewhat stilted in his manner.

When the cameo was in place, Peggy examined it through the mirror. But her eyes wandered from the brooch to the large black background upon which it had been pinned. She quickly looked away and ducked her head.

Donald put his hand to her wrist. "I think it looks very pretty on you, Peggy. You have such a lovely, creamlike complexion. And I don't believe I have ever seen hair the color of yours."

"And you've probably never seen anyone as big as I am, either," she said bitterly.

"On the contrary," Donald contrived. "I used to know a girl in Boston who would make you look diminutive. I was quite fond of her. She had an attractive singing voice, and the last I heard of her, she was well on her way to a career in opera. Most Wagnerian singers are large. They have to be to execute the vocal work expected of them."

"You were fond of her?"

"I was far more fond of her than she was of me," Donald continued. "I fear she thought me deformed—which, of course, I am. But accidents do happen. I can't help my deformity, so I've learned to live with it."

"A slight limp and the loss of an eye," Peggy remarked, "hardly seem deformities to me. In fact, I think you are easily as handsome as all three of my brothers."

"We all come from the same lineage," Donald commented.

"I come from the same stock, too, but look at me," Peggy returned.

"Long ago I learned to search for the beauty of a person beneath whatever facade they may have," Donald said. "Mayn't we go where we can sit? Standing becomes a strain on me after a while."

"Surely, Cousin Donald. We'll go into the parlor. There's a stout wooden chair in which I can sit," Peggy said.

From that time, there was the beginning of a friendship that would develop and grow over the years. As Donald became acquainted with Peggy, she began to feel less and less self-conscious and soon was at ease. It was as if they had known each other for a long, long time.

Paul Phenwick was a distinguished, handsome-looking man in his forties. His appearance was far more rugged than that of either of his brothers, Thadius or John. But he had always been more the athletic type, fond of the outdoors and adventure. Still there was no denying that he had inherited the Phenwick male attractive characteristics. Peter Phenwick had married twice and Paul was the next to the youngest child of his second marriage. Donald, on the other hand, was the grandson of Peter's eldest son of his first marriage. Although there was not that much difference in their ages, Paul was Donald's great-uncle.

"I've certainly enjoyed your visit to San Francisco," Paul said on the night before Donald's planned departure. "Mother would have liked me to have kept in closer touch with the Phenwicks of Boston and Greenfield, but I have been preoccupied with establishing my own empire. I do write regularly, and Mother keeps me informed about all the news. Will you have a second glass of brandy?"

"Thank you, no, Uncle Paul," Donald replied as he sat in the comfortable leather armchair in the library. "I promised Hayden that I would go out with him and see some of the night sights before I return to Boston. Then we're to stop in at a party given by some of his artist friends. It will probably be a long night."

"Ah, yes, Hayden and his friends." Paul rose and went to the silver coffee server. "In that case, will you have more coffee?"

"Yes, thank you, that might help me endure through that which is ahead of me." Donald laughed.

"Hayden is different from the twins. John Adam and Luke have their feet pretty well planted on the ground," Paul commented. "I sometimes feel that Hayden floats three or four feet above the surface. One wonders how a person like me could have fathered such a son who is so entirely different than I am."

"But you are vastly different than your brothers, Uncle Paul," Donald returned, "just as I am not in the least like any of my siblings."

"Admittedly, that is true. Still Hayden is almost alien to me."

"Then you should get to know my brother Richard."

"I see what you mean. Well, I'll simply have to abide Hayden and stop blaming the iceman for his idiosyncrasies." Paul laughed. "Not really. Lottie has always been a good and faithful wife. Besides, Hayden looks too much like a Phenwick not to be mine."

"And what of Peggy?" Donald dared to ask after a moment's hesitation.

Paul poured himself another glass of brandy and wiped

a handkerchief over his face before he replied. "Peggy? There are times I wish I could blame the iceman. No. I'm not serious. I feel sorry for Peggy, as does Lottie. The child has always been an odd one, and I do have compassion for her. She's seventeen and for the past five years she has been so self-conscious about her appearance that she hides whenever we have company. It's all we can get her to do to leave the house. We've had to have a private tutor for her because she refuses to go out in public—at least out where she will be around other children her age. It worries me. I fear she will spend her entire life right here in this house, becoming more and more inverse with each passing year."

"Isn't there something you can do for her?"

"Lottie and I have taken her to any number of physicians," Paul explained, "but she doesn't respond to treatment. The truth is, she doesn't follow instructions and conversely does just the opposite of what the doctors advise her to do."

"Does she have a death wish?"

"I beg your pardon?"

"A death wish. Dr. Joe—Joseph Ornby—once told me of his theory about people who don't help themselves. It's like they have a wish to die. He was speaking of those who drink excessively or take opium; but I should think the same would apply to a person who is overweight," Donald said. "Dr. Joe says that there is a mental or psychological factor involved."

"Then perhaps we should take Peggy to a psychiatrist," Paul suggested. "That never occurred to me."

"I don't think you can force her into it," Donald returned. "However, she and I have become well acquainted and close. Perhaps I can write to her from Boston and subtly attempt to give her confidence."

"If there is any way you—or anyone else—can help her, I would be eternally grateful. I admit I've come to think of helping Peggy to be different from what she is, as being a lost cause. I try not to think about it."

"May I suggest you do everything possible to help her lead as normal a life as she can?" Donald said.

"Normal? How can she possibly as she is?"

"I don't know. I'll speak with Dr. Joe about it."

Paul paced about the room and emptied his glass in a gulp. "I've tried avoiding thinking about Peggy and her condition because I don't know what in the name of goodness I can do about it. A man somehow feels helpless and, in a way, responsible."

"Adam Truff once told me that a child chooses his parents," Donald stated. "That is, before the soul is born, it somehow knows the life experience it needs and, therefore, selects where it must go. It could well be that Peggy is as she is because she has chosen to be, not consciously, but deep within her. And it may be part of her mission in this life to overcome whatever obstacles she has taken on. Take me, for instance, I must have chosen to be born into the family of Stuart Phenwick, somehow with the predestined circumstance of being a half-blind cripple. It's taken great effort, but I have overcome many of my limitations."

"Yes, that sounds like something Adam Truff might have said," Paul thought as an image of that longtime Phenwick family friend came to his mind. "I confess I don't understand any of that—and maybe I never will, but something instinctively tells me that what you say may just possibly be right. Please write to Peggy. You may be the one person in the whole world who can help her."

"Yes, I would like you to drive to the ferry with me," Donald said the next afternoon as he sat in the parlor alone with Peggy. "But I can understand that it is a warm day and that you would be uncomfortable making the trip."

Tears had come to Peggy's eyes. Her heart was heavy at the thought of Donald's leaving. "While it's true that it is a warm day, that is not the reason I don't want to go, Donald."

"Well, whatever the reason, it isn't important."

"But it is to me," Peggy said. "I don't like to leave the house—not during the day, hardly ever at night. People stare at me and make unkind remarks. Sometimes I can laugh them off—at least on the outside; but inside, I hurt, therefore, I avoid being hurt as much as possible."

"I love you just as you are, Peggy," Donald stated, "so please don't mistake what I say. I believe if you really want to change yourself, that you can."

"I've tried. I can't."

"Stop saying that you can't, because, if you really ever become determined enough, you can!"

"How can you know?"

"I've overcome many of my handicaps."

"You're still lame. You can never grow back your lost eye."

"True. So you see, you've got two points on me," Donald said. "But I've learned to see well with my one eye, and with a cane, I can get about perfectly well. Certainly I have limitations, but I face them head on and do all that I can. Do you understand?"

"I understand, but I can't—"

"No, I *can't*. You *can,* Peggy. And you will, when you really want to with all of your heart and soul. Furthermore, I believe you will . . . one day. We'll correspond."

"I very much would like that."

"And perhaps you'll one day come to Boston to visit the Phenwicks there."

"You mean to let them see their freak relative?" she bit.

"You're not a freak! Don't ever say that to me again, Peggy!"

"But I am."

"I told you not to say it," Donald returned. "Don't you realize what you constantly say and think is what you are?"

"I see what I am."

"Then look beyond appearances. I do. I see in you a beautiful, loving person. I see the real you."

"The real me, Donald? The real me buried under all this fat?"

"Yes. Now stop pitying yourself, and do something about changing what you appear to be to others," Donald declared. "Perhaps it will take time for you to come to the consciousness that you really want to change, but I believe it will happen. And when it does, you'll probably wonder why it took you so long to do so." He looked at his watch. "Now, dearest Peggy, forgive me for being so blunt. But you know I've spoken to you out of love and concern for your own good. Now I have to go or I'll miss my train."

Donald rose and reached his hand to help Peggy stand. Once she was on her feet, he embraced her and kissed her gently on the cheek.

A deep sob, mixed with a sigh, jerked up from deep

within her. Peggy placed her arms about him and held
him close to her like a child does with a favored toy. "I'll
miss you, Donald. I really will. And I'll write every day, if
you'll answer one out of seven."

"I may answer more than that, Peggy. Now let me go. I
promised that I would be back in Boston at a certain
time," Donald said as he kissed her again.

He was gone and Peggy felt terribly alone. Tears came,
along with heavy, convulsive crying. She went to her
room and locked the door securely behind her. Already
she sensed the emptiness created of Donald's absence. She
remembered his words. He had said that he loved her.
Surely, he didn't mean that he was in love with her,
merely that he had loving compassion for her. Still the
idea that a man, albeit her distant cousin, said he loved
her caused her to feel sorry for herself. More than anything in the world, she wanted to know what love was
about.

In Peggy's eyes, Donald was the most beautiful man
she had ever known. But she had known so few, none
really as close as she had been to Donald. While locked in
her room, she endlessly read romantic novels and
dreamed, trying to imagine what it would be like if she
were the heroines of the stories, if the Prince
Charmings—even just one—were hers.

She had confided many things to Donald, she would
continue to do so in letters to him. Rarely had she been
able to confide in any member of her immediate family.
Her mother was understanding, but she always seemed
preoccupied whenever Peggy attempted to explain her
feelings. There had never been a real closeness with Lola.
In time, Peggy had become so envious of her little sister
that she could not tolerate being around her. Especially

did she become jealous when Lola spoke of boys who flirted with her.

Lola went to a private school for young ladies. She learned all the social graces, how to dance, how to be the hostess, how to be a wife. Peggy never learned any of those things, and she deeply resented that Lola had the advantages she could never possibly have.

At times Peggy had wanted to speak her innermost thoughts to Hayden. But she believed that he would never understand her or the emotional problems she had. He had always been highly critical of her appearance. Once he had had to escort her to a party, only to escape from it feeling that he was the laughing stock of those present, not simply because he was with his sister, but because his sister was as she was. From that time on he developed an indifferent attitude toward Peggy.

Eight years younger than her twin brothers, Peggy had had little in common with them. Both John Adam and Luke had always treated her with respect. She could never speak to them about herself.

The fact is, Peggy felt she was simply tolerated by her family, something they had to put up with, and that was that. Maybe that wasn't far from the truth.

Peggy permitted only one small hand-mirror in her room. She didn't want to see her reflection in anything larger. When she went into other parts of the house where looking glasses were hung, she avoided them with a passion. The reason for that was that within her own mind she thought of herself as being not unlike normal people. In her mind's eye she was just herself, the real her—not the one others saw. When she identified with the heroines of romantic novels, she envisioned herself in the lovely gowns, slender and attractive. Hers was the lithe body in the hero's arms. She vicariously lived in a make-believe world; yet she would have given anything to know the truth of the real world, of passion and romance.

Then she was faced with the reality of the mirror, or the mirrored expressions in the faces of others when they beheld her. Why couldn't she die? Why did she have to endure such gross torment? Why couldn't she escape into some distant fantasy land and never have to be faced with reality again?

After she had exhausted her supply of tears and her clogged sinuses had cleared, Peggy pushed herself off the bed and went to the dresser where the hand mirror was kept. She examined her red and swollen eyes, her flushed cheeks, her still-trembling, pouting lips. Angrily she crashed the mirror onto the top of the dresser, and it broke into a dozen pieces. Then, she picked up one sharp piece of glass and tried to jab it into her wrist. The pain became too great before she could puncture the skin.

"Oh, God! Let me die! Let me die!"

Chapter Two

1900

The proud, stocky man of Italian descent examined his appearance in the shiny brass plate beside the column. The etched letters that spelled out Medallion Enterprizes, West only momentarily distorted his view. He was not particularly tall, but not short enough to be considered short either. Carrying himself erect, he adjusted the fedora on his black, greasy hair and tweaked his moustache before ascertaining that no wild hairs were out of place.

As the creaky elevator lifted him upward, Damien Brusco rubbed each of the toes of his shiny black shoes on the back of his trouser legs. The spats were meticulously in place. He fluffed the bright red handkerchief in his breast pocket, checked his matching red cravat and again adjusted his hat to what he believed to be a more rakish angle. The halting of the lift jolted him forward, and he gathered his poise as he grandly exited from the cubicle.

"Mr. Phenwick has an appointment to see me," Damien said with only a trace of a Sicilian accent. With a flourish, he presented his handwritten card to the bald, bespectacled man.

Abner Benson pushed from behind the desk, gave Damien the once-over and asked him to wait. Officious and resourceful, the secretary rapped lightly on the door before he entered Paul Phenwick's inner office. Without a word, Abner presented the card he had been given.

"Damien Brusco? Oh, yes, Mr. Brusco," Paul said. "Send him in. I'll see him at once."

Paul put aside the papers he had been going over and stood behind his desk while he awaited the entrance of Damien Brusco.

"Ah, Mr. Brusco, do come in," Paul invited. "Won't you have a seat?"

"Thank you."

"May I offer you a glass of wine or perhaps brandy?"

"The wine sounds tempting, Mr. Phenwick," Damien said after shaking hands, "but I make it a practice never to imbibe until after business hours."

"I was under the impression you conducted most of

your business during the night hours," Paul said without trying to sound sarcastic.

"Ah, the reputation of Damien Brusco is well known, heh?" Damien brushed his moustache and nonchalantly sat. "Where have you heard of me from, Mr. Phenwick?"

"From an Eduardo Anthony," Paul replied.

"Ah, Eduardo! I owe him money, he constantly sees to getting me employment. But I always make a point of being indebted to him, and—well, I think you know what I mean."

Paul strode about the room nervously. "Mr. Brusco, I've never—uh—well, encountered a man in your profession. This is all very new to me."

"I have been in my profession, as you call it, since I was fourteen—perhaps younger, but that doesn't count because it was a period of learning for me," Damien said confidently. "I am twenty-seven now. So you see, I know my business."

"And what precisely do you call yourself, that is, in your occupation?"

"Why, a gigolo, of course."

"Yes, well, needless to say, I've never dealt with your trade before," Paul replied awkwardly.

"You are a married man, are you not? Is it for your wife?"

"Why, the very idea is repulsive! How dare you, sir?"

"Forgive me, Mr. Phenwick," Damien said, making a calming gesture. "You would be surprised the number of husbands who require my services for their wives. Usually such wives are neglected because of the husband's interest in other ladies."

"That is not the case here," Paul hastened to add.

"What sort of—oh, dear—sort of women do you prefer, Mr. Brusco?"

"All sorts, Mr. Phenwick. I pride myself in being able to accommodate wherever accommodations are needed."

"But personally, don't you have a particular preference in physical types of women?"

Damien shrugged and made a gesture with his hands to indicate that he wasn't choosy.

"I understand—that is, by your name I would guess you are of Italian ancestry."

"Sicilian," Damien corrected with an arrogant expression.

"In any case, I've been led to believe that Ital—uh—Sicilians like large women."

"Ay, *mama mia!*" Damien returned with a big smile and squeezed together his thumb and first two fingers.

"Good." Paul turned his back to Damien. "I'll come to the point, Mr. Brusco, I have a daughter—"

"Not a small child, I trust. I do draw the line."

"No, she is twenty-five-years-old."

"And not married?"

Paul shook his head. "My youngest daughter, who is twenty-two, is just making plans to wed. But Lola is a beautiful young lady, lithe, petite."

"But you said?— Didn't you say *large?*"

"My older daughter, yes, Mr. Brusco, is quite heavyset. Mr. Anthony implied that you had a preference for such—well, damn it! I think you get the picture."

"Has your older daughter ever been with a man?" Damien asked.

"No. I'm certain she has not. Peggy has lived a rather sheltered life."

"Ah, then I am at your service." Damien clicked his heels together while seated.

"No, no, you don't understand, Mr. Brusco," Paul said. "I am an extremely wealthy man, and I come from an even wealthier family. I do not propose an illicit sort of arrangement between my daughter and you. That is not it at all. You see, I want Peggy to know what a normal life is like. In short, I want you to marry her."

"To marry her?" Damien stood up. "But I have a business!"

"And if you marry my daughter, you may retire from your business and live the rest of your life as a wealthy man."

"But you don't seem to understand," Damien objected. "I *like* the business I am in. Shall I say, I like the variety of it?"

"Then I take it that you are financially independent," Paul stated. "In that case, Mr. Brusco, I'm sorry that I have wasted your time. Mr. Anthony led me to believe——"

"Ah, Eduardo! Well, I confess I am not—shall we say—affluent. I have made much money in my time—but I've lost money as well," Damien explained. "Unfortunately, I am not getting younger—and, you see, older wealthy women like young men. Ah, at eighteen I made a fortune!"

"I've heard enough, Mr. Brusco."

"No, wait! You are a wise man, Mr. Phenwick," Damien said as he stepped nearer to where Paul was standing. "You could not have become as affluent as you are if you were not. Now, I preceive that you have a problem, especially if your daughter is untouched at twenty-five and is plump. Am I mistaken?"

"You are perceptive."

"And I further perceive that she is destined to remain in your house the rest of her life if she does not marry."

"Quite so."

"And you would like to have her flee from the nest, wouldn't you?" Damien questioned.

"Not that I don't love her."

"I understand, Mr. Phenwick." Damien went directly to Paul. "I have a reputation for being ultradiscreet. The left hand hardly knows what the right is doing. Sight unseen, your daughter sounds tempting to me. I have never considered marriage, but I confess I would not be radically opposed to it either. And, as I have said, I am both discreet and have a taste for a variety of pleasures. I would tell you from the beginning, before I agree to anything, that I would treat your daughter with the utmost of respect, satisfy her to an nth degree—but I would also continue with—what shall I say?—my profession—"

"But you wouldn't need the money."

"—on a gratis basis, then." Damien held a finger in the air. "There is a chance, of course, that your daughter could fulfill all of my desires, Mr. Phenwick. But should she not, I am telling you in advance of what could happen. I hope you understand."

Paul was blushing. "Yes, I guess I do. Very well. I will arrange for you to meet my daughter. You will come to the house for supper and be a perfect gentleman. Neither my wife nor any of my children must know of our arrangement. And if for any reason Peggy doesn't find you—uh—interesting or attractive, or whatever—than I will amply pay you for your efforts up to that time. You will be out nothing but time, and that will be financed. Are you willing to give it a try?"

"But, of course. And if your daughter does find me acceptable?"

"In that case, we will discuss financial matters to a letter. Isn't that fair enough?"

"Yes, quite fair, Mr. Phenwick. And you will not be dissatisfied with me, I assure you."

The men shook hands. Brusco clicked his heels together, adjusted his hat, and with the air of an impresario, he left the office.

Paul washed his hands. The doubts and apprehensions he had greatly disturbed him; but he had become desperate.

Although Hayden had taken an apartment of his own a short distance from the Phenwick house on Nob Hill, he spend a great deal of time at the family home. Like Peggy, he had kept up a regular correspondence with Donald Phenwick of Boston. When he first informed Donald that Lola had finally made plans to be married, his cousin began making arrangements to travel west again.

Over those eight years since Donald had first been to San Francisco, the exchange of letters between Peggy and him had come at steady intervals. Peggy had confided much to him, her thoughts, desires, frustrations and even her hopes. Several times during that period, at Donald's persuasion, she had attempted to lose weight. Her lack of success only caused her to gain more.

Peggy didn't write about meeting Damien Brusco, nor that he had become a regular caller at the Phenwick home. Partly because she did not know what was behind Damien's visits, and partly because she had developed a deep emotional feeling for Donald, and she sensed that he had similar feelings for her.

"Don't you find it peculiar," Lottie Phenwick said to her husband two weeks after Damien first came to dinner, "that that Mr. Brusco person comes so often to see Peggy?"

"Peculiar, my dear?" Paul questioned. "Why do you find it peculiar?"

"Well, he seems to me to be a man who is romantically interested in Peggy," Lottie replied.

"And why should you find that so unusual?"

"Paul, she's—well, Peggy has never before attracted a man's serious interest."

"Are you suspicious of something, my dear?" Paul asked.

"Yes, quite frankly, I am: his motives." Lottie went to her husband and put her hands to his shoulders. "I suspect he's only interested in the Phenwick money."

Paul embraced her. "Dearest Lottie, has it never occurred to you that there are men in this world who are attracted to heavyset women? Mr. Brusco has confessed to me that such is his case."

"Still I'm leery. You know I want for Peggy's happiness as well as you do, but I don't quite trust that man. Furthermore, he's Italian, and I'm certain he must be Catholic."

"Are we so staunchly religious that we would permit his being Catholic to stand in the way of Peggy's happiness?" Paul asked. "Besides, he's Sicilian."

"They're one in the same."

"Not to hear Mr. Brusco tell it. In fact, he becomes highly offended when such is suggested."

Lottie stared at her husband. "Paul, you didn't—"

"Didn't what, my dear?"

"No, I don't think you would do anything like that.

Forget I even mentioned it." But Lottie had become suspicious, and she would continue to be, simply because she intuitively didn't trust Damien Brusco.

Peggy had invited Damien into the parlor after supper as she had done for the past two weeks. She always took the sturdy wooden chair, and he pulled up a second chair beside her. Clever and aware of certain personality problems, Damien moved slowly in pursuit of his goal. He was in no hurry, despite pressure put on him by Eduardo Anthony.

"You've become practically one of the family," Peggy observed as he sipped at demitasse.

"Does it strike you queerly that I come to call so often, Miss Phenwick?"

"It does in a way," Peggy replied.

"Then put such queer thoughts from your mind, dear lady," Damien assured her. "I am here because I find you a particularly desirable woman."

Peggy clutched her breast. "As I am?"

"But, of course. There is so much of you to love," he said. "It offers me the challenge that Hannibal had when he crossed the Alps. I don't mean that in a derisive way. Not at all. Large women have always fascinated me. But I've never allowed myself to really know them as well as I've got to know you."

"How well do you know me, Mr. Brusco?"

"Quite well, I should think, by now. You are a lonely person who needs to be loved and fulfilled as a woman. But I can tell you are a very loving and devoted lady. You have read much and you are intelligent. You're everything I could ever want for a wife."

"For a wife?"

"Have you never thought of marriage?"

"Often."

Damien stood up, put his hands to her shoulders and bent forward to softly kiss her. Eagerly Peggy accepted his touch and kissed him as she had read heroines do in novels. In fact, she responded so frantically to the situation that it was all Damien could do to control himself and not carry his romantic desires beyond the point of propriety.

"I love you, Miss Phenwick, and I want you to become my wife."

"Are you certain, Mr. Brusco?"

"I am positive." The fact that he had earlier that day spoken with Paul and that they had come to a satisfactory financial arrangement made Damien all the more positive. "Will you marry me?"

"I must think about it—at least for a day. I'll let you know tomorrow," Peggy said. "But I must warn you that I will be very possessive. Jealousy is one of my negative traits."

Damien merely rolled his eyes and attacked her again with a kiss she could not resist.

Chapter Three

Love was not an issue. The H. Caswell Stockers of Nob Hill were one of the wealthiest families in San Francisco. Amanda Stocker was a leading figure in the social scene, a lady who considered herself among the elite, an

innovator and a leader. Caswell Stocker held large shares
of mining and railroad stock. Their son William was
doubtlessly the prize catch among the eligible bachelors in
high society. It might be mentioned that Hayden Phenwick was also considered in that category by everyone but
Hayden.

Lola Phenwick had become the beauty sought after by
many young men in the upper echelon. By the time she
had reached her early twenties, her time was largely occupied. Men wooed her with a passion. She had grown nonchalant in her attitude toward suitors in general.

When her mother, the former Lottie Wells, had married Paul Phenwick, she had no idea that he was from a
family of wealth and position. She had never been raised
with a comprehension of the social graces, but she quickly
learned. Therefore, she made a point of seeing that Lola
was properly instructed in finer matters. A casual conversation with Amanda Stocker at a formal charity tea had
brought to each of their attention that their children, one
of each gender, were marriageable. An exchange of invi-
tations followed wherein the Phenwicks entertained the
Stockers, then the Stockers returned the honor. Lola and
William were introduced and seemed somewhat attracted
to one another. Lottie pushed Lola to consider William
and what a marriage into the Stocker family would mean.
Likewise, both Caswell and Amanda prompted William
about the possibilities that would be opened to him by
marrying into the famous Phenwick family. Both young
people gave the matter sufficient thought before William
proposed and Lola accepted.

Peggy was never present at any of the meetings of the
two families. That was before Damien Brusco had come
into the picture. Once the engagement was announced,

the Phenwicks dared not keep Peggy closeted. Caswell, Amanda and William were noticeably shocked when they were introduced to Lola's sister.

Damien had been persistent in his proposal to Peggy, and she ultimately accepted it after a prolonged period of nearly a week after the question was asked. She had reservations about the man, although she had developed strong emotional feelings for him. If that was love, then she was in love. Twice she tried to speak to Lola about Damien, but her little sister was too preoccupied with her own affairs to have much of a reaction one way or another.

On the pleasantly warm May afternoon, Peggy had left the confines of her own room on the second floor, en route to make a pilgrimage to the kitchen for a snack, when she heard her name mentioned in the parlor. She stepped as close to the room as she dared and listened.

"I realize she is your sister," Amanda Stocker was saying, "but dear Lola, you must remember this is a society wedding, one of the biggest events of the season. Your bridesmaids should be debutantes who have already been presented. And certainly your maid of honor—well, my dear, the ceremony will be written up in all the newspapers along with pictures. I want you to know that I'm trying to be very tactful about this."

"I understand, Mrs. Stocker," Lola returned. "I've never been especially close to Peggy. We're of two different worlds it would seem; but she *is* my only sister."

"It's traditional that one's sister is her maid of honor, isn't it, Mrs. Stocker?" questioned Lottie.

"Traditional, yes," Amanda said, "but I would hardly call Peggy—no offense meant—*traditional*. I'm frankly quite surprised that you have allowed her to become as she is."

"We've tried, Mrs. Stocker, we've tried."

"Peggy is marrying in August," Lola announced, "and she has asked me to be her matron of honor. It makes a very sticky situation."

"Peggy is marrying?" Amanda gasped. "Whoever to?"

"No one of importance," Lottie said before she caught herself. "It will not be a social affair, just something simple and quiet."

"You do see the problem, don't you, Mrs. Stocker?" Lola asked.

"Yes, I do. I would like to feel compassion for your sister, Lola dear, but I've literally starved myself for years to maintain my appearance. That is beside the point, of course. It might be conceivable that Peggy could be one of your bridesmaids and be kept in the rear, that is, out of the center of things. I believe we could make that concession."

The door to the room, which had been slightly ajar, suddenly burst into the room. Red-faced and doing her best to control anger, Peggy barged in. She made an attempt at nonchalance, but her performance was unconvincing.

"Oh! I thought I heard voices in here," Peggy lied. "I presumed it was just Mother and Lola. Good afternoon, Mrs. Stocker. I trust I'm not interrupting anything."

"Yes, you are, Peggy," Lola scolded. "It would be better if you would excuse yourself."

"But I came to tell *you* that it will be best if Mr. Brusco and I elope and not plan to have a formal wedding ceremony," Peggy stated. "You see, I think I'm pregnant."

"Pregnant?" Amanda gasped.

Lottie fanned herself. "However did that happen?"

"The usual way, Mother," Peggy returned. "We'll wait until sometime in July to elope. We wouldn't want to steal the thunder from your wedding, Lola. And, since we're going to elope, you won't have to be my matron of honor. That way you and Mr. Stocker can take an extended honeymoon." Tears had come to her eyes. "And under the circumstance, I don't think it would be logical for me to be your maid of honor. It would be deceptive, since 'maid' implies that I've been untouched. Please excuse me, I'm going to get something to eat."

Lottie rose as Peggy hurried from the room. "She overheard our conversation."

"It's just as well she did," Amanda stated. "She has helped us resolve a nasty problem."

Lola was annoyed and angered. "Excuse me, Mrs. Stocker, I wish to speak with my sister."

"Certainly, Lola."

"Lola, you're not—?" Lottie asked as the girl reached the door. "I mean—"

"I simply wish to have a word with Peggy," Lola said as she left the room.

She found her sister in the kitchen nibbling on a piece of cake and washing it down with a glass of milk. "Peggy, I want a word with you."

"What is it?"

"That scene you just played in the parlor has me curious," Lola replied. "I want an honest answer from you. Are you really pregnant?"

"Of course. I said I was."

"I don't believe you."

"Don't you?" Peggy took a mouthful of cake. "Why don't you?"

"I believe I know you better than that."

"No, Lola, *you* don't knew me at all. You've never taken the time to understand even a little about me. Mr. Brusco swears he is madly in love with me. Yes, there are men who do find heavyset ladies physically exciting. He is a persistent man, and I gave in to his desires." Tears were streaming down Peggy's face.

"I don't believe you," Lola stated. "I think you overheard what was being said in the parlor and, to avoid being hurt, you contrived that tale. Isn't that the truth?"

"No."

"Isn't it?"

"Leave me alone, Lola. You don't understand me at all."

"Yes, I do, Peggy. I want to. Furthermore, I want you to be in my wedding party. If you don't wish to be my maid of honor, I can understand, but I insist that you be one of my bridesmaids."

"Lola," Peggy whimpered, "Lola . . ."

Lola went to her sister and embraced her. "Now tell me the truth. I won't even tell Mother, if you don't want me to."

"Lola . . . I lied. I've never been intimate . . ." Deep sobs came from Peggy, and she released all of her pent-up emotions in crying.

Lola, too, had become teary-eyed as she clung tightly to her sister. "How can I help you, Peggy?"

"No one can help me . . . no one!"

As planned, the Stocker-Phenwick wedding was *the* social event of the spring season. It was like a royal affair with the reigning nobility of Nob Hill and the rest of San Francisco society present. Peggy was a bridesmaid. She did her best to appear as inconspicuous as possible, but she was embarrassed and felt the unkind stares. Although she could not hear them, she imagined what the whispered comments were. Staring eyes quickly shifted to another direction when she became aware of them watching her.

Later the reception was held at the Stockers' palatial mansion. Again Peggy tried to remain as inconspicuous as possible and begged not to have to be in the receiving line.

"There you are, Peggy!" came the jovial greeting, and she looked up to see Donald Phenwick standing not more than ten feet from her.

Immediately Donald was beside her, a hand about her arm and whisking her into an adjoining room.

"When did you arrive, Donald?"

"Late," he replied. "I caught the end of the ceremony, standing at the back of the church."

"Standing? But your leg?—"

"I didn't have to stand that long. I tried to catch your eye, but you were staring down during the recessional. I confess I was surprised to see you in the wedding party."

"I shouldn't have been," Peggy returned. "Lola insisted that she wanted me. Oh, it was terrible!"

"You did remarkably well, dear cousin. I'm proud of you," Donald said. He studied her sullen expression. "I perceive something is wrong."

"Wrong?"

"Your last few letters had a different tone to them, as if you were concealing something from me," Donald commented. "Katherine was saying on the way out here that she had a psychic impression about you—and it had to do with some man."

"Katherine?"

"Katherine Phenwick, my niece. She's married to Thadius' son Philip," Donald explained. "They both rode out here on the train with me. Katherine is what you might call clairvoyant—at least she pretends to be." He laughed, then suddenly became serious. "Tell me about it, Peggy."

Peggy looked down and twisted her thick fingers together. "I'm—I'm planning to be married."

"Married?" Katherine had prepared Donald, but he didn't want to believe it until he heard it directly from Peggy.

"That comes as a surprise to you, doesn't it?" Peggy asked. "Well, to be perfectly honest, it came as a surprise to me, too."

Donald ran his finger over the silver head of his ornate cane. "I pray that it will make you happy, Peggy. Yes, I pray for your happiness."

"I saw Mr. Brusco at the church," Peggy said, trying to sound less disturbed than she had been. "I presume he got lost in the crowd here at the reception. He enjoys this sort of thing—I don't. I'm anxious to meet Katherine and—did you say her husband's name was Paul?"

"No, Philip. I know they are equally as anxious to meet you, Peggy." He gazed strangely into her face. "Why don't you wait here while I go find them?"

"Don't you want me to come with you?"

"It would be better if you remained here, I think."

Outside the room, Donald sagged against the wall. Katherine had forewarned him that he would receive depressing news upon his arrival in San Francisco. His niece also had perceived that he was considering to ask Peggy a crucial question. The love he had developed for Peggy had grown from the correspondence they had had over the years. Was it true love? Or was he simply being in love with the idea of love itself? They had never written about romantic feelings; perhaps he had only assumed many things. Why hadn't he expressed his inner emotions in writing? Why hadn't he been more aggressive? Then, it occurred to him that he had hoped to see a physical change in Peggy. There was a change, she was larger than he remembered.

"There you are, Cousin Donald!" exclaimed Hayden as he came up behind Donald and threw a healthy embrace about his shoulders. "I saw you at the church. Come, let's have a drink of punch. There are people I want you to meet. Oh, it is good to see you again!"

Peggy sat in the quiet of the room, listening to the sounds of the celebrating guests: a constant din of chatter, distant music and laughter. Such gaiety bothered her because she believed she would never be able to enjoy it herself. Rationalization, yes. It was easy to hate that which was not obtainable, and to become contemptuous of those who did participate and enjoy.

The door whispered open, allowing a rise in volume of the partying sounds. Peggy looked up, expecting to see Donald, returned. Instead she saw one of the most beautiful ladies she had ever seen. More than physical beauty, the intruder seemed to glow with a mystical aura.

"The party isn't in here," Peggy awkwardly said.

"May I come in anyway?"

"I spend much time in solitude. Standing through the ceremony tired me," Peggy continued. "My sister is the bride."

"You're Peggy Phenwick, aren't you?"

"I'm the Phenwick freak, if that's what you mean. But, of course, you could tell that just by looking."

"You mustn't say things like that. I was painfully shy as a child, and not particularly attractive. Permit me to introduce myself, I'm you're cousin, Katherine Phenwick."

"The clairvoyant of whom Donald spoke?"

"Did he tell you I was clairvoyant? I usually don't like to divulge that, it frightens people—only because they don't know what being clairvoyant or clairaudient means." She laughed and went to shake Peggy's hand. Her soft yellow dress rustled as she moved. Her smile was infectious and immediately set Peggy at ease. "Mayn't I join you for a while? There is something dreary being in the midst of such an aggregation of people. They swarm in pretentious confusion."

Peggy chuckled at Katherine's use of words.

"Do you know that you're really very pretty?"

"Me?" Peggy frowned. "Your attempt at being kind rings false. I don't believe you, Katherine."

"But, dear Peggy, I see beneath the surface. You have a very beautiful soul. Queerly as it may seem, you've taken on a particularly difficult cross to bear in this life—but not without reason. Still you are beautiful, and I predict that one day you will see the same beauty that I see as a reality."

"You're making fun of me."

"No such thing! No such thing! I'm perfectly serious," Katherine declared. "You'll find once you get to know me better that I am a very sincere person. And, dear Peggy, I wouldn't make fun of you for the world." She impulsively planted a kiss on Peggy's round cheek. "There is a lesson to be learned in being as you are, and as you have been thus far in your life. But that is going to change. I'll not frighten you any further by saying such mysterious things. I know that if I were in your shoes, I'd be terrified if a virtual stranger came up to me and started to say the things I've already said to you."

"You are a descendant of the illustrious Augusta Phenwick, aren't you?" Peggy asked in hopes of changing the course of Katherine's thoughts.

"I am the—" Katherine caught herself. "Yes, I am one of Augusta's descendants, just as you are."

"And you've been accepted as a Phenwick Woman?"

"Very much so."

"May I tell you that I like you, Katherine? There is something about you that makes you seem very familiar to me," Peggy said lightly. "And furthermore, I love your perfume. It suddenly has become very pungent."

"My perfume? I forgot to bring perfume with me, and there wasn't time to purchase any here in San Francisco," Katherine explained. "I simply splashed on a bit of violet toilet water. I don't see how it—"

"No. It's the scent of roses," Peggy corrected. "I've been particularly fond of roses. I would know that fragrance anywhere."

"Roses?" Katherine glanced around the room. With clairvoyant vision, she perceived the outline of a man seated a short distance from Peggy. "Oh, I see. You've chosen—" She turned her gaze back to Peggy.

"Yes, and we must do something about this, mustn't we?"

Peggy had not heard the voice that Katherine had. The latter simply nodded her head in consent and returned her full attention to the large woman.

"Is there something wrong, Cousin Katherine?"

"No, not at all. I had no idea that a certain party was here in San Francisco."

"Which party is that?"

"Never mind. Perhaps I had better go have a look." Katherine stepped to the door. "Oh, if you really wish privacy, Peggy, you would do well to go upstairs. You're certain not to be interrupted there. We'll speak again later."

How peculiar, Peggy thought. Still, that interlude with Katherine had somehow picked up her spirits.

After Katherine was gone and she sat in contemplative silence for nearly five minutes, Peggy became aware of an almost overpowering scent of roses. She wondered how it could be, since Katherine was no longer present. Then an eerie sensation came over her, and she felt as if she had sprouted with goose bumps. The door slowly opened, but no one was standing there. Now alarmed, she got up and hurriedly made her way to the exit. As she reached the door and it opened wider, the fragrance of roses was overpowering. She moved from the room faster than she had moved from anywhere in years.

An urgent impulse came over Peggy to climb to the floor above. As she moved with alarming swiftness for her, she kept looking down at her feet. Something was terribly wrong.

Upon reaching the second floor landing, Peggy had a compulsion to climb to the floor above. Whatever had come over her? Normally, she would have had to rest after going up a flight of stairs as quickly as she had; but she was hardly winded. The next group of steps were taken equally fast. She did have to stop at the third floor balustrade and get her bearings. What was happening to her?

As she stood there, contemplating what had occurred, Peggy thought of Joyce and Carol Phenwick, her sisters-in-law, the wives of her twin brothers. They had been pleasant to her and kind. They, too, were in the wedding party.

Suddenly a feeling of fatigue came over her, a dizziness. Her one thought was to find a room where she could lie down. The climb had been too much for her.

The first door she tried was locked.

When she went to a second door, she thought she heard sound coming from within. Putting her ear to the door, she listened.

"Ay, *mama mia,* you are a resplendent beauty!"

The voice was familiar, she knew it. Reacting out of curiosity, Peggy opened the door to behold Damien Brusco in bed with one of the chambermaids. At the interruption, Damien grabbed for a sheet to cover his bare backside and stopped in mid-action as he glanced up to see Peggy watching him.

"Mr. Brusco?"

"Oh, goodness!" the maid squealed. "I'll lose my job for this!" With that, she jerked the sheet from Damien, got up and wrapped it around her slender, but attractive, body.

Damien wildly reached to find a cover. "Perhaps you don't think I have a logical explanation for this."

"If you have, Mr. Brusco," Peggy snapped, "I don't care to hear it." She stepped back and slammed the door behind her.

Moments later Damien came scurrying out of the room, vainly trying to pull into his clothing, barefoot. Seeing that Peggy was only halfway down the flight of stairs, he took time to slide into his shoes without stockings.

"Stay away from me!" Peggy exclaimed as he caught up to her on the second floor.

"*Cara mia,* you must listen to me!"

"To you and your logical explanation?" she fired.

"I know it has distressed you, finding me as you did," Damien said. "It must be a shock to unexpectedly see your intended husband unclothed under such circumstances. But you must let me explain."

"No explanation is necessary, Mr. Brusco. A picture expresses a thousand words. And the picture I saw was ugly, and the words were profane. And all of the other words you've said to me since you've been courting me, they too re-echo in my ears as filthy profanity! You are a hypocrite, Mr. Brusco, and I want nothing more to do with you—*ever.*"

"No, no, that is not true! You must grant me the favor of hearing what I have to tell you," Damien said. "You will find it most enlightening."

"Enlightening? I daresay!"

"Let us go into this room where I can explain to you," Damien urged as he opened the door. His hand had connected to her upper arm. "Grant me just five minutes, *cara mia.* Please, you must do that for me!"

The look in Damien's eyes, the expression on his features were so tormented and troubled that Peggy relented, although she didn't believe there could possibly be any explanation that would erase that which she had witnessed.

Damien held the door for her, and she entered.

Chapter Four

Damien took a few moments to straighten his attire and make himself entirely presentable. He was always concerned about his appearance. The interlude gave him time to gather his wits and organize his thoughts. When he finally turned to Peggy, he was composed, a charismatic person who had taken charge of the situation. His smile was warm, appealing, with just a touch of studied innocence; yet he wore an expression of self-confidence.

"*Bella mia,* eyes do not deceive," Damien began. "I am deeply sorry that you discovered what you did. Had I any notion that you might have climbed to the third floor, I would have never— No, that doesn't sound right, does it?"

"I don't believe there is any way you can excuse your behavior, Mr. Brusco," Peggy said coldly. "There is no possible means by which you can explain away what I saw. Facts are facts."

"Ah, facts! I am glad you said that," Damien replied. "We must examine facts. I will be blunt with you. The facts are that I am a normal man with normal desires for normal women."

"Do you call that sleazy chambermaid a normal woman?" Peggy fired, rage seething within her.

"I do."

"You told me you preferred large women," Peggy bit. "That—that person is as thin as a broomstick."

Damien chuckled. "Not that thin, *cara mia*. I *do* find large women attractive—but then, I confess I find most women attractive. I asked you to marry me. That means I have chosen you above all the other women I have known."

"Whom you have had relationships with?"

"I am a most prolific man with a ravenous appetite for women," he explained, "as you obviously have a ravenous appetite for—" He caught himself. "I did not mean to say that in a derogatory way."

"As I have a ravenous appetite for food?" Peggy questioned. "And I obviously have, haven't I, Mr. Brusco?"

He nodded his head.

"Are you suggesting in some perverse way that we deserve each other because of our individual ravenous appetites?"

"In a sense, yes."

"Your logical explanation isn't very logical to me, Mr. Brusco." Peggy started for the door.

"Wait! Please hear me out," Damien begged. "There is something I had not planned to tell you, but I think I must."

"What is it?"

"I am a professional man." Damien stood erect and clicked his heels together.

"And *what* precisely is your profession?"

"I am a gigolo, a man who accommodates women." He made a casual gesture with his hand, accompanied by a shrug.

Peggy gasped in shock. "I never dreamed . . ."

"Nor would I have permitted you to know, had you not found me in the uncompromising position with the chambermaid," Damien continued.

"I don't wish to hear any more."

"But you must. You see, I was hired by your father."

"Hired by my father? For what purpose?" she asked incredulously.

"Too woo you and convince you to become my wife," Damien replied simply. "A friend told him of me, and he learned of my versatility. You see, your papa feels sorry for you."

"So he hired you to accommodate me? Is that the expression you used?" Peggy said. "And all this time you've been playing on my emotions, trying to make me fall in love with you. It was only a game with you—correction, a business."

"Your papa wants me to marry you, *cara mia,* not to illicitly accommodate," Damien assured her. "I must tell you the truth. I have fallen in love with you."

"Because you were paid to do so?"

"No, not for that reason. I could have pretended." He reached for her hand, but she jerked it away. "*Cara mia,* I know you can't understand what motivates a person like me. Do you think my profession is easy? It is not."

"How can you boldly stand there and say that you have fallen in love with me aware that I discovered you with that thin excuse for a chambermaid?" Peggy snapped.

"How can I make you understand?"

"I don't believe you ever can, Mr. Brusco." The hurt she felt at that moment was grinding at her innermost parts. Her stomach had become so tense with gnarling pain that it was all she could do to keep from doubling over. "Excuse me, Mr. Brusco. I do not understand you, and I *don't* ever want to understand you. My emotions have been slapped about all my life, more than you can possibly comprehend. Rejection—gross rejection—is sheer torture!"

"Yet you reject me."

"Because your behavior and your attitude is highly objectionable to me. Whatever else I may be, I do possess a moral consciousness," Peggy stated. "What you are and what you stand for is repulsive to me . . . absolutely repulsive! Please do not follow me out of this room. I want no further part of you, and that is final!" With a look of defiant rage, she pushed him aside and stomped from the room.

As Peggy reached the top of the stairs leading down to the first floor, and the music and chatter from below became prominent, Hayden climbed the steps in her direction. Obviously he had seen her. She remained where she stood and let him come to her.

Even if he weren't perceptive and sensitive, Hayden could have readily seen that his sister was in a negative mood. The few drinks he had had put him in a jovial frame of mind. "Well, well, have you been hiding on the second floor, Peg?"

"Hayden . . . I . . ." Tears were lining her face in glistening streaks.

Hayden frowned. "What is it?" He put his arm about her shoulder.

"I want to kill myself! I want to die! I can't take any more of this life! It's intolerable to me!"

"Hey . . . hey, Sister, something has really got to you hasn't it?" Forcefully he guided Peggy to a nearby room, opened the door, and finding it unoccupied, he assisted her into it.

Peggy sat in a sturdy chair and cried. She was inconsolable. Throwing her head back, pounding her fists on the chair arms, stamping her feet on the floor, she gave vent to the tortuous emotions that had accumulated over the years that had never truly been released. Through fitful sobs, she blurted out about her discovery of Damien Brusco and subsequently the revelation that he had been hired by their father.

"Frankly, old girl," Hayden said without trying to sound unsympathetic, "Father was only thinking of your good and of your happiness. Undoubtedly Damien could have made you very happy had you not discovered the truth about him. With his experience, he might have been able to transform you into a different woman."

"Hayden, for goodness' sake, don't make a mockery of me!" Peggy countered.

"I'm not mocking you in the least. I'm stating a simple fact," Hayden replied. "Surely, you're not stupid enough to believe you are like other women. This may hurt you, Peg, but, believe me, I'm saying it for your own good."

"I don't want to hear it!"

"But you're going to, anyway," Hayden declared. "You're twenty-five, a virgin, and there appears to be little hope that you will attract a man even for a casual affair. Be realistic. I love you, Peg, because you're my sister. You won't believe this, but I've cried more than once feeling sorry for you. I would give anything to see you happy and to live a normal life."

"Hayden—don't . . ."

"Please listen, baby, listen. You're my little sister. I've tried to find men who might be interested in you—not gigolos. I haven't found any. Both John Adam and Luke have attempted the same. We're all concerned about you. Don't you realize that when others hurt you with unkind remarks or curious looks that it hurts us, too? Despite her sophisticated exterior, Lola feels it, too. If I were you, I would forget what I had inadvertently discovered—meaning Brusco and the chambermaid—turn the other cheek, as it were—and go ahead with him. You know, maybe he *does* love you."

Peggy shook her head. "No, I could never stand to have him hold my hand again, much less kiss me, knowing about him what I do. That picture will always remain in my mind—and I will hate him with the most contemptuous hatred."

"Only because you first hate yourself," Hayden flew back at her. "Hatred only breeds more hatred. Forgive Brusco. Somehow try to find forgiveness in your heart and overlook his weaknesses."

"You don't understand, Hayden. Nobody understands me." Peggy touched a handkerchief to her face, blew her nose and wiped her eyes.

"I think you're being silly," Hayden said softly, revealing compassion.

"And I think you just don't know," Peggy replied. "Please leave me alone. I feel as if I'm going to cry again, I'd rather you weren't here."

Hayden kissed her lightly on the forehead. "Be kind to yourself, Peg."

Once Hayden was gone, Peggy glanced about at the enormous room. She was seated in a large armchair in front of the fireplace. She presumed the room was the library, since there were several shelves of books. In fact the room was so large, it was divided in four distinct sections with groups of chairs in each area. A strange premonition came over her that she was not in the room alone. As the feeling increased, she was about to rise when she heard a tapping sound.

"Who—who's there?" she asked in a husky voice.

"I overheard your conversation. I came in here to get away from the throng, too. It's your cousin Donald."

"Donald?" Peggy pushed herself from the chair with effort. Fear plunged through her. Had Donald overheard all of her confession to Hayden? Then fear turned to embarrassment. She wiped at her eyes again.

"What your brother said is true, Peggy. Hatred only breeds more hatred," Donald said as he started to get up.

"Stay where you are, Donald, I'll come to you." She felt as if she were a hundred pounds heavier as she moved across the room to where he was seated.

"Perhaps Hayden cannot comprehend what those of us who are structured differently have to endure," Donald commented as he gazed up at Peggy. "But I can. Why, do you know I often cross the street to avoid encountering a group of children at play so I won't have to put up with their thoughtless remarks. And if I've been asked once, I've been asked a million times, how I lost my eye; and usually before I can answer, a sarcastic or belittling suggestion is made as to how it happened. People can be very unaware of another's feelings."

"I know you understand, Donald." She took his hand and sat in a chair beside him. "We are kindred spirits, aren't we?"

"You must not think badly of your father for what he tried to do," Donald said a short while later after Peggy had reiterated about the incident concerning Damien Brusco. "I fear that because Paul was inexperienced in such matters, he made a poor choice."

"I was humiliated," Peggy stated. "Father must have realized my desperation. I can see what he was trying to do. It was an ill-executed plan. Father really must have deep concern for me."

"That is an intelligent observation," Donald remarked. He squeezed her hand. "I spoke briefly with Katherine, and she made what I believe is a marvelous suggestion."

"What is that?"

"That you come to Boston with us."

"I couldn't leave San Francisco."

"Why not?" Donald asked. "A change of scene could well do you an extreme amount of good. Besides, there is someone I would like for you to meet."

"My family are all here in San Francisco," Peggy argued, but the idea had begun to intrigue her.

"How close are you to your family? Really?" Donald inquired. "For that matter, you have far more family in Boston. True, they are not as closely related to you, but they are family—and we would see that you were well taken care of."

Peggy thought a minute. "No, I couldn't. I don't think Boston is ready for me. It's bad enough I cause a spectacle here."

"Dearest Peggy, you've got to stop thinking like that," Donald coaxed. "All right, so people look at you. Has it ever occurred to you that they might be looking in admiration?"

"What a foolish thought!"

"Is it? If Damien Brusco has proclivity toward ladies of abundant pulchritude, doubtlessly there are others like him," Donald suggested. "You might be surprised at the number of men who let their fantasies wander when they see you. Oh, I don't say there are a multitude of them, but there must be a select few."

"You're only trying to boost my morale, Donald." She

laughed faintly, cynically. "Who—? Who is it you would like me to meet in Boston?"

"Ah, then that sentence didn't escape your attention," Donald said as he studied her expression of interest. "She is perhaps the grandest Phenwick Woman of all: Millijoy. There's none other like her—and most of the clan say 'thank goodness' for that."

"I've heard of Millijoy Phenwick," Peggy remarked. "As a matter of fact, Joyce mentioned her earlier today. I would like to meet her—sometime."

"Then go back to Boston with Katherine, Philip and me," he eagerly said. "We would enjoy having your company. And I think after what you've been through, unless you wish to reconsider your attitude toward Damien Brusco, a change of scene could do you a world of good."

"I can never change my attitude toward Mr. Brusco, not after what I saw," Peggy said. "He lied to me, misrepresented himself. No, I could never encounter him without remembering."

"Good. Then forget him and come to Boston with us."

"It can't be done that easily."

"But it *can*, Peggy, if you make up your mind. Anything can be accomplished once you honestly make up your mind to do it," Donald insisted. "You're an adult. Your father has given you abundant funds to live comfortably the rest of your life. Let me speak with him."

"I like Katherine very much," Peggy commented as she considered the matter. "I'm certain we could become good friends. And, of course, you'll be there."

"Yes, I'll be there." Donald sighed.

Chapter Five

"You will never know how helpless I feel about being unable to give the beautiful things of life to Peggy that I have presented to my other children," Paul said two days later when Donald went to his office to see him. "She's so unlike the others. It really is a puzzle to know what to do for her."

"Give her a letter for unlimited funds and send Peggy to Boston with Philip, Katherine and me," Donald stated. "She'll be with us and we'll look after her."

"Send Peggy to Boston? But she hardly leaves the house here."

"All the more reason to have her visit another city," Donald argued. "She knows if she goes out on the streets in San Francisco that she will be recognized as a Phenwick—your daughter, Uncle Paul. But in Boston, I believe she can be convinced that even though she attracts attention, no one will know who she is, hence she wouldn't feel the criticism was reflected on her family. You may not realize it, but Peggy has confided to me in her letters that she is very proud of her family, certainly of her brothers, and even of Lola. Despite the rejection she has felt, she has a deep love for all of you. Besides, Aunt Millijoy is in Boston."

"Aunt Millijoy?" Paul laughed. "I'm afraid Aunt Millijoy, in all her sophistication and splendor, would take one look at Peggy, throw her hands in the air and send her back on the next train."

"You don't know Aunt Millijoy very well, do you, Uncle Paul?"

"I haven't seen her in years. I always liked her. She was something else! I think she taught me more things than any other adult did when I was a boy."

"Perhaps Aunt Millijoy can teach a thing or two to Peggy, too." Donald stroked his chin. "Why don't you simply give Peggy part of the money you were going to pay Damien Brusco, and tell her to go and enjoy herself."

"How do you known about Brusco?"

Donald explained the situation and how Peggy had discovered him with the chambermaid.

"Why, that two-timing scoundrel!" Paul exclaimed.

Donald folded his hands before his face and looked up at Paul. "*Weren't* you aware of his proclivities, Uncle Paul?"

"Why do you say it like that?"

"You hired the man. Surely, you investigated into his background before you arranged for him to meet your daughter."

Paul ducked his head. "Yes, I knew about his tastes. I acted out of desperation. My heart has ached for Peggy over the years. I wanted her to have something—someone. You must believe me, Donald, what I did was in an attempt to make her happy. It didn't work. I made a poor choice."

"Then make a choice now to send Peggy to Boston. You see, Paul, I am very fond of her—and not just as her distant cousin. I've learned to know the real Peggy, the heart and soul beneath the exterior. She has a fascinating mind, and wonderful observations about life—except some of them are a bit distorted because of her experiences."

"Are you in love with Peggy?" Paul asked, his eyebrows scowling in disbelief.

"I wonder if you would understand the ramifications of my love, Uncle Paul. I doubt that you can." Donald toyed with the silver head of his walking stick. "I live with Mother. Her health is not what it was. Edward House is a big, rambling old building, as you well know. When Mother goes—or even now in her declining years of ill-health and being confined to bed—I will be virtually alone in that old monster. It is very lonely, Uncle Paul. Although I've been close to many people in an abstract way, such as my niece Katherine or any number of others, I have no one to call my partner in life."

"Surely, as handsome as you are, Donald—and there is no doubt about your good looks in my mind—you could have your choice of the finest women in Boston," Paul stated.

"Perhaps you're correct, Uncle Paul. But what perfectly normal, attractive woman would honestly want to be saddled with me? Dr. Joe has suggested that I undergo a series of operations on my leg. You see, the bone is deteriorating at the ankle. If I did go through with the operations, I still might never be able to walk again. Even if they removed the leg and gave me an artificial limb, I might be able to hobble around for a few more years, but I could never stand straight because my spine has grown misshapen. In other words, I have nothing to look forward to but being a cripple the rest of my life."

"Therefore, you would forgo marrying a normal, beautiful woman," Paul suggested, "and consider a misfit."

"Don't call Peggy a misfit!"

"What else is she?"

"She's not a misfit. I've not explained myself very well, have I, Uncle Paul?"

"I think you've explained yourself quite well, Donald." He put his hand on the young man's shoulder. "And I *do* understand. Very well, I'll consent to allowing Peggy to go to Boston with you. And who knows what will come out of it?"

Donald rose, left his walking stick behind and threw himself into his uncle's embrace.

The Phenwicks had four compartments on the train out of Oakland. Katherine and Philip shared one, while Donald and Peggy each had one to themselves. The fourth compartment was used as a kind of parlor where the four of them could sit during the daytime. The ride was long and seemed endless. Meals were served in the communal compartment. Had there been more time to make arrangements, they would have had a special car to themselves. They made do with what they had.

Joyce and Luke Phenwick were on the same train as far as Denver, Colorado. It wasn't until after the lovely young couple disembarked that Katherine had the opportunity to spend time alone with Peggy. However, before they departed, Peggy had many hours alone with her brother Luke; it was a chance for the two to really get acquainted for the first time in their lives. Furthermore, it was the closest that Peggy had ever become to any of her siblings. Luke caused her to begin to have a change of outlook.

"What are you thinking?" Katherine asked the afternoon the train neared Chicago, and Donald and Philip had gone to stroll about the rest of the cars. "You seem to be in quite a pensive mood."

"Shall I be honest with you?" Peggy returned.

"Please do," Katherine said. "I would know if you were attempting to deceive me."

"Oh, yes, I forgot about you," Peggy remarked. "Very well, I was thinking of Damien Brusco. I can't get over my bitterness about him and the entire situation involving him. I even still hold a little resentment toward my father."

"Uncle Paul did what he did because of his love for you, Peggy, don't you realize that?"

"I realize it. But it seems he was interfering. Oh, I've forgiven him. That's the thing about me that is disturbing. I can mentally forgive, but emotionally I still find that I hold resentment," Peggy confessed. "I guess it's because I've been hurt too often."

Katherine smiled as she studied her cousin's face. "Have you ever wondered what it would be like if you were physically different?"

"How many waking hours have there been in my life this far?" Peggy asked. "That is how many times I've thought about it. I often daydream. In fantasies I try to imagine what it would be like if a fairy-godmother were suddenly to appear, wave a magic wand and change me into a sylphlike beauty. It would make me blush to tell you where my imaginings have taken me. But ultimately I come back to reality—well, a kind of reality."

"A kind of reality?"

"For instance, suppose I were transformed overnight into the beautiful me I long to be," Peggy continued. "In the first place, no one would know me. How would I even convince my family who I was? What would I wear? This dress would fit me like a sack. Maybe I could borrow a few of Lola's things to wear, but I wouldn't even know how to act—or how to walk and move like a lady."

"Then you must make your transformation slowly," Katherine commented.

"My transformation?"

"It will happen," Katherine stated. "I know that as well as I'm sitting here."

"Slowly. *That* is the word that makes me impatient."

"And if a magic wand were to be waved over you and you changed very quickly, what would you do?"

"I would make up for everything I had missed these years," Peggy declared. "I would catch up with the outside world."

"Would you?" Katherine asked enigmatically. "And, I daresay, it would not be long before you found yourself back where you are."

"Why so?"

"Because, in your attempt to make up for everything you imagine you've been deprived of, you would overdo," Katherine said. "If you think about that for a moment, I suspect you would have to agree."

"Then there would be no purpose of changing."

"On the contrary," Katherine returned. "Were you to have had a taste of the other life, you might make a valliant effort to obtain it again—that is, if you found it pleasant to you."

"I'm certain I would."

"Think of this a moment," Katherine continued. "Suppose when you had altered in appearance, you attempted to leap into a romantic affair and your hunger to know the fullness of it overpowered the man—or men—of your interest. You could well react with far greater hurt than you've known as an outcome of your situation with Damien Brusco. There are some things you can't catch up on."

"I've thought of that," Peggy admitted. "Maybe I'd become a *femme fatale,* and have a string of men dangling behind me."

"And a string of emotional problems," Katherine said. "You're far too sensitive a person to become so careless and uninhibited."

"Am I? I wonder." Peggy frowned. "This is so foolish! The two of us daydreaming together!"

"But isn't it fun, Peggy?"

"Fun?" Peggy thought a few moments. "I admit I feel much more lighthearted than I have in a long while. Even when Mr. Brusco was courting me, I didn't feel quite this giddy. Maybe beneath his grand airs I detected a strain of deceit. Oh, I don't want to get back to thinking of him."

Katherine stood up to stretch. "I'll only be a few minutes. Are you certain you don't wish to join me?"

"I know my limitations, Katherine. I'll sit here like a great glob and sulk."

"Don't sulk, Peggy. You must learn to be happy doing what you're doing wherever you're doing it at the moment," Katherine said. "This moment is all you really have, so you might as well enjoy what it holds. I'll not be long."

Peggy considered Katherine's parting words. And she came to the conclusion that she really had no idea what happiness was. The thought saddened her, and she pouted as she caught a glimpse of her reflection in the window. As was her usual reaction, she quickly turned away.

A strange thing happened.

The clacking sound of the train wheels crescendoed,

then the noise died away until Peggy was only aware of a distant rumble. A singular brightness seemed to permeate the compartment, a hazy glow that distorted the walls, the luggage rack, the other seats. Then it came, that unmistakable smell of roses she had sensed on that first day she had met Katherine. But Katherine wasn't there, and she hadn't been wearing rose-scented perfume anyway. As she braced herself, believing that she might be having an attack of some sort, her skin became prickly with an eerie sensation.

"*You* have *been chosen, Peggy.*" The man's voice was a light baritone with an ethereal quality to it.

"Who—who said that?" Peggy's eyes had widened, which was most unusual for her.

"*It is not important who. What is essential is that you know and accept the truth of what I say.*"

"Am I to believe a voice out of my own imagination?" Peggy asked.

"*Am I only in your imagination? I wonder.*"

"You must be. I'm alone in this compartment."

"*Not entirely.*"

"Then, where are you?"

"*Look out the window.*"

Peggy turned, and instead of seeing her reflection, she saw an opaque image of a handsome man smiling at her. His hair was dark, and his face was almost too beautiful to be real. (You'll forgive the immodesty of the narrator.) She shook her head.

"*I'm beginning to get the hang of this. When I had heard tales that Augusta had been able to do it, I thought it was pure fabrication. Now, I must say, it is quite an interesting diversion.*"

"You're the wrong gender to be a fairy-godmother," Peggy stammered.

"I wouldn't be too certain of that." I laughed. *"But, rest assured, I have no magic wand to wave at you."*

Boldly Peggy asked, "What have I been chosen for?"

"Why, dear child, to become a Phenwick Woman. That's what this is all about, don't you know? Oh, well, we'll meet again. Maybe then you'll be more disposed to believe. I hope you like the roses, dear heart. There will be more."

The hazy glow suddenly was gone from the compartment. The clickety-clack of the train wheels had returned. And Peggy was incredulously staring at her own reflection in the window.

"Are you all right, Peggy?" Katherine asked when she returned to the compartment.

Peggy was sitting with her mouth agape. She blinked twice and adjusted herself in the chair. "How did you do that?"

"How did I do *what?*" Katherine asked as she took a seat.

"No!" Peggy shook her head. "It was just my imagination."

"You're not making a great deal of sense, Peggy."

"Neither did that—I mean, what I imagined happened." Peggy glanced again at the window and quickly turned back as she saw her own likeness.

Katherine breathed deeply and smelled a faint trace of roses. She smiled and leaned back on the seat to relax. She knew what had happened.

Chapter Six

The day was sultry, humid, when the train arrived at the Boston railway station. All four of the Phenwicks had grown weary of the ride, but they had done their best to keep their spirits up. Katherine always seemed to be happy, even when there was no apparent reason to be. Philip, likewise, had such a pleasant disposition that his presence had a way of making others completely at ease. Peggy admired Katherine's husband and felt a bit envious of her for having married such a wonderful man.

Peggy had become edgy and she had difficulty in disguising her anxiety. Whenever she became too tense, Donald would do what he could to break the tension. She came to lean on him for a tremendous amount of support, little suspecting the true motivation behind his actions toward her.

"I was once a very strong, active lad," Donald related in the carriage, after they had left Katherine and Philip and were en route to Edward House. "I was far more athletically inclined than my brother Richard—than any of my brothers, for that matter."

"Do I have it right?" Peggy asked. "You have three brothers."

"Richard is my only full brother," Donald explained. "That is, Richard, Polly and I have the same mother. My eldest brother Daniel and my late sister Ann Marie were children of my father by his first wife Marcia. Alexander, whom we call Xan—he's Katherine's father—has a singular history. Suffice it to say that he was the son of Barbara Phenwick and my father. I dearly love both Daniel and Xan, as if they were my full brothers."

"There was one more child in your family than there was in mine," Peggy commented, trying to show interest in Donald's narration. "Then you had the accident, and that interfered with your athletic ability."

"There were actually two incidents which brought about my present physical condition," Donald replied. "That is an old story, and I don't particularly care to reiterate it."

"Is your sister Polly here in Boston?"

"Both Polly and Richard are here," Donald replied. "Fortunately, because of his peculiar religious persuasions, Richard spends most of his time in Cambridge. Polly is married to a distant cousin, Albert. They are extremely happy. And I confess that I've become closer to Albert than I have to Richard."

Donald continued telling bits and pieces about his family as the carriage moved toward the large mansion on Beacon Hill known as Edward House. Soon the vehicle was approaching the house, and Donald pointed it out to Peggy.

"It is a monster, isn't it?" Peggy commented.

"Edward House was built in a time when mansions of this size were fairly common," Donald said. "Actually, the first structure, which was called Barrywell House, was built on another site at the direction and under the supervision of old Augusta Phenwick, who started the clan of Phenwicks." He laughed. "Then Patricia Phenwick came along—she was married to Augusta's adopted son, Edward—and had the old house torn down and rebuilt to the same exact design that it had been. Of course, by then, Beacon Hill had become the fashionable place to live. She renamed it Edward House. It's not really as dreary and gloomy as it looks, once you get used to it."

"How long do you suppose it takes getting used to?" Peggy asked lightly, amused by Donald's explanations.

"That, I suppose, is a very subjective matter, and entirely up to the individual," he replied. "I've known no other house, so I've been used to it for as long as I can remember."

The carriage pulled up to the front door, and the driver assisted both Donald and Peggy out of it. Peggy climbed the steps to the door while Donald paid the driver.

An eerie feeling came over Peggy as she looked up at the building. Why was it vaguely familiar to her? Had she dreamed of the mansion, only to have it materialize a reality? The thought left her with a bizarre reaction. She ruminated over past dreams which she could remember, but she could not find a reference in any of them. Yet, remembering the nature of dreams, she could well have dreamed about it years and years before, the memory of which had all but vanished even from her subconscious mind.

"Ready?" Donald asked as he took the key from his pocket and unlocked the front door.

"I never carry keys at home," Peggy said as she watched him. "I simply ring for the butler, and he opens it for me."

"There is no need of disturbing Hoxley," Donald returned. "He has enough to keep him busy without bothering to let me in and out of the house, when I'm perfectly capable of doing it on my own. I did telegraph ahead and asked him to prepare the guest room on the second floor for you. I suspect it will be ready."

The tall, efficient Mortimer Hoxley appeared at the sound of footsteps in the entrance hallway. "Ah, Mr. Phenwick, you've arrived." He stared for a moment at Peggy before he caught himself. "Is your luggage here?"

"You'll have to send Craig to the railway station for it," Donald said, handing the butler the claim receipts.

"Very good, sir."

"Oh, Hoxley, this is Miss Phenwick of San Francisco," Donald introduced. "She will be occupying the guest room for an extended stay."

"Yes, sir." Hoxley glanced again at Peggy and quickly looked away. "If there is nothing more you wish of me at the moment, sir, I'll give instructions to Craig immediately."

"You do that, Hoxley." Donald directed Peggy to the stairs. "They're a bit steep, but one gets used to them."

"Did you see the way he looked at me?" Peggy asked.

"Hoxley has a way about him," Donald said. "He studies people as if he attempts to determine the sort of person they actually are."

"He stared at me in sheer amazement, unable to believe that I was actually a Phenwick," she returned, bitterness in her voice. "I fear it was a mistake of me coming to Boston."

"Nonsense, stop imagining such things."

"It wasn't my imagination, Donald."

"Up the steps, if you please, or I'll prod you with my walking stick," he teased.

By the time Peggy had reached the next-to-the-top step, the door opened to the room to her right. A large, bulky-looking, nearly bald man with gray hair around the

back part of his head came out. He looked over his wire-
framed glasses at Peggy, a perplexed expression covering
his face. Then he brightened as he saw Donald trudging
up the stairs behind her.

"Ah, Donald! So you've returned from San Francisco
at last, have you."

"Dr. Joe!" Donald exclaimed as he pushed passed
Peggy. "I hadn't expected to see you here."

"Just having a routine look-in on your mother, Donald," Joseph Ornby said. "She's about the same as she
was when you left. I don't anticipate any great improve-
ment. Then again, she might surprise us. I don't believe
I've had the pleasure of meeting this young lady."

"Excuse me, Dr. Joe, this is our cousin, Peggy Phenwick of San Francisco," Donald introduced. "This is your
distant cousin, Joe Ornby—the one I told you about. He's
a doctor."

"Somehow when you say it that way," Joseph replied,
"it deflates my ego. I'm pleased to meet you, Cousin
Peggy."

"Thank you, Dr.—uh—Cousin Joe." Peggy tried to be
gracious, although she imagined that he looked at her
with a criticizing attitude.

"May we go in and see Mother now?" Donald asked.

"I see no reason why you shouldn't," Joseph replied.
"I'll go down and have Hoxley fix me a cup of tea and
take it in the library. If you have a few minutes, Donald,
I'd like to speak with you."

"Certainly," Donald replied. "I won't be long with
Mother."

"Do you think I should meet your mother right away
before I've had a chance to freshen up from the ride?"
Peggy asked after Joseph Ornby went downstairs.

"It's as good a time as any," Donald assured her. "She sleeps much of the time. Now she is certain to be awake." He took her hand and squeezed it. "Don't be so apprehensive. She is an invalid who has very few visitors. She'll welcome you."

Peggy felt the encouragement of Donald's touch, braced herself and went toward Ruth Phenwick's room.

While Donald went to kiss his mother, Peggy remained near the door. She observed that Ruth was pale and looked helplessly feeble against the pillow which supported her head. Then, while Donald spoke softly to Ruth, Peggy let her eyes wander around the room. A large painting of the late Stuart Phenwick dominated it. It was not difficult to see where Donald got his remarkable good looks. Other photographs of Stuart were placed at various positions, all directed so that Ruth could see them from where she lay. On a dresser to her right, Peggy saw several other photographs, some of which looked to be quite old. There were pictures of all of the Phenwick children: Daniel, Ann Marie, Alexander, Richard, Polly and Donald, taken from different periods of their growing up. She would have liked to examine them closer, but she did not move from the spot she had hit when Donald left her.

As she watched Donald stroke a gentle hand over Ruth's brow, Peggy turned her attention to a photograph which was placed apart from the others, as if it had a special position of importance. With a faint feeling of recognition, she moved nearer to where it was placed. The face was extremely familiar, but she could not place it.

"Peggy, forgive me for getting so occupied with Mother," Donald said as he rose from the bed and motioned for her to come to him. "Mother, this is Cousin Peggy Phenwick from San Francisco."

"The one who writes you all of those marvelous letters?" Ruth asked. Her voice was weak, and her eyes had a glazed-over appearance. "I am pleased to make your acquaintance, Cousin Peggy."

"Thank you, Mrs. Phenwick."

"No, no, Cousin Ruth, please," the woman said.

"I've asked Peggy to stay with us here at Edward House," Donald explained. "I promised Uncle Paul I would personally look after her."

"And he will," Ruth uttered. "I hope you will come in often and sit with me so that we can become well acquainted, dear Peggy. I have so little company."

"And it's just as well, Mother. Dr. Joe says you need all the rest you can get."

"Doesn't he think I'll get enough rest in my coffin?" Ruth asked.

"Please, Mother, don't say such things."

"But I'm being realistic Donald." Ruth turned her attention to Peggy. "He thinks I'm naive and don't understand about my condition. Rest assured, dear son, I'm completely cognizant of what is going on. Why shouldn't I be? Only a dummy would believe otherwise. I dream of my late husband. Stuart seems to come often to me. And, to be perfectly frank, I look forward to the time when I can join him."

"Enough of that, Mother, I won't hear it," Donald exclaimed. "Why don't you take a few minutes to get acquainted with Peggy now, while I go downstairs and have a few words with Cousin Joe?"

"Does Joseph wish to speak with you?" Ruth asked.

"I saw him frown when he checked my pulse. There must be a reason he wishes to confer with you."

"Never mind that. You just get to know Peggy."

"Won't you take a chair, my dear?" Ruth offered after Donald left the room.

"I fear that chair may not hold my weight," Peggy replied.

"Nonsense. Joseph sits in it all the time, and it doesn't even creak when he does. It's the sturdiest chair in the house," Ruth stated.

Peggy braced herself against the back of it. "I'll stand just a little longer, if you don't mind."

"Not at all, Cousin Peggy. You do whatever you wish in this house. After all, you're a Phenwick, and this house has only been occupied by Phenwicks for the last hundred years or so," Ruth explained.

From where Peggy was standing, she got a better look at the photograph which had attracted her attention. "That man . . ." She pointed. "He looks so very familiar to me."

"Which is that, dear?" Ruth tried to raise her head, but she lacked the strength. "Oh, Adam. My, my, I shouldn't think he would look familiar to you. He's gone now, you know."

"Adam Phenwick?"

"No, no, Adam Truff. He might as well have been a Phenwick, as close as he was to our family," Ruth said. "Yes, dear Adam. It was such a shock when I heard of his death. He was the sort of person who you would imagine would live forever. Adam was the first man I ever loved."

"Your—?" Peggy caught herself.

"My very good friend. Oh, I would have liked to have

married him," Ruth admitted. "I would have even consented to have been his mistress, if he had desired that. Not Adam. Many women fell in love with him, but he was aloof to all of them. At least, that is what he led us all to believe. That made him all the more of a challenge. Oh, the stories Adam used to tell. He should have been a writer. Still, with all of his wild tales, I wondered how much of it was the truth, and how much was fabrication. I suspect none of us Phenwick women ever knew the truth about Adam Truff. He and Stuart were close friends. Oh, the stories I could tell you about Adam. And if I know a volume of them, I can't begin to guess the number of them that Millijoy knows."

"Millijoy?"

"Millijoy Phenwick. She's your cousin, too." Ruth sighed. "I know Millijoy was deeply in love with Adam, but she would have never married another man and forfeit the Phenwick name. It is too important to her. You see, she was married for a short while to my husband's brother. We're sisters-in-law, I suppose you would say. I always knew that she had strong feelings for Stuart, too. Stuart was my husband. But I am as certain as I know I am lying here, that neither Stuart nor Adam ever—well, Millijoy is an attractive and an appealing woman—but never Stuart or Adam."

"May I get a closer look at the photograph of Adam Truff?"

"If you like, dear. It was taken years ago when he was a young man."

Why was the likeness of Adam Truff so very familiar to her? And why couldn't Peggy place where she had seen the face before?

*　　*　　*

Joseph Ornby was seated in a comfortable leather-upholstered Queen Anne chair in the library. It had been his favorite seat for years. Donald sat opposite him. Both men had remained silent while Hoxley served the tea.

"Is it about Mother?" Donald questioned when the butler left the room. "She hasn't taken a turn for the worse, has she?"

"No. Ruth will basically be as she is right now," Joseph replied. "I suspect she will simply fade away in her sleep. But, as I have said in the past, that may not be for a considerable length of time from now—or it could be tomorrow. I simply can't guess at it."

"If not about Mother—?"

"There are two matters," Joseph stated. "First, I have conferred with Dr. Elmo Johnson at Boston Hospital, and Dr. Michael Fitzpatrick, a bone specialist in New York. Both Johnson and Fitzpatrick have reached the same conclusion, and that is that they feel time may be running out for you."

"Running out?"

"Concerning your ankle and the proposed operation," Joseph said. "Or, more to the point, a series of operations. Fitzpatrick warns that if you wait much longer, it may be too late to correct the condition, which could mean that you will no longer be able to walk."

"What are the chances of success for such operations if they are performed in time?" Donald asked.

"I would guess you'd have a fifty-fifty chance of being able to walk at least as well as you do now."

"There was suggestion made that the leg might be removed and an artificial limb be used in its place."

"That would be an extreme measure to take, Donald," Joseph replied, "a most extreme measure. My advice is that you submit to the operations. Fitzpatrick is one of the best bone surgeons in the world. If anyone can perform a miracle with surgery in your case, it would be he."

Donald thought a moment. "How soon would it be necessary?"

"As soon as possible," Joseph returned. "I would say within the next three months at the latest."

"Let me give it further consideration."

"Don't think too long about it, my boy," Joseph warned. "The longer you wait, the less likely of success your chances will be."

"I see. Thank you for telling me that." Donald looked down at the teacup and studied the liquid in it before he drank. "There was another matter?"

Joseph fumbled in his inside coat pocket. "Yes. I received a letter from Paul Phenwick just this morning. While it is congenial in nature, I perceive it is a desperate plea of a concerned father."

"A desperate plea?" Donald looked startled. "Meaning?"

"Can't you guess?"

"Is Uncle Paul apprehensive about Peggy's being in Boston?"

"Not so much about her being here," Joseph replied. "But it is her physical condition that worries him. I don't have the letter with me, or I would let you read it. Basically he voiced his concern over Peggy, a concern he has had since she was a small child. He feels helpless to know what to do about it. In short, he wishes for me to examine her and see if there is anything I can do for her."

"Will you?"

"I will with her permission," Joseph returned. "You see, Donald, Peggy is a grown woman—an adult. Were she a minor, her parents could request treatment for her. Now that she has reached the age of consent, and gone beyond it by a few years, such treatment would have to be entirely up to her. I had only to meet her to see that she has an acute problem. And I thought, since Paul mentioned your interest in her, and you had told me of the communication you had had via the post, that *you* might be able to persuade her to consider letting me examine her."

"That is a very touchy matter, Dr. Joe," Donald replied. "She is extremely sensitive."

"No doubt. Yet, I believe that if anyone can convince her of the need to do something about her condition, it is you," Joseph stated. "Oh, it isn't something that you have to do within the next twenty-four hours. But I must stress there is an urgency."

"An urgency? What sort of urgency?"

"In his letter, Paul mentioned that she had lost consciousness a time or two in the last year," Joseph replied. "That would indicate to me, even without examining her, that certain of her vital organs are being inhibited by fat. And, according to the letter, she has a pattern of gaining rather sizable amounts periodically, which she finds almost impossible to shed. That, too, is an indication that she is in trouble."

"I never dreamed it could be that serious. Was it a mistake that I insisted Peggy come to Boston with me?"

"No. If she will listen to me and permit me to help her," Joseph said, "it might have been the best thing in the world for her. On the other hand, if she doesn't alter her condition, I suspect she will be returned to San Francisco in a coffin within a relatively short period of time."

"You're not serious?"

"I'm most serious, Donald." Joseph rose and went to the mantelpiece. "Paul assures me that he will spare no expense to see that Peggy is helped. If you cannot convince her of the importance of this, then I know of only one other person who might."

"Who is that?"

"Need you ask?" Joseph questioned. "Why, Millijoy, of course."

"I had planned to take her to meet Aunt Millijoy at the earliest possible convenience," Donald said.

"In which case, I'll make a visit to the grand lady as soon as possible. In the meantime, I suggest that you exert whatever pressure you feel you can to persuade Peggy to come and talk to me at my office."

"I will do what I can," Donald replied. "But, it is a delicate subject. I don't wish to alienate her."

Joseph chuckled to himself. "You do what you can." He started to leave. "Something curious happened when I came in the library a little while ago."

"What is that?"

"Well, I thought there was someone else in here," Joseph replied. "In fact, since the room is so dimly lit, I thought a man was standing over there in the corner of the room, running his finger over book titles. I spoke to him, but got no answer. Then, when I went over to investigate after I had lit the lamp, I could see that I had been mistaken."

"A figment of your imagination?"

"Perhaps. Yet for a few minutes after I reached that part of the room, I was aware of a most pungent aroma of roses."

"Roses?" Donald laughed. "It must have been your imagination."

"Yes, I wonder." Joseph paced back to the corner of the room he had mentioned. "The scent is no longer here—not even a trace of it. Well, enough of my imagination for one day." He shook Donald's hand. "I'll let myself out. But think on those things I've told you."

"I will, Dr. Joe."

Ruth had fallen asleep in the middle of a sentence as Peggy sat in the sturdy chair beside the bed. The older woman had begun to ramble, and Peggy had let her mind drift away from her words.

Grunting as she got from the chair, Peggy went again to where the photograph of Adam Truff was placed. She lifted it and stared deeply into his handsome face. Her first impulse was to take the picture with her that she could study it closer. She wished she had asked Ruth permission to do so. Since she had not, she replaced it where it was. Then she left the room and waited at the top of the stairs for Donald to come and show her to the room she was to occupy.

Chapter Seven

On the third day after her arrival in Boston, Peggy made arrangements to go to Triumph House to meet Millijoy. She had had several conversations with Donald in the meantime, and although he had broached the subject Dr. Joseph Ornby had wanted him to do, he had made little headway. Since Donald had to undergo an extensive examination on the day Peggy wished to see Millijoy, it was arranged that Katherine would accompany Peggy to the mansion on the coast.

"You're not putting me out in the least," Katherine said after she had greeted Peggy. "I love going to Triumph House. I'm the one who should apologize to you for not coming sooner to visit you."

"I've been resting up from that harrowing train ride," Peggy commented. "Besides, I've been getting acquainted with Cousin Ruth and, through her, with the Phenwicks of Boston for as far back as she can remember. I didn't realize that I was a descendant of such an interesting family."

"There are many things that might surprise you about the Phenwicks, if you were to learn about them," Katherine said mysteriously.

"I presume, from things Ruth has told me, that Old Augusta was really the most eccentric of all," Peggy said, "wasn't she?"

Katherine smiled. "The carriage is waiting."

Triumph House was constructed in a circular design, and it was considered one of the most unusual houses in the entire area of Boston. Peggy was amply impressed when she saw the mansion rise on the horizon and Katherine informed her that that was their destination.

"You'll want to speak with Millijoy by yourself," Katherine said as they neared the place. "She is quite outspoken; but it is far more desirable to meet her on a one-to-one basis."

"If she's so outspoken, I don't know that I'm really that anxious to meet her," Peggy replied.

"No one is coercing you to see her."

"What a curious thing to say," Peggy remarked.

"Well, it is the truth." Katherine appeared preoccupied. "I'll simply drop you off and come back later in time to take tea with you and Millijoy. That should work out quite well."

"Katherine," Peggy said a few moments later, uncertain how to take her cousin's remarks, "what do you know about Adam Truff?"

"Adam Truff?" Katherine glanced at her with a cautious expression before she smiled. "Why do you ask?"

"Cousin Ruth has a photograph of him," Peggy said. "And every time I see it, I have the feeling that he is very familiar to me . . . but I can't place him."

"I wouldn't worry about that, if I were you," Katherine commented. "If you really want to know about Adam Truff, you must ask Millijoy about him. They were the best of friends."

"Oh." Peggy thought about that. She had other questions, but she would save them for the illustrious Millijoy.

Katherine dropped Peggy at the front door to Triumph House, explaining that she was late for an appointment, so she would not stop in to see Millijoy until she had fulfilled her mission.

The door was opened to Peggy by the stoic Victor Samson, the longtime head servant of Triumph House. Muscularly handsome, although marked with indications of age, the man was as proper as a person in his position should be.

"I'm Miss Peggy Phenwick," she introduced. "I believe Mrs. Phenwick is expecting me."

"Won't you have a seat, and I'll tell Mrs. Phenwick that you are here."

Peggy did not sit. Instead she stood in awe of the fabulous round entrance hall with the circular staircase at one side. The enormous crystal chandelier next attracted her attention. She stared up at it from the side, then she stood directly beneath it and slowly turn around as she gazed up. The effect was dizzying. A purple blotch flashed across her vision, and she suddenly felt as if she were about to lose her equilibrium.

"Are you all right?" a pleasant voice asked.

Peggy vaguely was able to focus on the dark-skinned, attractive young lady who had come up beside her. "I guess I was staring too intently at the chandelier. It has an hypnotizing effect."

"Yes, it has. May I help you?"

"I'll be all right in a moment," Peggy stated. "Are you one of the servants?"

"No. I'm Mrs. Gordon Thomas Phenwick."

"But you're—"

"Black? Yes, I am part Negro, but I am also Mrs. Millijoy Phenwick's granddaughter. You see, Negro blood runs in our side of the family. My given name is Melany, they call me Lanny."

"I am—I am your—I guess I am your cousin Peggy Phenwick."

"Oh, yes, from San Francisco." Lanny shook her hand. "You've been expected. Has Samson announced you?"

"He's just doing it—if the butler is named Samson."

"I am busy doing a few chores," Lanny explained. "I just happened to come through here when I saw you. As long as you've been announced, I'll go on about my business. We'll get to know each other better at a later time. It's good to have met you, Peggy."

"Thank you. It's been—I've enjoyed meeting you, too, Lanny."

Peggy watched as Lanny gracefully walked from the

room. What she would give to have a figure like that, white or black.

"Mrs. Phenwick will see you now, Miss Phenwick," Samson announced a short while later. "Come this way."

Samson led Peggy up the stairs. He had to stop twice to permit her to catch her breath. Then he directed her to Millijoy's private rooms.

The elegant lady of Triumph House was gowned in red satin. In essence it was a lounging garment, but it was so stylishly designed that it could be worn anywhere. Silver was in predominence in her black hair, and more and more signs of age had crept into the artistic beauty of her face. She held herself grandly and seemed to straighten even more as she heard Peggy enter.

"So you are Paul's little—Paul's daughter," Millijoy exclaimed as she turned to see the visitor.

"Yes, I'm Paul Phenwick's daughter," Peggy said, getting off on the wrong foot. "My baby sister Lola is his little girl. I'm generally referred to as the other one."

"I was always so very fond of Paul," Millijoy exaggerated, purposefully avoiding a retaliation to Peggy's attitude. "And, of course, I've dearly loved his brothers Thadius, John and Daniel Louis. Daniel Louis, of course, is gone now; but John is a particularly good friend with whom I intrust all of my legal matters."

"I don't know my uncles," Peggy said.

"You must get to know them, Peggy. Both Thadius and John are two of my favorite people," Millijoy said. "Won't you sit? Not there. I'm afraid that chair is far too fragile to hold your weight."

Peggy closed her eyes to gain control over the anger that wanted to spew forth. "I must be careful where I sit."

"I should think so," Millijoy returned. "I don't believe I've ever seen a woman as large as you."

"Nor are you apt to again," Peggy fired back. "A lady elephant may come close to my size, but I shouldn't think that you, of all people, would often attend the circus. And, speaking of circuses, another few pounds increase and I'll consider looking for a position in the freak show. I thought I would save you the bother of suggesting that."

"My, my, you are on the defensive, aren't you?" Millijoy moved away from the girl. "I suspect you've suffered a lifetime of abuse over your size."

"I have learned to live with it," Peggy rejoined. "One has to adapt."

"I should think that would take a terrible amount of adapting," Millijoy stated. "Certain conditions can be altered, if a person is so inclined."

"Have you ever been as heavy as I am?"

"No. Never."

"Then you can't begin to comprehend how difficult it is to alter the condition," Peggy said. "I think I must be wasting your time, Cousin Millijoy. Furthermore, I have no intention of remaining here to take your abuses."

"Do you find me abusive? I don't see how I could possibly be near more abusive to you than you've been to yourself."

Peggy turned heel and went toward the door.

"Where do you think you're going?" Millijoy demanded to know.

"Away from you. Most people are kinder and far more tactful than you are, Cousin Millijoy," Peggy retaliated.

"Perhaps I am less tactful," Millijoy returned, intensity in her voice, "but I suspect I'm being kinder to you in the long run than most people are."

"Kinder? Speaking of my size?"

"Your size is very visible, it cannot be avoided. You present a constant reminder of your condition," Millijoy said, a little enjoying the opportunity to express herself so blatantly. "To avoid it, I would have to close my eyes."

"Then I'll help you avoid the sight of me, by leaving your presence as quickly as possible!" Peggy was infuriated. She felt her blood pressure rise and throb at the top of her head. Again the dizzying sensation came over her, and she reached to brace herself against the wall. She wanted to cry, but she was too angry to do so. "Furthermore, if I ever return to Triumph House again, it will be too soon!" Her vision became clouded, and she felt a sharp pain in her chest. "I find your attitude contemptible!"

"Good! I'm pleased that you do," Millijoy fired back. "That means I've got under your hide."

"I was told you were a gracious, understanding lady," Peggy said. She needed to take the weight off her feet, but she could not tolerate being in Millijoy's presence another moment. Yet, when she tried to move, the dizziness became more pronounced. "I—I have to—I need to . . . sit. I feel funny."

Millijoy was immediately beside the young woman. She put her arms around Peggy and tenderly led her to a nearby chair. "Dear Peggy, you must pull yourself together. I apologize for baiting you as I did."

"*Baiting* me?" Peggy had eased down onto the chair. She was aware of Millijoy's arms still about her.

Once she was certain Peggy was comfortable, Millijoy went to pour a small glass of brandy. "Here, I want you to sip on this. It will help you relax."

"I don't care for brandy."

"Would you rather die here on the spot?"

"Yes, as a matter of fact, I would gladly do that if I could," Peggy snapped.

The older woman held the glass to Peggy's lips and coaxed her to take a sip or two of it.

"It's bitter."

"The bitterness will help bring you down off of your high horse," Millijoy stated. Then, after leaving the glass with Peggy, she went to the small table beside the large chair and took a bottle of smelling salts from it. A moment later she was passing the opened container beneath Peggy's nose.

Peggy coughed. "Oh, I can't stand that either."

Millijoy put the smelling salts to the girl's nose a second time. As Peggy coughed again, she pushed the bottle away. Millijoy was smiling when Peggy glanced up at her. The smile was warm and compassionate, even understanding.

"What did you mean when you said you had baited me?" Peggy asked. She was beginning to feel less uncomfortable.

"I wanted to see," Millijoy replied, "just how well adjusted you were to your girth. You're *not* at all. I thought maybe if I were to anger you enough, you would permit me to help you."

"Help me?" Peggy stared incredulously. "How can you help me?"

"Perhaps I can give you the incentive to want to alter your present state," Millijoy said. "Joseph Ornby came to call on me last night, especially to speak about you."

"About me? I've only met Cousin Joseph once."

"True. He told me that," Millijoy said. "Why don't you come and sit on the sofa."

"It looks fragile."

"It'll hold you," Millijoy assured her. She assisted Peggy to the sofa. "Joseph received a letter from your father. You may not realize this, Peggy, but Paul is deeply concerned about you. He is at his wit's end to know how to help you. The truth is, neither Paul nor Joseph, nor anyone else can help you. Only *you* can do that."

"It's impossible!"

"Is it? I think not." Millijoy took a seat opposite Peggy. "I've always been a person who has accepted challenges. I welcome obstacles, because they are things to be surmounted."

"I can never change."

"Change is the only constant thing that there is, Peggy," Millijoy stated. "Every minute of every day each of us changes a little. Not always for the better—but we do change."

"I am the same as I've always been for as long as I can remember."

"That is *not* true," Millijoy disputed. "You have progressively gained more and more weight, for one thing. You have become more and more bitter toward the outside world because people do not unequivocably accept you for what you are. Well, the fact is, you haven't accepted yourself for what you are."

"How can I not have?"

"That I can't explain," Millijoy said, "but you obviously haven't accepted yourself, or you would have altered your condition long before this. A condition accepted as unchangeable can never be changed. You think that you are stuck as you are and that there is no hope for any difference. That is not true."

"How do you know?"

"Listen, my dear, I have spent a lifetime altering conditions around me, but first I have had to make up my mind that things needed to be changed," Millijoy said. "Hear me out. I was born a bastard as the result of my mother, who was just a child at the time, being raped by a black man. The man was hanged, and my mother was forced to watch the hanging. The entire matter affected her mind. She died insane many years later. I was raised, through the benevolence of a benefactor, by a fairly well educated black woman. I could pass for white. But she used to tell me that I could accept myself as a Negro and live like one, or I could choose to live as a white and make something of myself. And when I chose to be a white, because whites had the opulent luxury that I desired, she told me to go to it, change my attitudes, make up my mind and go after anything and everything that I wanted. Well, I did. Triumph House is the result of a poor little mulatto girl's effort to alter the conditions of her life. That is why it is called Triumph House, because it is a monument to all that I have achieved. I wanted something so desperately that I would not permit anything to stand in my way of getting it. And if you really want to alter your physical condition, or any of the circumstances in your life, then you simply have to make up your mind to do something about it and do it."

"That's easy for you to say."

"Easy?" Millijoy made a contemptuous sound which was somewhere between a chuckle and a derisive moan. "Yes, *easy* because I have accomplished. I have lived in opulent luxury for years and years because I have literally pulled myself up by the bootstraps. No one did it for me. I did it myself. And if what I have done and my way of life is looked on by others with scorn and envy, that is *their* problem, not mine! Life is meant for overcoming, accepting challenges and meeting them head-on. You said you wanted to die. That is the coward's way out. But I believe, and you may find this difficult to comprehend, that if a person does not overcome the challenges of one lifetime, they must return to meet the same obstacles again—and perhaps, in the next, those conditions will be far more profound and difficult to resolve."

"You're speaking of other conditions."

"I'm speaking of any conditions, Peggy," Millijoy stated. "My life is coming to an end. When the time comes for my transition, I will die with a triumphant smile on my face. I only hope and pray that you will someday come to the realization of what I am saying. I cannot transmit confidence to you, or determination. Only you can do that for yourself. But I can be beside you with support and encouragement."

"Encouragement?"

"Moral support, if you like." Millijoy smiled broadly. "I believe in miracles. I've seen too many happen, not to believe otherwise. But miracles happen only when a decision to permit them to do so is first reached. One makes a decision to reach a desired goal. Next they erase all doubt that what they desire can be accomplished. It's called belief that it will happen. And third, one goes about expecting the miracle to come about, despite appearances which would make it seem otherwise. If you want to be transformed into a new woman, you must expect that it is possible."

"Transformed into a new woman?" Peggy's eyes brightened. "Oh, if only that were possible."

"It is! Anything is possible when you make up your mind that you want it," Millijoy stated. "All of my life

I've accepted challenges, as I said. I quite frankly think my days in this body are numbered—and the number isn't large. Don't mistake that for a desire for death, it isn't. No, no, it's an awareness I have that my days are nearly fulfilled. When I've accomplished everything I was meant to accomplish, I will no longer need to occupy this form. But, until then, I will. Yet there is a challenge or two more that I would like to accept. And one of those, Peggy, is to help you."

"Why should you want to help me?"

"Because, instinctively, I know you are destined to become a Phenwick Woman," Millijoy said. "Don't ask me how I know it, I just do."

"Katherine said that," Peggy remarked. "And he—that is, someone else mentioned that I was meant to be a Phenwick Woman."

"*He?* You said *he.*"

"Actually it was no one, merely a figment of my imagination," Peggy replied.

Millijoy smiled to herself. "Have you sufficiently caught your breath and gathered your wits to go into the next room with me?"

"I believe so."

Millijoy led the way. Then, when they entered the adjoining room, which was delicately decorated as a kind of study, she put her arm around Peggy's and led her to a large portrait which was hanging in good light.

"Cousin Ruth has a photograph of him," Peggy said. "It's Adam Truff, isn't it?"

"Then you've met him."

"Only through Cousin Ruth's photograph. He was certainly a handsome man, wasn't he?"

"I believe I loved Adam as much or more than I loved

any other man," Millijoy stated. "He had a way of calling me 'dear heart.' "

"Dear heart?" Peggy puzzled. "But I—"

"Yes?"

"Nothing." She had remembered thoughts or an image that had appeared to her on the train en route from California.

Again Millijoy smiled an enigmatic smile. "I believe Adam comes to visit me often. I sense his presence."

"Tell me about him."

Millijoy motioned for her to sit on a love seat, then she squeezed in beside Peggy.

"In life Adam was a man of mystery and magic, melodious flamboyance and mystical depth," Millijoy recited, as if they were thoughts she had previously put into words. "He was in this world, but he wasn't quite of it. It was as if he could never permit himself to be limited by the confines of convention and the restrictions of society. Turning his back on tradition, and sometimes propriety, he dramatically walked the paths of his own choosing. Oh, he was unorthodox, Adam was. Yet he had a kind of magnificence that could not be matched. I was certainly not the only one who loved him. The number must have been legion. But one does not love and capture a god in a little pen of confinement. The very nature of a god is to express himself in an uninhibited way, because his overview of life is far more sensitive and profound than the views of mere mortals. A man of mystery and magic? No. He was a miracle!"

"You paint a remarkable picture of the man," Peggy commented. She could sense that Millijoy was trembling with excitement when she spoke of Adam Truff.

"He was a god who permitted himself to be a human

for a while," Millijoy continued. "It was his human aspect to which I tried to relate. But he was a god who appreciated the splendid wonders around him. He loved nature, refreshing brooks, majestic mountains, the beauty of flowers."

"Flowers?" Peggy glanced curiously at Millijoy.

"Pansies, lilacs . . . roses."

"Roses?"

"Adam was especially fond of roses," Millijoy informed her. "On the day he died—and I'll never know how he did—he arranged for me to receive an enormous bouquet of red roses. When they arrived, I knew he was gone."

"Red roses?"

"I don't know if you've ever been aware of it," Millijoy said, "but red roses have a far more pungent aroma than any others . . . a rich, velvety scent. I know his spirit is present when I perceive the odor of roses when there are none around."

Peggy was staring at Millijoy, but her thoughts had returned to the train ride from San Francisco, to the compartment when she had been left alone, and to the reflection of the handsome man she had seen in the window glass. No wonder the likeness of Adam Truff seemed so familiar! But how was it possible?

Millijoy was chattering on, but Peggy's mind was elsewhere.

"So naturally with Tommy playing in Vienna," Millijoy was saying a few minutes later when Peggy's mind returned to the present moment, "I would like to accept the challenge of making one last trip to the Continent. I do love Germany and Austria—the entire of Europe, for that matter. I used to keep a town house in London, which I have since given to my son Tommy and Evelyn his wife.

You must meet Tommy and Evelyn. They are both really marvelously talented people—if I do brag on them."

"Tommy and Evelyn?" Peggy had missed the transition in Millijoy's train of thought. "Vienna?"

"And since I'm accepting challenges again," Millijoy continued, "I think it would be perfectly delightful for you to accompany Lanny and me to Vienna."

"I couldn't go to Europe," Peggy protested.

"And why not, may I ask?"

"Well, look at me."

"You look at you, and make up your mind to change that which you behold," Millijoy stated. "You have lovely features, a very pretty face beneath the bloat. And you have lovely, sparkling eyes, which are overshadowed by the puffiness that obscures them. Once you make up your mind and accept the challenge to change, you won't mind how people stare at you. Why, you can simply say to yourself, 'just wait until they see me transformed.' It will be marvelous! Now, I'll not take no for an answer. You *are* going to Vienna with us."

"I am?" Peggy was dubious, still a surge of fascination seemed to percolate within her. Did she dare consider going to Europe? Could she tolerate the staring and the unkind comments that would surely follow her? In her heart she wanted to set her mind on a new goal. With Millijoy's determination and confidence, she might just possibly be able to overcome that which had been a problem for her all of her life.

Tea was served in the upstairs sitting room when Katherine arrived from doing her errands. Lanny joined in the tea party.

Samson wheeled in the tea cart with a single red rosebud in a slender crystal vase among the tea things. He set a small table overlooking the terrace with one of the prettiest views of the ocean from Triumph House. Gulls were soaring, sweeping down in the wake of a small boat that was moving toward the city. A soft afternoon breeze whispered in through the open terrace doors. It brushed against the draperies to move them ever so slightly.

"Philip is very busy now," Katherine said as tea was being poured. "We couldn't possibly go to Vienna with you."

"Then, you come by yourself," Millijoy suggested.

"I couldn't leave Philip for that long a time," Katherine replied.

"You two young people are still so very much in love, aren't you?" Millijoy's question was more of a statement. "You richly deserve each other. Love is perfectly marvelous. I was in love myself once—several times."

"I wouldn't upset Philip for the world by even suggesting that I would be away from him for an extended period of time," Katherine said.

"Perhaps I'm not as strongly in love with Gordon Thomas as I should be," Lanny interjected. "I've lost track of the time that he's been away with the army. I do miss him; but I know that the only way to keep a love is by letting it go. He must be his own person and do what he feels he must. Still I envy the kind of love you and Philip have, Katherine. It is ideal."

"There is a reason for that," Katherine replied. Then she turned her attention to Peggy. "This talk of love, romance and husbands must be a little boring for you, mustn't it, Peggy?"

"I am interested in what you have to say," Peggy replied.

"I'm afraid that Katherine and I have chattered so much over the years," Lanny observed, "that when we get together, we monopolize conversation. It's that way with good friends."

"Peggy looked down at the teacup. She tried to smile. "I've never really had any close girl friends, no one with whom I could confide as you two must in each other. There's my sister Lola, of course, but we never really confided much when it came to intimate matters. As a matter of fact, I've often thought that Lola and I were strangers under the same roof. Still I have to admit it is a large roof."

"Well, since Katherine can't leave her precious Philip to travel to Vienna," Lanny said, "it will afford us the opportunity to get to know each other and become good friends."

"You would like that, wouldn't you, Peggy?" Millijoy asked.

"I'm cerain I would—that is, if I decide to go," Peggy replied.

"I thought that was already a foregone conclusion," Katherine remarked. "I mean, if it isn't, it should be."

"It has come up so all of a sudden," Peggy said, "that I haven't had adequate time to meditate upon it."

"What better have you to do?" Lanny questioned.

"Indeed," Millijoy echoed, "what better?"

"Is this a conspiracy?" Peggy inquired as she looked from one to the other.

"A conspiracy? What a notion!" exclaimed Lanny.

"Conspiring for your own good?" Millijoy asked.

"Then it is," Peggy said.

"We would not conspire to anything," Millijoy included, "unless we felt it would be to your benefit, Peggy.

Undoubtedly it won't be easy for you at first. And you may be stared at and hear little singular remarks about yourself. You must learn to use all that for your own welfare. Let such incidents give you incentive to conquer the windmills of your own confusion."

"My confusion?"

"You are confused, Peggy, that is all," Katherine inserted. "When you learn who and what you are, you'll find that things will be radically different for you."

"I'm confused by the confusion," Peggy said softly.

After tea and the conversation had pretty much played itself out, Katherine accompanied Lanny to her room to examine several new gowns which she had purchased. Peggy was invited to join them, but she declined.

"I've had no reason ever to be interested in fashion, have I, Cousin Millijoy?" Peggy asked when she was alone with the older woman.

"I can see where you might not," Millijoy returned. "You've really been blocked off from the outside world, haven't you?"

"Far more than I had realized in the past."

"Then it is time you emerged from your protective closet and see what the world is really like."

Millijoy excused herself for a few minutes, explaining that she wished to see Samson about some matter.

Peggy thought Millijoy's tactics peculiar, since it would seem logical for her simply to ring for the servant and have him come to her. Still she did not dwell on the matter.

Once alone, Peggy rose and went to gaze out at the water. A singular thought lighted her mind, as if she knew beyond a doubt that she was on the brink of a dramatic transformation about to take place in her life. The thought both amazed and amused her.

Leaving the terrace, Peggy went into the study where her attention immediately went to the portrait of Adam Truff. If only, she thought, a man like that could come into her life. What a notion! Then the thought came that even if such a man were to enter her life, he could only react negatively toward her because she had accepted herself as a grotesque creature. *Accepted herself?* Had she? Was that precisely what she had done? If that indeed was the case, she had better make up her mind to do something about it.

Was the portrait of Adam Truff smiling at her?

As she stared incredulously at the painting, Peggy again became aware of the scent of roses. This time she was not startled. A curious thought came, a man like Adam Truff *had* come into her life—but not in the way that she ever had imagined could possibly be.

Chapter Eight

Donald had always had a fine rapport with Millijoy Phenwick; there was a mutual admiration and respect between the two. After receiving the report from the specialists, Donald spoke with his mother and sister about the prospects of undergoing the required operations. Polly and Albert agreed to stay at Edward House with Ruth while Donald was hospitalized.

John Phenwick was the only other member of the

family who was told about the impending plans. He offered all the support to Donald that he could give and promised to make whatever special arrangements were necessary. However, he did suggest that it would be well for the young man to take Millijoy into his confidence.

"I'll cancel the trip to Vienna," Millijoy exclaimed on that warm afternoon when Donald called at Triumph House.

"You'll do no such thing, Aunt Millijoy," Donald replied. "I love you dearly and appreciate your concern, but there is absolutely nothing you can do here in Boston while I'm undergoing the ordeal."

"I can give you moral support," Millijoy charged.

"And I would appreciate that. But it is unnecessary," Donald returned. "I will sense your moral support from wherever you may be."

"You have many of your father's characteristics," Millijoy said. "Stuart had a stubborn streak, too. I will not enjoy the Continent knowing the agony you must be suffering."

"But only I can suffer, dear Aunt Millijoy," Donald observed. "I have heard that Peggy is planning to travel with you. It may be difficult for her."

"I'm well aware of that," Millijoy responded. "It is my hope that it will be so uncomfortable for her that she will finally take the bull by the horns and do something constructive to alter her appearance. Needless to say, Lanny and I will be there to give her all of the support that we possibly can. Like you she will have to face the ultimate eventuality by herself. I have great plans for her."

"Dear Aunt Millijoy, the grand manipulator!" Donald commented.

"Isn't that what life is all about: manipulating to one

extent or another?" Millijoy took a pose as if she had pronounced an edict. "Unfortunately, all persons do not have
the basic gumption to motivate themselves, nor to handle
their own manipulations."

"And that's where you come in?"

"Precisely. I like to think of myself more as a motivator than a downright manipulator," Millijoy said. "I suppose one is simply a degree of the other, still motivator
has more of a subtle quality to it, don't you think?"

Donald laughed.

"I'm glad you still have a sense of humor, Donald, in
spite of what you must face."

"A person such as me requires a sense of humor."

"Do I detect a note of self-pity?" Millijoy asked.

"I try to avoid self-pity. But I have accepted the reality
of my physical being," Donald said. "Well—I've adjusted
to it." He looked out the window to the ocean beyond. A
melancholy expression came over his handsome features.

"What's troubling you?" Millijoy asked after studying
him.

"Troubling?"

"Don't try to pass it over with naiveté," Millijoy returned. "There *is* something troubling you. And I perceive
it is not the forthcoming operations that concern you at
this moment."

"Always perceptive, aren't you, Aunt Millijoy?"

"I try to be."

Donald repositioned himself. "I think I've fallen in
love." He stared straight into Millijoy's face until the
reaction in her eyes became too intense and he turned
away. "I suppose that sounds strange, doesn't it?"

"Why should it sound strange? It's a perfectly normal
thing to happen."

"For other people," Donald said, "those who are whole and can function properly."

"I was right. You *are* nursing self-pity!"

"No, not self-pity, I think. I am simply facing facts."

"Are you attempting to tell me that you're impotent?"

Donald laughed. "No, not that. But my leg—"

"Poppycock! That's what I say it is! It is self-pity poorly disguised," Millijoy observed. "I've known of amputees who have had a perfectly marvelous romantic life."

"Many?"

"No, *one,* but that proves my point."

"Not to me, Aunt Millijoy."

"Well, it should." She thought a moment. "Who is the young lady of your interest?"

"You may think it peculiar, but it is Peggy."

"Peggy Phenwick?" Millijoy asked with amazement.

"Yes."

Millijoy turned her head away for fear a singular expression might betray her immediate reactions. "Peggy has an interesting personality, Donald. And I believe, beneath her padded exterior, she has beauty and perhaps a lovely personality, but—"

"But—?"

Millijoy rose and walked about the room as she spoke. "Do you actually love her—romantically love her—or do you only feel sorry for her?"

"I love her."

"You answered that too quickly," Millijoy said. "Think about it for a minute."

"Peggy and I have corresponded for the last several years. I believe I know her better than anyone else. She has deep thoughts and warm emotions."

Millijoy crossed to where he was seated. "Are you physically attracted to her?"

"I—well—I believe I am."

"Your hesitation tells me more than your words." Millijoy put her hand to his shoulder. "You feel sorry for her, don't you?"

"I told you that I love her."

"Pity isn't love."

"I don't pity her!"

"Don't you?" Millijoy patted his cheek. "I understand, Donald. I can see what's going on in your mind. You think of yourself as a cripple and, therefore, you would settle for another who is a cripple in her own way, rather than seek a woman who is completely attractive to you. How long do you think a relationship would last on pity? Eventually that pity will be used against you and develop into contempt, frustration and God only knows what else! You're not blind in both eyes, Donald. You can see what Peggy is. However, suppose she were to change, completely change and emerge an elegant lady, slim and lovely in every way. Would you suddenly feel incompetent, inadequate to her?"

"I—I don't know."

"That is exactly what I thought, you don't know," Millijoy replied. "Or consider another supposition, that your operations are thoroughly successful and you can walk as straight and upright as any other man, but Peggy does not succeed in making a physical transformation. How would you feel toward her then?"

"I would still only have one eye."

"The patch merely augments the mystique of your appearance," Millijoy commented. "It gives you an air of fascination."

"But suppose neither of us changes for the better?" Donald said.

"That only time will reveal," Millijoy said. "I don't say your feelings of love toward Peggy are wrong, only that they are not on a firm basis for what true love is."

"And what is that?"

"Complete physical, spiritual and mental attraction," Millijoy replied.

"You speak as if you know that for a fact."

"I know it as a theory," Millijoy confessed. "I have been in love. You know, of course, that I was very much in love with your father for years. The fact is, I settled for becoming his close friend and confidant because he was already married. I was deeply disappointed when he took your mother for his second wife. And, while I'm baring my soul, I might as well admit that I was deeply in love with Adam Truff. That love, too, developed into a special friendship and closeness. Apparently in both cases, there was never a complete physical, spiritual and mental attraction for each of us. Well, both Stuart and Adam are dead. I've continued on. Believe me, Donald, I know what love is—I simply haven't been able to accomplish it fully."

"And you would wish to deprive me of a little love?"

"Not deprive you, Donald. If you told me at this moment that you were madly in love with Peggy and wanted to marry her at the earliest possible time, I would give you my blessings and best wishes. Furthermore, I would do everything in my power to help each of you."

"Can't you see that I have strong feelings for Peggy as she is right now, for what she is?"

"I see that perfectly well, dear boy," Millijoy rejoined.

"But I am aware that strong feelings and love are two different matters. Take time to meditate on that."

"I shall." Donald stood up, embraced Millijoy and hobbled from the room. "Thank you for finding time to speak with me."

"And thank you for coming to speak with me."

Millijoy was concerned. She had given much thought to Donald and his physical state. She tried not to feel sorry for him, but it was as difficult not to feel pity for Donald as it was not to so for Peggy. Perhaps they could make each other happy.

Later that day, Lanny entered Millijoy's second floor rooms. Although she had every right to the title, she was not known as a Phenwick Woman. Still she had taken her rightful place as Millijoy's granddaughter and heiress apparent to Triumph House, since Tommy and Evelyn had purchased property in England and France, where they preferred to live.

"Ah, Lanny! I was hoping you would come in to see me," Millijoy exclaimed upon seeing the pretty swarthy-skinned young lady. "Is something troubling you? You appear to have the weight of the world on your shoulders."

Lanny smiled, but her turgid lips quickly reverted into a petulant expression. "The world has a certain heaviness from time to time, Grandmother."

"Have you received word from Gordon Thomas?"

"He is being sent to Africa, whatever for, goodness only know."

"No wonder you're wearing such a concerned expression."

"I've accepted the fact that Gordon Thomas is a soldier," Lanny returned. "And I refuse to be a typical soldier's wife. He chose to go into the army, I suspect in defiance of his father's wishes."

"*Your* father's wishes," Millijoy corrected.

"How strange it is to be married to a man who was raised by a man he had known as his father, only to discover that Tommy is *my* father and not Gordon Thomas'. I hope I never have to explain that to my grandchildren." She laughed.

"You would do well not to have children," Millijoy stated, "much less grandchildren."

"Why? Because the Negro strain you tried to eliminate would still be there?" Lanny questioned. "You and I have so much in common, Grandmother, yet we have such different views about things. I would welcome having mulatto children and raising them as the individuals that they are, not in a patronizing way because they were born a combination of two races. Frankly, I've discussed it with Gordon Thomas, and we agree that the truly strong persons in this world will eventually be those of mixed races. The world is progressively becoming smaller. In time, I suspect that long-distance travel will take only a matter of hours. Races and nationalities ultimately will be forced to join for the survival of all."

"Profound thoughts, Lanny."

"Yes, aren't they."

"And are such thoughts what are troubling you?" Millijoy questioned.

"Such thoughts are always with me," Lanny returned. "I usually don't wear them so obviously on the surface. But, as usual, Grandmother, you are perceptive. My concern is about Peggy."

"How so?"

"I took her shopping today," Lanny replied. "She was

so conspicuous and drew so much attention that I was embarrassed for her. Then, when I took her to the seamstress, the woman could not help but make derogatory comments about Peggy's size. I tried to catch her attention before the damage was done. I was too late."

"You must learn to use such embarrassing moments to Peggy's advantage."

"I?"

"In a roundabout way," Millijoy continued. "I am of the opinion that every incentive must be given to help Peggy see the necessity for changing herself."

"Interfering as usual, Grandmother?"

"Some matters require interference."

"What would you have done were you in Peggy's place?"

"I would have simply told the seamstress that the dress was only to be worn temporarily, and that it would doubtlessly have to be taken in before long, that I was determined to change my size."

"That would be you, Grandmother. At this point, it would not be Peggy." Lanny moved about the room. "We've become good friends. I think I can understand and relate to her far better than Katherine can."

"I'm pleased to hear that," Millijoy commented. "And have you thoroughly convinced her that wonders can be done for her in Europe?"

"Not *thoroughly*."

"I've written to Augustus Ornby, whom you've never met," Millijoy said. "He's quite a famous doctor in Vienna. He has achieved worldwide fame as a psychiatrist."

"And how do you suppose a psychiatrist can help someone like Peggy?"

"Very simply in that much of her problem is mental

and the emotional attitudes with which she reacts to various things," Millijoy explained. "Dr. Joseph told me that. Augustus is Joseph's brother, you know."

Lanny stretched. "You know, I don't comprehend how you're going to do it, Grandmother, but I'm convinced you'll manage to see that Peggy makes a transformation—one way or another."

"You can be certain of that," Millijoy stated. Then, catching a curious look in Lanny's eyes, she laughed too.

Chapter Nine

Most journeys have an element of monotony about them. Despite the activities designed to occupy one's time and make sea voyages less tedious, there was still a feeling that one was confined to the vessel, ergo unable to experience a true sense of freedom. Then, too, there were the changing seas and unusual weather conditions which made for alterations in plans to accommodate the sudden and unexpected.

Because of her extensive travels, Millijoy used the time aboard ship to lounge about and rest up for the active schedule she anticipated ahead. Much of her time was spent reading or napping. The sea air agreed with her, which seemed to have an invigorating reaction on her. Since they were traveling on a Medallion ship, the captain was familiar to her; and at times when she was not acquainted with the captain of a particular ship, it was a certainty that she would know him quite well before they reached their destination.

Lanny, on the other hand, had done little traveling overseas. This was a relatively new and exciting experience for her. Of course, being with Millijoy, she was bound to encounter many situations the average traveler would not meet. Intensely pretty, Lanny's beauty had a way of attracting all sorts of people, who looked on her as some exotic creature, probably of nobility. Since she was gowned in fashionable luxury, speculation arose about her.

Eagerly Lanny moved about the ship with ease. Graceful and as aristocratic as a princess, her dark skin added to the texture of mystery about her. Her eyes met many different sets of eyes, many of which reflected intrigue and fascination. Men continuously stared, and there was little left to the imagination as to what most of them were contemplating when they surveyed Lanny. She had a coy way of returning such glances which could easily be construed as being flirtatious.

While on occasion Peggy had observed her sister Lola maneuver among men, tease and lead them on, she was astounded to see with what ease Lanny was able to arouse interest, entice and as quickly let the man know precisely where his place was. With the exception of her experience with Damien Brusco, Peggy had had no association with men. They simply had never been attracted to her. And after the fiasco with Damien, she had a bad taste in her mouth about men in general. Still she was absolutely amazed to watch Lanny as she handled herself among them.

"Every one of those men has a desire to be intimate with you," Peggy observed on the third evening out as the two were taking a quiet supper in the cabin which they shared.

"Men are predictable," Lanny replied. "Grandmother warned me that men—especially single men—aboard ship are notorious for their behavior. A shipboard romance is a part of a game they like to play. There are even married men who during such times are out for a little adventure on the side, especially if they have a wife who is on the sickly side, going to Europe to take a cure of some sort or another." She laughed. "But men are basically harmless as long as you know to handle yourself. They have the reputation for being the aggressors, but it is my observation that they are rarely aggressive unless they have been incited by the female to do so."

"I don't understand," Peggy said innocently.

"It is the man's basic nature to be eager, always ready for stimulation," Lanny commented, "but it is only when the woman is provocative and alluring that they really ever make a move. That is why men are so easily manipulated by conniving women."

"Obviously I'm far from being provocative and alluring," Peggy said. "I know when I had that situation with Mr. Brusco, I was flabbergasted to know what had attracted him to me. When he explained that he liked large women, I suppose something innately within me responded. I had never previously attracted a man in such a way. I really must have been a fool, and Mr. Brusco could not have helped but realize that. He must have laughed at me and my eager attitude. Now that I know my father had hired him to do what he did, I look back and see how stupid I was." She sighed. "But you see, it was all so very new to me."

"You should have married him in spite of his persuasions," Lanny remarked.

"No. Never. I'm basically too possessive," Peggy returned. "I could never share my toys with Lola when I was a child—what was mine was solely mine. If I was that way with such insignificant objects, imagine how I would be with a husband."

"You would possess him to death," Lanny commented. "I dearly love Gordon Thomas, but I know how foolish it would be of me to attempt to hold him and keep him from doing what he wants. When he first announced that he could get a commission in the army, I was left speechless. The idea of his being away from me for long periods of time, or my following him about living in makeshift accommodations was repulsive to me. I had a choice to let him go, or to follow him. I let him go—and I believe our love for each other has become stronger because of that. Oh, I once thought I would be terribly possessive with a man—no longer. I, too, enjoy my freedom."

"Do you—I mean, have you ever been with other men?" Peggy dared to ask.

"Do you mean since I've been married?" Lanny smiled curiously, which, if Peggy had been more worldly wise and perceptive about such matters, would have been all the answer needed. "I enjoy the company of other men in a social sense, Peggy. I'm certain, for instance, that Grandmother will have a list of gentlemen of nobility and the like for me to meet and perhaps allow them to escort me to various events. She has already said as much—or should I say 'promised'?" She giggled. "You mustn't look so shocked, Peggy. Simply because I permit myself to be escorted, shouldn't necessarily imply that anything— well—romantic is to happen."

"Were I in your place," Peggy admitted, "I fear I would do everything in my power to incite them to—you know."

"Ah, but you've not had the—I don't mean to make an issue of this, please forgive me—you've not had the opportunity and experience. I suspect you would react from a basic need within you—a basic hunger, if I may say so." Lanny sipped from her wineglass. "I *do* understand you, Peggy. And I realize that I merely eased into my overall experience with men as naturally as I learned the other basic ingredients of life. You, on the other hand, have not had the chance to grow naturally into the experience of human relationships. I think of you as a person who has been imprisoned, and upon your release, you're liable to try to make up for lost time."

"I'm a long way from being released," Peggy said with a shrug.

"But you will be, Peggy. I only pray that you will be able to handle the newfound freedom."

"Let me know the freedom first, then I'll let you know if I can handle it or not."

Lanny placed her hand on Peggy's and squeezed.

On the next to the last day at sea, Peggy was seated on the deck in an isolated place where she felt she would not attract the attention of the curious. She enjoyed solitude because she had been alone for so much of her life. Impossible dreams filled her fantasies, and she thought of several different stories which Lanny had told her. Life was so easy and uncomplicated for her distant cousin. She accepted it as it came, made the most of it and catalogued

it in the book of her memories. Conversely, it seemed that
Peggy had been fighting life and every experience in it.
Yet she had many, many unfulfilled dreams, wishes,
desires. Why shouldn't she? Her fundamental being was
as normal and responsive as Lanny's. She hated being different, despised feeling that she had to hide from normal
activity and from the critical glances of those who func-
tioned in such accepted ways.

A shadow fell across Peggy's face, although she was
wearing a broad-brimmed straw hat. She gazed up to see
a pair of trousered legs standing a few feet from her. Following the line of his trousers in an upward sweep of her
eyes, she met the curious expression of a somewhat small
man with black hair and a small moustache. Dark brown
eyes were like those of an animal. He was staring; and
even when his eyes met hers, it took him a moment or
two to react. Peggy smiled as she had observed Lanny do.

"Ah, ma'moiselle, I have never seen so much of heaven
in one place," he blurted.

Peggy pointed upward. "Heaven is in *that* direction."

"That depends on one's definition of heaven," he replied with a noticeable touch of a French accent. "I believe that one's heaven can be another's hell, and vice
versa. But, of course, I am not speaking in an ecclesiastic
sense. I am not a religious man. Are you a religious
woman?"

"I attend church."

"But that has nothing to do with being religious," he
returned. "I still go to confession, simply because I like to
imagine what the expression is on the dear priest's face
when he hears all I have to tell him. Then he says he will
pray for me and to go and sin no more. At that I say,
'surely you don't call what I have told you sinning.' There

is usually a long pause of silence before I am abruptly dismissed. When I was a child, I used to love making up the wildest tales to tell in the confessional booth. Most of them were sheer fantasies—*then*." He smiled down at Peggy with a twisted, twitching smile. "Do you mind if I sit with you for a while?"

"I was meditating."

"Ah, then *you* must be religious."

"Not meditating on spiritual matters," Peggy hurriedly clarified.

"Then permit me to introduce myself. I am Andre Ceillo." He touched his hat and clicked his heels together. If he had not made the last gesture, Peggy might not have become suspicious; but the clicking of heels reminded her of Damien Brusco.

"I am Miss Peggy Phenwick."

"Ah, Phenwick!" Obviously he had recognized the name. He pulled up a chair and sat facing her from the side. "I confess you delight my imagination, ma'moiselle. I have a fascination for women who are larger than I. But then, I am a diminutive man. In the part of France from where I come, all of the people are generally small. It is characteristic of us. But that does not keep me from admiring large people."

"Before you go any further, Mr. Ceillo," Peggy said, "I wish to know one thing. Are you acquainted with my father, Mr. Paul Phenwick of San Francisco?"

"Never! I do not know San Francisco," he replied with a look of disdain. "Of course you have a father, but I do not know him. I confess to you that I am a man of few words and a great amount of action, if you know what I mean." He touched her upper arm and reacted with a giggly shiver. He smiled, pursing his lips, and gave the impression of a naughty little boy. "I am easily stimulated."

"You've only just met me, Mr. Ceillo."

"I believe in predestination," Andre said. "And I believe that we were predestined to meet on this voyage. I have watched you from the first day aboard. You were always with that dark young lady, so I observed from afar." He put his arm around her shoulder and inched over until he had one hip on the chaise with her. Then he scooted up so that he could look deeply into her eyes. "Don't you find me stimulating? I may be diminutive, but I have—how do you say?—potentialities." Quickly he glanced in each direction before he lunged his face at hers.

The abrupt movement augmented by the additional weight on the wooden frame chaise caused it to groan, creak and eventually snap. The piece of furniture collapsed just as Andre's lips touched Peggy's. She shrieked as she plunged the eighteen inches to the deck, and Andre landed sprawling on top of her. Without reacting to the shock, he pursued the object of his desire.

A cabin boy had heard the crash and, bringing assistance, ran to see what had happened. The sight the two young men beheld was so ludicrous that they both broke forth with convulsive laughter.

Andre glanced up, moving his eyes but not his lips. Infuriated by the audience, he suddenly jerked up and with the ease of a gymnast, he was on his feet. "How dare you spy on us?"

"You've broken the chair, sir," the cabin boy said. "This is hardly the place for that sort of thing. And that chair was meant for casual sitting, not energetic activity, sir. I'll have to report this to the captain, sir, and you'll probably receive a charge for the furniture on your bill, sir."

"The effrontery of the plebians!" Andre all but screamed. "Do you happen to know that this lady is Miss Phenwick, herself, of the Phenwicks who own the Medallion ships?"

Peggy was like a turtle who had been turned onto its back. She was unable to roll or thrust herself into a position so she could push herself upright. Furthermore, part of the chaise was prodding her uncomfortably in the back.

"Do you mind helping me up?" Peggy asked.

Both the cabin boy and Andre reached a hand down to Peggy. They each pulled, but she jerked them down so that they both landed on top of her.

"Ah, the capacity of big women!" shrieked Andre as he took advantage of the situation and rolled from side to side.

"Get me up from here!" Peggy demanded.

The cabin boy scampered to his feet and motioned for the other young man to come and assist. Peggy had to knock Andre to the side. Then, with two pulling her and the third pushing from the underside, they finally managed to get her into a sitting position and ultimately to her feet.

Embarrassed by the circumstance, and in pain from the actual physical abuse, Peggy asked the cabin boy to escort her to her cabin. He complied despite the protests of Andre Ceillo, who ardently desired to see her to her accommodations. Peggy had had all of the man that she could take for one day.

That night there was a concert aboard ship. Peggy attended it with Lanny. Halfway through the program Lanny called her attention to the figure of a little man moving from seat to seat. When she got a closer look, Peggy realized that it was Andre Ceillo. Although he peri-

odically sat, shortly after there came an offended sound
and Andre abruptly rose.

"That's Andre Ceillo," Lanny whispered to Peggy.
"He's a pest. And he fancies himself a gigolo. Wait until
after the concert and I'll tell you some of the stories I
heard about him this afternoon."

Peggy quite frankly did not want to hear tales about
Andre Ceillo. He was an unprincipled opportunist. It disturbed her to think that she had almost fallen for his line.
But she still remembered the touch of his lips on hers,
and how she had responded to such stimulation. It both
fascinated and worried her.

Chapter Ten

Wherever Millijoy went in Europe, it seemed she
was either personally well known, or her reputation was
so fabled that her name was whispered in the salons as
one of the—to put it mildly—most interesting women of
international fame. She had hobnobbed with royalty and
pretenders, the extremely wealthy and the elite. To many
she represented the epitome of American aristocracy. An
international investor, she had multiplied her fortune into
an overwhelming sum, which put her among the capitalis-
tic giants of the early twentieth century.

It was an era when monarchies were beginning to
crumble and royalty were scratching out whatever they
could to maintain themselves. Hence, it was a time when
many an impoverished noble desperately sought to marry

into wealth, whatever the price to his pride and his basic desires. When it had been announced that the notorious Millijoy Phenwick was planning to visit Vienna, Zürich and several other European cities, those individuals who had need to bolster their sagging fortunes—if they had any at all to speak of—made every effort to maneuver to be thrown into the vicinity of the great lady. Such methods and approaches were familiar to Millijoy, and they amused her. Even she was romantically pursued by men of all ages.

Millijoy always took a certain fascination in the machinations of such would-be suitors. They invariably had polish and class, manners and distinctive good looks; and not all of them were vacuous ninnies and idle fops. The young men who tried to gain her favors, some of them thirty years her junior, most intrigued her. Yet she felt certain compassion for them and their needs. Although her romantic interest in men had somewhat diminished, she was flattered by the attention she received, and needless to say, she took advantage of it.

Naturally, because of the notoriety of the Phenwick name, those persons associated with Millijoy were, in their own ways, considered as celebrities, too—especially if they had the Phenwick name. And the name that attracted most attention on most invitational lists was that of *Miss* Peggy Phenwick.

When Millijoy and her party arrived in Vienna and were settled into the Franz Josef Hotel in an elegant suite of rooms, old friends and acquaintances began to call. Naturally there was great curiosity about the unmarried Phenwick lady. Once Peggy was met, however, the grapevine quickly carried the news that she was not particularly physically desirable, but that she was a Phenwick and doubtlessly an heiress to a considerable fortune. To make matters interesting, Millijoy let it be known that she herself would offer a considerable dowry to the man who won Peggy's affection.

Consequently, the men came and tried to overlook appearances. Peggy had never received such interest in all her life. At first she was absolutely amazed by the attention. Yet she would have been utterly nonchalant not to be aware that there were unscrupulous motives behind the interest which was shown her. It was the attitudes of the women that bothered her. She often heard the usual whispered comments about her appearance and she could not help but observe the attitudes of disdain and critical appraisal of her.

"Of course I find most of the men terribly attractive and interesting," Peggy confided to Lanny at the end of their first week in Vienna, "but I am not naive. I know what they are after, and it isn't the lovely Peggy Phenwick, the freak from San Francisco. They're nothing but gold diggers, which is an unkind expression used at home. Even Lola has been pursued by such men."

"You are right, Peggy," Lanny remarked as she sat back in a comfortable chair and studied her cousin. "But I do wish you would stop referring to yourself as a freak."

"That's what I am," Peggy replied. "Frankly, it saddens me to think that so many men are so desperate that they would have to stoop to such tactics—and be willing to settle for me."

"But I know you, Peggy. I'm aware of the kind of person you are," Lanny said. "You could undoubtedly make a man extremely pleased, to feel well loved. I'm certain you have the capacity to give—well—spiritual compassion and comfort to a man."

"Spiritual compassion?" Peggy bit. "How many of those men are looking for spiritual compassion? Furthermore, there are few, even if they were, who would settle for that to compensate for what they truly desire."

"All right, they're leeches," Lanny explained, "but they are men."

"Do you know it is that very fact that has made me make up my mind to change myself?" Peggy stated.

Lanny sat forward. "You have?"

Peggy's eyes met the deep brown, almost black eyes of Lanny. Her jaw tightened as a defiant expression came to her face. Then there was a look of determination. "I cannot say precisely what has caused me to reach such a decision. I suspect it has been an accumulation of several things. Perhaps the first thing that comes to mind is the fact that I find myself very much attracted to men. I keep thinking how wonderful it would be if any one of them were to like me—really like me because I was me and not simply because I am a wealthy Phenwick. It seems my curiosity has been whetted to the point I want to find what it would be like to experience life as other women do."

Lanny rose, went to Peggy and hugged her. "That's a beginning, dearest cousin, a very good beginning."

The office of Dr. Augustus Ornby was in a newer building in Vienna, near the opera house. The interior was done in paneled oak, lightly stained and varnished. The furniture was covered in deep velvet in shades of light blue and soft rust. The atmosphere was pleasant and conducive to making a person able to relax quite quickly. Diplomas and honorary certificates of award were on the walls, and he always made a point of having a fresh bouquet of flowers on a library table.

Bearded and ruggedly handsome, Augustus Ornby was not as stockily built as his brother Joseph of Boston. He had a kindly father appearance, which in itself set many of his patients at ease and made them open up to him. His understanding face represented the understanding father who possessed spiritual compassion. He was an authority and deeply involved in his work.

Peggy was shown to a large, comfortable armchair after Augustus warmly greeted her, more than just another patient, but as a member of the family. They chatted briefly as a matter of getting acquainted before he opened a file on his desk and hurriedly scanned the letter which lay on top.

"I feel as if I know you, Peggy," Augustus stated as he glanced up from the handwritten page. "I have been well prepared for your arrival."

"Prepared for me. Cousin Millijoy?"

"Admittedly I had tea with dear Millijoy two days ago," Augustus replied. "She is a person with a vast and wonderful personality. I've always enjoyed the times we two have had together."

"Well, at least the ice has been broken, hasn't it?" Peggy commented, a bit uncomfortable since she wondered what exactly Augustus had been told about her.

"I will tell you that I have also received several letters from my brother in Boston, Dr. Joseph Ornby," Augustus continued. "And I have here two epistles from your father and another from your cousin Donald. It seems there is great concern over you."

Peggy looked down at her thick fingers.

"I will be perfectly honest with you," Augustus said,

"and tell you precisely what I wrote to my brother, which was basically the same thing I told Millijoy. And that is, although I would gladly interview you and listen to your problems, I will make no attempt to do anything to help you alter your condition until you wish beyond a doubt to do something about it. Perhaps I can motivate you to a certain point, but only you can have the desire to make a change. Without such a desire, everything you attempt under coercion would fail. A person must desperately want to alter circumstances before they can be improved."

"I'm fully aware of that, Doctor."

"Please, we're cousins, you must call me Aug as the others do."

"Very well, Aug." Peggy felt awkward and inadequate to the situation. Still she realized that she had to put forth her best effort and be as honest as she possibly could be under the circumstances. "I believe I do want to change."

"What has brought this decision about?"

"For years I have remained closeted away from the outside world, Aug," she related. "I've actually hidden. Now I have been given a taste of what life is really like—not what my fantasies have created, rationalized because of my physical condition. I will honestly say that I have wished to die."

"To escape?"

"Yes, to escape." Peggy swallowed hard. "This is difficult for me."

"I am well aware of that, Peggy." Augustus folded his hands and sat back in the chair. "You have a sister, haven't you?"

"Yes. Lola."

"She is quite the opposite of you in physical appearance, isn't she?"

"Yes, very much so."

"Do you resent her?"

"I suppose I do—I must have always done so."

"Did you feel that Lola received more love and attention when she was a little girl?"

"Her personality was such that she simply took whatever attention she wanted," Peggy replied. "I think our parents and our brothers loved us equally well, it's just that Lola was able to get a more explicit show of interest. I was always plump, Lola was little and cute. We were so very different."

"And to augment your difference, you did everything you could to perpetuate it," Augustus suggested. "Isn't that so?"

"I don't believe I was consciously aware of doing such a thing," Peggy replied. "But, when I think back, I am convinced that I must have."

"Do you feel that you actually felt hatred for your sister?"

Peggy thought a moment. "Yes, I probably did—at least when we were children. I know I terribly resented her. I can recall having thoughts that I would be entirely different if she had never been born."

"But she was, so there was nothing you could do about that—other than to yourself."

"I know what you're saying. I understand."

"Yet you believe your problem is much deeper than your surface relationship with your sister, don't you?"

"I suspect it must be."

"Do you have any idea what it is?"

"No."

"Then that is what we must discover, mustn't we?"

"Yes."

"Peggy, I am going to make a radical suggestion to you," Augustus said after giving a few minutes to thought. "I want to suggest a drastic course for you. We will start with several sessions of probing into your subconscious mind to see if we can't find exactly what has motivated you to become as you are. At the same time we will examine your motivations for desiring change. That, however, is merely preliminary work. The difficult part will come later."

"You make it sound a horrendous ordeal."

"It well may be, Peggy," Augustus replied. "But if you truly desire to change—and it will be a change that takes place both within as well as without—such drastic measures must be taken."

"Such as what?"

"It will require a dedicated six-month period of severe programming," Augustus said. "I have a colleague in Germany who operates a spa designed to help persons like you. He is both a medical man and a psychologist. Dr. Kristofer Werner is his name. He only works with patients who have an acute problem, such as you have. It quite frankly will mean a six-month period of rigid routine and strict confinement. I should imagine that, at least at first, it would seem like a rendition of hell, pure and simple. You may find it extremely unpleasant and not at all to your liking. Still I wonder if it can be much different from the closet in which you have put yourself for most of your life."

"You make it sound like a prison," Peggy said.

"Confinement, yes; but the prison you are in, Peggy, is of your own making. You carry it around with you all of the time. You have constructed your own prison walls over many years. Can't you see how you've locked yourself in?"

"Yes, I can. There was a time when I would violently deny that; but in my heart of hearts, I know that it is true," she said softly, surprised to hear herself uttering such thoughts.

"Then, if you can come to think of it as a more concentrated form of confinement for six months, and cooperate to the fullest of your ability to do so, I believe you will emerge like a gorgeous butterfly from an ugly cocoon. You'll have to keep your mind on that goal constantly and not on the physical, mental and emotional battle you must wage to accomplish it."

"You frighten me."

"I cannot deceive you and tell you that it will be an easy matter to accomplish," Augustus said. "There will be times when you will want to abandon the project, to run away, to slip back into your old way of doing things. But, believe me, anything worth accomplishing was never done easily. You must thoroughly understand before you consent to go through with this."

Peggy frowned. "I must think about this. I've already begun to tremble with apprehension."

"Of course you must reach the conclusion, beyond a doubt, that you want to put yourself through all of it," Augustus said. "I will see you again tomorrow."

When Peggy returned to the hotel that afternoon, she found a letter waiting for her from Donald. He had undergone the first of several projected operations and was in the process of recovering from it. He wrote: "I am confined to bed; but if all this will help me improve my condition, it will be well worth the agony I must endure."

Donald's words, more than any other, convinced Peggy that she would submit fully to the treatment and all that was involved in it. She had no concept what hell would be like, but she had her suspicions.

Chapter Eleven

Peggy stood before the long window on the third floor of the hotel, which overlooked a garden courtyard. The flowers of summer were blooming in profusion. The bright colors, especially the reds and yellows, caused her to reflect on the life she had known in San Francisco. Flowers had always fascinated her. In a sense, they were a means of escape for her. She could admire their beauty, their graceful splendor and let her mind wander to an ideal world of her creation wherein all things were lovely—even her.

She counted up the months. It was July. Six months from then, it would be January, the ground would be covered with snow. Was it possible that she could possibly evolve into another person by then? The thought both intrigued and terrified her.

Peggy had received another letter that day from Donald. After initially perusing it, she reread it several times. In some ways his words were puzzling, as if a hidden meaning lay behind them. At other places, he expressed encouragement and extreme optimism. "I was asked: What is it that I most want to accomplish? If I keep doing the things that I am doing, the way that I'm doing them, will they get me to my goal? And when I finally analyzed what that was all about, I realized that I simply had to change what I was doing and the way that I was doing it. I *do* have a very definite goal now, and I intend to accomplish it."

A smile touched Peggy's lips as she reread Donald's affirmation. Yet she wondered what his specific goal might be. In thinking back, she had never recalled his speaking of any women in his life—other than his mother and sister. Although Polly had been in a way responsible for his physical disability, he adulated her. Peggy decided that Donald's goal was not a woman—but she could have been mistaken.

"A goal?" Millijoy questioned later that same day when Peggy went to take tea with her. "Of course I have always had a world of goals, far more, perhaps, than I could ever hope to accomplish in one little lifetime. One goal initiates the next and still the next after that. In fact, I can think of no accomplishment that is achieved without first it was goal, a thought perceived and worked toward. But one must be minutely specific about whatever goals one has in mind."

"Specific?" Peggy questioned.

"Most certainly. The mind has to have formed an exact image of that which one wishes to accomplish," Millijoy replied. "It is not enough, for instance, for one to desire money or wealth. A dollar is money. No, it is absolutely necessary to know precisely how much money one wants. Or if one desires a lover, one must know the qualities and the sort of personality he wishes to see in such a person. Otherwise, if one doesn't specify exactly what he wants, he has to settle for what he gets—and that may be something far removed from what he would idealistically want."

"You're speaking in abstract terms," Peggy commented.

"Not necessarily," Millijoy rejoined. "It has been my experience that most people do not know exactly what they want. Oh, they may have some vague idea or a notion about what they might like to have, but they rarely give it scientific thought—that is, outline the ingredients of their desires. Take yourself, for instance. You would like to have a satisfactory arrangement with a man. Out of your desperation, you have merely sent the thought 'a man' out into the creative Mind of the ether; and what you have got back was simply 'a man' or a series of several men of almost identical makeup. I should think, were Augustus to know of your past experiences in attracting men of basically the same ilk, that he would diagnose that you have projected thoughts out of your frustration and disappointment. Yet, were you to specify *precisely* what your ideal in a man would be, and hold your thoughts steady on such, then you would find a different sort of person—the sort who would actually make you happy—coming into your life."

"Such notions are far above my ken, Cousin Millijoy."

"Because you so desperately want to know the fulfillment of a relationship with a man that you are willing to settle for anyone who falls into the masculine category," Millijoy stated.

Lanny had been seated at the writing table in the far part of the room where a refreshing afternoon breeze brought a cooling sensation to the warmth of the day. She had been half listening to the conversation. "Peggy is such a complex and emotional person," she said as she rose and crossed to where the others were seated, "that she would surely fall emotionally in love with any man who played up to her; and, in so doing, she could easily become hurt."

"That is the case, isn't it, Peggy?" Millijoy questioned.

"I'm afraid it is," Peggy replied. "But you simply don't understand what my life has been like."

"Don't start with that lack of understanding attitude again," Millijoy fired. "That's self-pity, and I'm quite frankly tired of listening to you nurse it."

"Self-pity?" Peggy thought a moment. Taking time to reflect before reacting was something she was forcing herself to learn to do. "Yes, you're correct. It is self-pity, isn't it? I don't know how to react otherwise."

"Well, then, that's something you're going to have to work on, isn't it?" Millijoy stated.

Peggy simply nodded her head. She had learned the futility of attempting to argue with Millijoy. "Still I have about reached the point where I would be willing to take a chance," she said a few minutes later.

"Take a chance?" Millijoy asked.

"On what?" Lanny added.

"Whatever man or men whom I might attract," Peggy said softly. "Neither of you can possibly comprehend how badly I want to be loved."

"Badly?" Millijoy questioned. "I suspect that was a poor choice of words."

"Should I have said how wonderfully I want to be loved."

"*That* would be far better and decidedly to the point," Millijoy returned.

"I don't understand any of your philosophy, Cousin Millijoy."

"You will. I have faith in that," Millijoy said. She

glanced at Lanny, altered her position, then returned her attention to Peggy. "I received another letter from Donald today. It seems that he has been permitted to return to Edward House, where Polly is looking after him with the meticulous care of a loving sister. Poor girl, I know she is ridden with guilt, feeling herself responsible for the loss of Donald's eye. Yet Donald is the first to admit that he had provoked whatever action Polly had taken from which the accident and subsequent loss of eye was brought about."

"I received a letter three days ago," Peggy said. "I'm pleased to hear he is no longer in the hospital. He was uncomfortable there."

"What are your feelings concerning Donald?" Millijoy asked as she gazed directly into Peggy's face.

"My feelings?" Peggy made a sound halfway between a laugh and expression of surprise. "Not only is he my cousin, but I consider Donald my best friend in the entire world. I like him very much, but I have the feeling he treats me as he does because he feels sorry for me."

"Feels sorry for you? For goodness' sake, I hope you don't think either Lanny or I feel sorry for you," Millijoy stated. "I, for one, comprehend your problem and wish to help you do something about it, but I certainly don't feel sorry or any sort of pity for you. Don't come to me looking for that."

"I haven't. I'm certain understanding is far more important than pity," Peggy said.

"You've come a long way if you're beginning to think like that," Lanny interjected.

"I wonder if you may be mistaken about Donald," Millijoy commented as she glanced first at Lanny and then back at Peggy. "Have you ever considered that he might have a deep emotional feeling for you?"

"Donald?" Peggy registered a look of surprise. "Oh, I think not."

"If I were you, I would consider it a possibility," Lanny said. "Reread his letters. You may discover an altogether different attitude in them."

Peggy's lower jaw had sagged.

"You spoke earlier of the chance of having vicarious liaisons with other men because you so *badly* want to be loved," Millijoy remarked. "Suppose a fine young man like Donald, or any other who might want to develop a deep and engulfing love for you were to learn of such liaisons, how do you think he would feel?"

Peggy thought a second. She laughed. "This hypothetical conversation is perfectly silly. I've read Donald's letters over and over again. He is simply a concerned friend. Furthermore, the very idea of my having a relationship or even an affair with—well—with anyone is perfectly absurd. I know what I am. Although I avoid mirrors with a passion, I still have seen what I am."

"And you've decided to go to Dr. Werner's spa, haven't you?" Millijoy added as a means of throwing her a curve.

"How did—? Oh, Dr. Augustus must have told you."

"He may have."

"Are you certain you want to go through with such a program?" Lanny asked.

"I believe I am."

"*That* is important. You have your desire or goal," Millijoy said. "Belief is the second step."

"If only Lanny—" Peggy hesitated.

"If only I could do *what?*" Lanny asked.

"It would be nice if you were to accompany me to the spa."

"But totally out of the question," Millijoy inserted before Lanny had an opportunity to respond. "Lanny has a husband who will be expecting to see her before long. And, for that matter, I need her to travel with me back to Boston. Put that notion from your head at the outset."

"It was only an idle hope," Peggy replied. "I guess I feel as if I'll need moral support."

"I suspect Dr. Werner and his staff will give you all of the moral support that you'll require. After all, the spa and treatments are enormously expensive. They will surely have a thoroughly trained staff to fulfill your needs."

"I could take the train ride with Peggy and see that she gets well situated," Lanny suggested.

"Nonsense," Millijoy declared. "Once Peggy leaves us here in Vienna, she will be entirely on her own. If she makes it to the spa, that is her business. If she weakens and feels she can't go through with it, she can simply turn around and come back."

"Isn't that being negative, Grandmother?"

"It's being practical and, I daresay, realistic," Millijoy returned. "I, however, have faith that Peggy intends to see this matter through and emerge from it with flying colors."

"You have more confidence in me than I have in myself," Peggy said.

"Then, by heaven, I suggest you start putting more effort into working up your confidence," Millijoy stated.

Lanny accompanied Peggy back to the room they shared. She thought perhaps Peggy would want to carry on the conversation other than in the abrasive way Millijoy had attacked it. But Peggy had become pensive and simply thanked Lanny for being with her.

Later, before Peggy prepared herself for supper, she

dug out the three letters she had received from Donald while in Vienna. She reread each of them several times. Certainly he expressed concern for her, but he always had. He was a loyal friend and a loving cousin, and that was all. Wherever had Millijoy got the mistaken impression that he might have deeper feelings for her?

Later, after she had dressed for supper, her gown being a variation of the other practically formless garments she wore in a dark blue, nearly black shade, Peggy merely glanced over at the bundle of letters, neatly tied with a ribbon. Her thoughts returned to Donald. For the first time she realized that she did have a very strong feeling of love for him. But, as she analyzed it, she realized it wasn't a romantic type of thing at all. It was the kind of love she had for her brothers, John Adam, Luke and Hayden. Donald was simply one of the family; and perhaps the most understanding of all. Certainly she felt extremely close to him, even closer than she seemed to be to her brothers.

Resolving to give the matter contemplative thought at another time, Peggy put the letters back into the drawer where they were neatly kept.

As she waited for Lanny, Peggy sat in the large armchair near the window. Doves were fluttering through the evening air. Twilight was one of her favorite times of the day. The presence of doves made it seem somehow different.

Peggy wondered what Dr. Kristofer Werner would be like, how his spa would be, and what sort of treatment she would receive there. Apprehension came over her and she thought of Millijoy's words.

No! She was determined to see it through, regardless of how difficult it might be. Augustus had convinced her that it was now or never, and that if she didn't see the treatment through to successful conclusion, she might as well resign herself to an early death.

How different it would seem, she thought, if she had someone other than herself to be undergoing the change for. Someone she loved. Someone who loved her. Why were her thoughts so constantly on love and the frustration she felt due to a lack of it in her life? Romantic love. Not family love—and the love that Donald must have for her because he was her cousin. Still it was a form of love.

Love? Peggy didn't even know what love was—and it hurt her.

Chapter Twelve

The train wound through the pine-covered hills as it went northwest from Vienna. The luscious German countryside was like a broad plain, white-daisy-dotted rolling mounds, verdant green and straw yellow. Lakes, streams, rivers. Wide-eyed children stared at the passing spectacle and waved. When twilight came, Peggy had been nodding, and she was desperately fighting sleep. But sleep was better than the myriad confusing thoughts which had cluttered her mind throughout the day. Confusion. Temptation to get off, catch another train going in the opposite direction and return to Vienna. Or—and she had given serious consideration to the idea of going directly west and ultimately returning to San Francisco.

She had watched the continual parade of passengers enter and exit from the train compartment. Round, sturdy, sometimes harsh German faces. Dowdy women, pudgy men, a handsome Prussian officer with a sharp scar on his cheek. People observed her with a passing glance and tried not to gaze in amazement. Peggy generally looked away and out the window.

The train was scheduled to pull into the station shortly after nightfall. It was late.

The gaslamps along the platform whizzed past at first; then, as the train slowed, they were no longer indistinguishable streaks of brightness. The conductor helped Peggy with her luggage. She had been the only person left in the compartment by the time she had reached her destination.

A desolate atmosphere hovered around the train station. Few people had disembarked. Then a short man with a bowlegged walk came trudging toward her. A round-faced, turned-up-nose individual, he made a beeline for Peggy.

"Fraulein Phenwick?" he asked.

"Yes."

He rattled several sentences in German before realizing that she did not understand him. "Excuse me," he said in broken English, "I am Franz Heiken. Herr—Dr. Werner sent me to fetch you. The carriage is this way. I'll get your valises."

While Franz gathered the portmanteau, a smaller suitcase and a satchel, again Peggy had thoughts of simply inquiring about the next train away from that place. It was a mistake, she thought, the very idea of attempting such a vast project was an error. She could never make it. Still she was there and chances were that there was not a train out before morning.

Franz held the door to the ancient carriage for Peggy

to enter, then gave her a boost up. The vehicle creaked and groaned with the invasion of her weight. The door was firmly closed, and she likened it in her mind to the feeling one must have when one is put in a prison van to be taken to a place of incarceration. A dreary, dismal sensation came over her, and before she reached her destination, she had resigned herself to accept her fate. A sullen expression covered her face as Franz opened the door to her and reached a hand to help her down.

"The fraulein will be shown to her room," Franz instructed as the front door to the sanitarium-spa was opened to Peggy and she was greeted by a stern-faced woman of stout and obviously muscular proportions.

"I am Frau Schtricker," the large woman announced in far better English than the chauffeur had used. "I am what you would call the head matron, Fraulein Phenwick. You will come this way, and Franz will see to your luggage."

"Am I to see Dr. Werner tonight?"

"Nein. Tomorrow," Frau Schtricker replied. "Tonight you will be fed a light meal and expected to get a good night's sleep."

"My last meal?" Peggy asked.

Frau Schtricker looked at her from the side without a change of her stoic expression.

"The condemned is usually given a last meal," Peggy added.

"Condemned?" Frau Schtricker made an amused sound, at least that is what Peggy interpreted it to be. "Your condemnation obviously began years ago. But you are free to think of it as whatever you like. This way, please."

Peggy reluctantly followed the woman down a long cor-

ridor. The place was like an old castle or at least a villa of
mansion proportions. It appeared to have been standing
for centuries. Perhaps that was her imagination. She had
been given the impression that a sanitarium-spa would be
far more modern and cheery looking than this place. Why
did she feel it had a sinister, almost malevolent quality to
it?

Frau Schtricker showed Peggy to a comfortably furnished room on the second floor. The lamps were glow-
ing, and it was far less ominous appearing than the
corridors leading to it. A bowl of fresh flowers was on the
table, and the comforters had been turned down on the
bed, which was in a niche in the wall. The curtains had
been drawn.

"Am I to be shown to the dining room?" Peggy asked
after Frau Schtricker had pointed out the features of the
room.

"Nein. What meals you have will be taken in here."

"You make it sound as if I am to be starved."

Frau Schtricker merely shrugged. "You will know better about that after you have seen the herr doktor. I can
tell you nothing more. Helga Krankenschwester has been
assigned to you, fraulein. She will be with you first thing
in the morning. Once you have had your interview and initial examination with Dr. Werner, Helga will be able to
explain about your regime. It really is not my place to tell
you anything more."

Abruptly Frau Schtricker left the room, and Peggy felt
suddenly alone and despondent. She had been led to her
prison cell and she feared there would be no escape.

Supper consisted of several kinds of fresh fruit, a hand-
ful of nuts and a cup of tea. Fortunately, she thought, she
had eaten in the train dining car in the early evening.

Having difficulty sleeping that night in a strange bed and worried about what the next day would bring, Peggy was up a large part of the night. She positioned herself near an open window where the refreshing summer night breeze helped to ease her anxiety. Ultimately she managed to get a few hours' sleep.

"Good morning," Helga Krankenschwester greeted as she entered Peggy's room the next morning. Like the matron Peggy had met the night before, Helga was a large-boned, solidly packed woman in her late thirties. Her stride was firm and decisive, but she possessed a sunny disposition and a cheerful smile. Full, round, rosy cheeks glistened with a healthful appearance, and her laughter was loud and jovial. "I am Helga."

"Pleased to meet you, Helga. I am—"

"Fraulein Phenwick," Helga quickly inserted. "We will come to know each other well in the next weeks and months. I always warn my patients that they will probably dislike me in the beginning and think that I am some sort of agent of torture. But, despite my strength, I am basically a gentle and compassionate person. In time, it is hoped that you will come to feel close to me and consider me your good and understanding friend."

"You used the expression 'agent of torture.' Whatever did you mean by that?"

"Being here is not easy, not for the patient," Helga explained. "Dr. Werner takes only extreme cases. But he gets tremendous results. Yet to go on his program and endure the grueling experience of sticking with it can be an unpleasant ordeal."

"Am I to have breakfast?" Peggy asked.

"You may have an apple and a cup of tea."

"And that is all?"

"It will be more than enough," Helga replied. "You will find that Dr. Werner's first technique is to reduce the amount of your food intake."

"Drastically?"

"That well may be. I cannot speculate on that at this time," Helga said as she went to get the promised apple and tea.

Dr. Kristofer Werner was a tall, slender man with a good face and a distinguished profile. Blue-eyed and blond, he possessed the dignity and austerity of his heredity. He had been going over a report which had been submitted to him by Dr. Augustus Ornby of Vienna.

"Do sit down, Fraulein Phenwick," Dr. Werner invited as Peggy entered his somber office and registered an expression of bewilderment. "I am pleased to meet you."

"Thank you, Doctor Werner."

"I have here a report from Dr. Ornby, who, I've been led to understand, is your distant cousin."

"He is."

"Good. This morning you will undergo a series of tests," Dr. Werner stated. "They will all be basically harmless, so I do not wish you to become apprehensive about them. They are simply to give me a thorough picture of your overall physical condition. I will advise you from the outset that, with rare exception, I usually put my patients on a thirty-day fast, during which time you will experience daily enemas and massages. The first three days will be rigorous for you, and, perhaps, unpleasant. However, after that initial period, you will begin to feel much different, and all pangs of hunger and even the desire for food will disappear."

"What is the alternative to that?" Peggy questioned.

"There is *no* alternative."

"But you said 'with rare exception,' " Peggy returned.

"True. Do you consider yourself an exception, Fraulein Phenwick?" the doctor asked as he sat and leaned against the desk.

"I've never gone without food."

"That is quite apparent—and that is also at the root of your problem." Kristofer Werner stared for a moment before he smiled. "Let me tell you that during that thirty-day period you will lose a considerable amount of weight, which in the long run will be encouraging to you. Furthermore, you'll feel remarkably better than you have in a long while. At that time you will be put on a very light diet, which will be adjusted from time to time as you begin to make progress. Dr. Ornby advises me that you were informed you would probably have to be here for a period of at least six months."

"He did, but he gave me no indication that what I would have to endure would be so drastic."

"Drastic? Ah, that is an interesting word," Dr. Werner commented. "You are physically in a desperate situation. Other measures have failed over the years. Drastic devices must be taken. But I promise you that you will see unbelievable results for your persistent endurance."

"I assume it isn't too late to change my mind about this."

"On the contrary, it is, Fraulein Phenwick," the doctor said coldly before he brightened with a smile. "Anything worth accomplishing is never achieved by running away from it. I've no doubt that you will scream and call me the vilest names you can think of before it is over. I have told you all that I have because I wanted you to be forewarned. Perhaps I have accentuated the negative aspects of the course that is ahead of you," Dr. Werner said.

"Now I will tell you that much of your thirty-day fast will be spent asleep. You will be periodically awakened to take liquid, massage and whatever other measures are necessary. The result after the first month is that you will see noticeable progress and you will find that you have a renewed amount of energy, both of which you will find are highly encouraging."

"And there is no turning back?"

"The outside doors are locked to you until you have emerged the lovely lady you are destined to become. I will speak periodically with you and personally examine your progress." He smiled again as he stared deeply into her face. "And, dear Fraulein Phenwick, you may scream and call me any name you wish. I guarantee that, in the end, you will come to me and apologize for any negative attitude you've had toward me. Now, you will find that Helga is waiting outside to take you to where you will be tested."

Peggy pushed herself up from the chair. Her attitude was that of a recently condemned woman, sentenced with no chance of parole until the ultimate goal had been accomplished. Dejected, even forlorn, she walked to the door. Taking hold of the knob and bracing herself, her back tightened before she slowly turned her head around. She stared with sad eyes.

"What is it, Fraulein Phenwick?"

"Dr. Werner, I don't know any vile names," she said quietly. "Could you give me a list of a few?"

Werner smiled. Then he stood erect and clicked his heels. "You may start with 'savior,' then there is 'emancipator.' "

"I don't consider those as being vile words."

"You will think they are before this is over, dear

fraulein." He smiled again, attempting to put more encouragement into it. "Helga is waiting for you."

"Perhaps she has a better vocabulary selection." Peggy turned and left the doctor's office.

Dr. Kristofer Werner stood a moment gazing at the closed door. He considered what had transpired between the patient and himself. Then he moved to behind the desk and opened the file folder which was labeled 'Peggy Phenwick.' He took a scratchy pen and wrote: *Initial reaction—excellent!* After which, he again thumbed through the pages sent to him by Augustus Ornby.

Peggy glanced at Helga, who quickly got to her feet and came to join the patient.

"Was it as bad as all that?" Helga asked.

"Worse."

Helga put her arm about Peggy and led her down the hall. "We will first weigh you, then take a bit of blood and—"

"Don't they simply have a guillotine here, or a congenial firing squad?" Peggy asked cynically. .

Helga laughed and squeezed Peggy encouragingly. "I'm afraid not."

"In that case, would you mind telling me the vilest words you know?"

Chapter Thirteen

The only vile words that Helga allegedly knew were in German. The words which she taught to Peggy were actually expressions of endearment; but unfamiliar with the German language, Peggy thought she was being terribly profane and bordering on obscene. When she growled them, or yelled them at Dr. Werner, her tone was anger—the words were quite the opposite.

As Dr. Werner had predicted, the first three days of the fast were the most difficult. The second day was the worst, and Peggy had such a thundering headache that she was in complete agony. Helga responded to her distressed cries, and when she was not massaging her, she cradled Peggy like she would a small child.

Fortunately, the headache had subsided by the third day. Only the gnawing hunger pain persisted. Again Peggy required the loving response of Helga. It was comfort she dearly needed.

By the fourth day, remarkably both head and hunger pains had diminished, and Peggy began to feel a returning surge of energy. Sleep had not come easily the first part of the ordeal, now it was not difficult at all for the patient to sleep most of the day and the night. A mild opiate was administered to induce slumber.

Helga remained with Peggy twelve hours a day; then she had a room in the vicinity to which a bell was connected with Peggy's room. Peggy would ring if she needed anything during the hours which were designated as Helga's own.

"I don't know what the day is," Peggy said when she regained consciousness at the end of the first week. "And quite frankly, I don't care."

That night Peggy awakened before it was completely dark outside. It took several minutes for her to gain her bearings and identify the sanitarium room. As if she were jolted to full awareness, she sat up and curiously looked around the room. She was wearing an issued white nightgown, which she pulled out in front of her to see if there was less of her beneath it. Unsteadily she arose and went to the window from which she could see the high wall that kept the patients in the sanitarium grounds.

Helga had explained that Peggy would be able to go outside within the next few days and sit where it was warm. As the result of being without food, Peggy was perpetually cold. Only heated mineral tubs warmed her, or the sauna, which was kept quite hot.

The grounds were lovely, well tended and luxuriant with shades of green trees and shrubbery. Summer flowers were everywhere in bloom, although at that time of the day some of them were closing their sunny faces for night. A heavyset man was swimming in the large outdoor pool. An attendant appeared and coaxed the man from the water.

A short while later, as night had nearly fallen, and the grounds had been vacated, Peggy was still standing at the window. She felt a bit weak, she thought; yet, on the other hand, it seemed she had a larger charge of energy than she had had in a long time. There was no doubt that she had lost an appreciable amount of weight. Stepping to the mirror, she gazed at her reflection, pulling the gown tightly about her. Yes, she definitely had become slimmer.

After admiring her accomplishment, Peggy returned to the window. It seemed the breeze had whispered her name. During her long hours of sleep those days, she had had endless dreams, many of which were nightmares. Sometimes when she was awake, she sensed that she was still existing in a dreamlike state. Things were distorted, not quite real. And, at times, it was difficult for her to distinguish whether she was actually awake, or if she was still asleep dreaming.

The figure of a man emerged from behind a row of hedges. He was dressed in white. Too slender to be a patient, she thought. She assumed he must be an attendant or a technician. He stepped with a remarkable self-confidence, as if he liked to think of himself as a man of the world. That being the case, Peggy decided that he was too important to be merely a man in the employ of Dr. Werner.

The man glanced up at Peggy's window. She sensed that she could feel the penetration of his gaze. How mysterious! Then, as she became aware that darkness had completely enveloped the entire out-of-doors, it struck her peculiarly that she could still see him as if the white of his suit was luminous. She could not see his features well, but she received the impression that he was fairly good-looking, a man of manners and style.

A few moments later the mysterious individual walked toward the building and seemingly entered. What a remarkable experience, Peggy thought. "Yet, perhaps he is all part of these interminable dreams I've been having," she said aloud.

The next afternoon Helga accompanied Peggy downstairs to the grounds. The patient was placed in a large lounging chair and covered with a comforter, despite the warm temperature.

"I will leave you for a short while," Helga advised, "while I call on Dr. Werner. He wishes to see me. You remain here and I'll come back for you."

Peggy opened a book and ran her eyes over sentence after sentence of words. However, her mind was seemingly elsewhere, and she soon realized that she was getting nothing from the exercise. Putting the book aside, she turned her attention to two squabbling bluejays. Their raucous chatter was enough to disturb anyone's concentration.

Near where the birds were hopping about and carrying on what sounded to be a heated argument, Peggy saw the approaching white trouser legs. Although it didn't fully register with her at first, the man got remarkably close to the bluejays without their reacting to his presence. He stepped between the birds, which apparently didn't bother them in the least, then he moved to where Peggy was seated.

Peggy's eyes ran up to the man's face. His hair was black, both atop his head and his beard and moustache. Dressed immaculately in white, he appeared as enigmatically as he had the night before when she had seen him from her window. That was strange. She had not fully seen his features earlier, yet she knew beyond a doubt that it was the same person.

He glanced down at her and smiled. There was something terribly familiar about his expression. His features reminded her of someone, but she couldn't remember who.

"Good afternoon." His voice was soft, but the sound of

it had a singularly unusual quality. "Do you mind if I join you?"

"Are you a patient here?" Peggy asked, uncertain how she was to react to the man.

"I am a visitor here. May I sit?"

"By all means," Peggy replied. She tried to remember how Lanny had invited men to sit when they asked to join her aboard ship.

The stranger drew up a chair, which did not appear to be particularly comfortable. He smiled before he lowered himself onto it and properly crossed his legs. "Allow me. I am Collin Williams."

"Collin Williams?" Peggy asked, finding herself more and more fascinated by the person.

"I sometimes reverse the names and go by William Collins," he said. "Whatever suits my whim at the moment."

"And at this moment your whims dictate Collin Williams, is that the case?"

He smiled broadly. "And you?"

"I'm Peggy Phenwick," she replied. "And they're not reversible."

Collin laughed.

"You're obviously not a patient here."

"What makes you say that?"

"You're remarkably slender," she said.

"It could be that I have lost the weight required of me," he returned, "and am here simply to get myself prepared to go back to the outside world."

"Oh, I hadn't thought of that." Peggy had been instructed that even after she had lost the required amount of poundage, she would have to remain at the sanitarium until she was psychologically fit to leave. Losing weight was one thing, mentally adjusting so that the weight loss could be maintained was very much another matter. "You speak English too well to be a German."

"So I do," he replied. "Actually, I've come recently from America."

"I'm an American," Peggy said. "What a strange coincidence."

"Is it?"

"Is it what: strange or a coincidence?" Peggy asked.

"That is a rather perceptive question," Collin returned with a ripple of laughter. "I suppose it could be either."

As Collin chattered on about himself, a peculiar sensation came over Peggy. She suddenly felt thin and she perceived that he was looking at her as a normal man scrutinizes an attractive woman. Even when she gazed down at her body, it seemed she beheld a form that was quite different from what she knew hers to be. It caused an eerie reaction.

"What is it, Miss Phenwick?" Collin asked as he observed her bewilderment.

"I can't explain the reaction that has come over me except to say that I feel remarkably different. Does it appear to you as if I have changed any?"

"Not particularly. You are still the same lovely and attractive lady who caught my attention a short while ago."

"Lovely? Attractive?"

"Most definitely. As I observe you protectively covered, I suspect that you are dressed in an elegant ball gown beneath. There is no doubt in my mind that you have an exciting figure."

Peggy looked down at herself again. "You're making fun of me, aren't you?"

"Not in the least." He looked serious. "Sometimes one

must look beyond apparent appearances to see the real beauty. And, as one learns to do that, one's sense of perception alters drastically."

"Then you were only jesting—"

"Nonsense. I was describing what I see. Often what one sees on the exterior is not at all what one sees with his perceptive eye. I have trained myself to see what people really are."

"I can't quite follow you."

"I know I seem to speak in riddles. Why should I settle for the mundane world of appearance when I can perceive the image a person has of himself, even before that image materializes."

"Ah, then you are in some way psychic?"

"You might say that."

"Very well, but why do I feel as if I have changed, that I am different—the way you have described me?" she asked.

"Because you have obviously subconsciously formed that impression of yourself. You must be idealizing a dream and holding steadfast to the image of it. Or should I say to the image of yourself?"

It was Peggy's turn to laugh, because she didn't know what else to do. "You have quite a line, Mr. Williams."

"You must call me Collin." He stood, reached down to take her hand and gently placed a kiss on the back of it. "You must hang on to that image. I've no doubt it will become a physical reality. Now, I must depart." He bowed, smiled, then turned and walked down a path leading away from the sanitarium. Shortly thereafter, he was out of sight.

Peggy stared after him, even to the point that she repositioned herself.

"Is something wrong?" Helga came up to Peggy from the direction opposite to which she was staring.

"Oh, Helga! You startled me."

"I didn't mean to do that," Helga stated. "I had been watching you from the doctor's window. He tells me that you are progressing surprisingly well. He is pleased. Tomorrow he will examine you."

"Then you saw Mr. Williams."

"Mr. Williams?"

Peggy looked at her curiously. "Well, you certainly couldn't have been watching me very carefully from the doctor's office if you didn't see Mr. Williams. Such a handsome man, although I must say he struck me as being quite mysterious. He had a worldly quality—and, now that I think of it, he also had an other-worldly quality."

A singular smile came to Helga's lips. "I think you've had enough fresh air for one day, Fraulein Phenwick. It is best not to overdo it your first time out." She helped Peggy up. "Did Mr. Williams tell you his other name?"

"Why, yes, it's Collin." Peggy laughed with a somewhat giddy attitude. "What an interesting man he is. Sometimes he goes by the name of Collin Williams and other times by William Collins."

Although Peggy's energy had increased now that she was used to being without food, she still leaned on Helga for support. Led to the sauna room, the masseuse prepared the patient to take the heat for twenty minutes.

During her period of baking, as she thought of it, Peggy could not get thoughts of Collin Williams from her mind. What an extraordinarily handsome man he was. Yet, as she thought of him, it struck her that there was something terribly familiar about him. Had she seen him somewhere before? Try as she may, she could not put her finger on anywhere that might have been.

A while later, when Helga was massaging Peggy, the latter lapsed into long periods of silence while she again considered the enigmatic Mr. Williams.

"You realize, don't you, Fraulein Phenwick," Helga said as she made long rubbing strokes across Peggy's back, "that during a time like this, when you are undergoing such an extreme physical change, that the mind sometimes plays tricks."

"Plays tricks?"

"Causes hallucinations."

"Hallucinations?"

"The mind imagines things," Helga explained.

"Are you suggesting that Mr. Williams—?"

"I was standing very near to the window while I was in Dr. Werner's office," Helga explained. "Although my attention was given to him most of the time, I periodically glanced out to watch you in case you needed assistance."

"And you did *not* see Mr. Williams?" Peggy asked.

"I saw only you seated by yourself."

"But that's impossible!" Peggy stated. "I was fully awake, and I both saw him and spoke to him."

Helga patted her gently and continued massaging.

Chapter Fourteen

By the end of the third month at the spa, Peggy had lost four stone (fifty-six pounds). The loss made a dramatic change in her appearance, to say the least, and it had conspicuously altered her mental condition. It had been an extremely difficult three months. Had it not been for the constant loving encouragement of Helga Krankenschwester with both physical and moral support, Peggy might have attempted to escape the sanitarium and return to the United States. Now, with such a substantial loss, although she had another three stone to go to reach her ideal weight, she had proved to herself that such a change could be accomplished.

After the first thirty days of fasting, Peggy was put on a liquid diet. Not until the third month was she allowed to have any solid food, and that consisted of mainly fruits, nuts, vegetables and occasionally eggs. Even then she was given such small proportions of food that, to the average person, it would seem like starvation. She walked at least two hours a day and participated in regular exercises which were meant to give her muscle tone. Twice a day she took the mineral baths, followed by a sauna; and she had a minimum of three massages a day.

Dr. Kristofer Werner regularly interviewed Peggy, closely monitoring her progress. He was enthusiastic about her accomplishment, kind and understanding.

"You still have a way to go, Fraulein Phenwick," Dr.

Werner said on a warmish autumn afternoon. "I anticipate that you will lose a stone to a stone and a half a
month. Ideally, by the end of the fifth month you will
have reached your goal, so that the last thirty days can be
spent working strictly on your rehabilitation."

"Rehabilitation?" Peggy asked.

"You will now begin a course of learning to adjust to
your new condition," Werner said. "Already you have noticed that you carry yourself and move differently."

"Surprisingly so," Peggy admitted. "And I seem to
have so very much more energy."

"And, I daresay, a greater enthusiasm for life," Dr.
Werner inserted. "That is all well and good, but it is time
for you to begin refining your ways. Your progress has
been extremely good. I am proud of you. How do you
feel about yourself now?"

"Much different than I did before I came here," Peggy
replied. "There was a mountain before me, and it discouraged me because it was like facing it with the frustration
of trying to move it with a teaspoon. I will admit it has
not been easy, or comfortable, to go through with what I
have; but the results have caused me to have a new outlook. Now I want to achieve my goal!"

"And you will, I have no doubt about that." Dr. Werner rose from behind his desk and went to stand before
Peggy. He studied her attractive features where the bloat
had subsided. "You are already emerging a good-looking
woman. There is no reason for me to believe that you will
not ultimately evolve into an extremely lovely woman."

"Extremely lovely?" Peggy questioned. "Encouragement is one thing, Dr. Werner, but don't you think you're
overdoing it?"

"Not in the least. I have seen this process in the past,"

he commented. "You have delicately proportioned features, which, I might add, are artistically ideal. I have dealt with other persons who, although they accomplished phenomenal transformations, did not have the basic excellent structure and refinement that you have. When you finally leave us, I expect to see a gorgeous woman who will turn the head of everyone who sees her."

"I fear you are being overly optimistic, Dr. Werner," Peggy returned. His words had made her feel warmly proud and had touched her deeply. Still, despite the transformation she beheld in progress, she was not thoroughly convinced that she was destined to become a raving beauty.

"You will begin working at least two hours a day with Frau Mueller," the doctor instructed, "who is an authority on poise and regal social graces. You have told me of the resentment toward and the envy you have of your sister Lola, not only because of her beauty, but because of her social education. Frau Mueller will teach you as much or more than Lola has ever learned. There is no doubt in my mind that by the time you leave here, you could be accepted in every royal court throughout the world as well as into every aristocratic social situation. The Phenwicks of Boston are the epitome of the heights of society. I suspect that you are destined to take your place among the most accomplished and sophisticated of them."

"Your statement overwhelms me, doctor," Peggy said. "I will confess that I have always had a dream of becoming the most glamorous Phenwick Woman of them all. I used to think it was an impossible notion, a dream of bizarre fantasy which was quite unobtainable. I would like to believe every word that you have told me."

"Then, by all means, dear Fraulein Phenwick, *believe!*"

Peggy left Kristofer Werner's office with a motivated sense of elation. Her thoughts were soaring toward situations which she had always felt would be improbable for her to accomplish. Her footstep was lighter than it had been for as long as she could remember. She hummed a Strauss waltz and felt as if she could dance along with it.

Stopping before a full mirror, Peggy examined herself. Where she had avoided looking glasses in the past, she now enthusiastically sought them out to study her progress. Certainly she had a distance to go, but she was at least on the right track.

A plumpish woman in her late thirties observed Peggy's self-admiration. An attractive person with a round face, blond hair and wearing a patient's gown, she stepped to where Peggy was watching her reflection.

"I do not speak German," Peggy said when the lady spoke to her. "I am an American."

"Ah, so!" the woman returned in broken English. "I speak only a fair amount of German myself. My native tongue is Dutch. I'm Agnes Van Cleff from Amsterdam. I only arrived here two days ago. I come every year at this time to spend a month."

"How do you do, Miss Van Cleff? I am Peggy Phenwick from San Francisco."

"It is a pleasure to meet you. Allow me to correct you, it is Frau—that is, Mrs. Van Cleff. I am married."

"I am Miss Peggy Phenwick, and I've never—" Peggy caught herself. "I am still a maiden lady."

"Ah! Then you must have been very much overweight when you came here."

"I was—and still am."

"But you are so pretty—fleshy, but pretty. I do hope we shall become friends. I always make a point of establishing one good friendship each time I come to the sanitarium. I think this time it will be yours."

"My friendship? But you hardly know me."

"I can see who you are," Agnes replied. "And I have very strong impressions about people. I often make predictions which come true. Which room is yours?"

"204," Peggy said in English.

Agnes translated it into Dutch. "I will remember that. And, if you don't mind, I'll come to visit with you. Now I am on my way to see Dr. Werner—a man I adore. We shall speak again soon."

Peggy found Agnes Van Cleff extremely interesting, and thought it peculiar that she should have singled her out. Although there were thirty some patients at the spa, there was little contact among them, especially in early stages of treatment.

That night, after Helga retired to her own room, Peggy found herself wide awake and brimming with energy. That in itself was a completely new experience for her. She tried to read, but her mind was racing with a rampant excitement. She could not imagine why such rushes were coming to her. Pacing about the room, she periodically stood at the open window. The wind was cool, but she let the windows remain open.

The soft rap at the door was almost indistinguishable at first. It was a woman's knock, Peggy thought, and it occurred to her that it was probably Agnes Van Cleff come to call as she had promised. Checking her appearance in the mirror, she stepped to the door with a kind of assurance she had never felt before.

"Miss Phenwick."

"Oh! Mr. Williams!" Peggy exclaimed. Then, as she conquered the sensation of surprise that had come over her, she lightheartedly said, "Or is it Mr. Collins tonight?"

"Ah, you remembered. I'll assume the title of Collin Williams tonight. Mayn't I come in?" The handsome man had such amazing eyes that for a moment Peggy thought she was being hypnotized by them.

"I would be honored to have you visit for a while," Peggy returned. "I've been about to crawl out of my skin from boredom, unable to hit upon a particular thing to occupy my time. Come in and have a seat. I have little to entertain you with except conversation."

"That will suffice nicely."

As Collin entered, Peggy turned again to get a quick glimpse of her appearance in the mirror. When she turned back to the door, she was surprised not to see the man standing there. Instead he was on the opposite side of the room, near the window. Had she been so occupied examining her attitude that she had not seen his reflection as he passed behind her? No doubt that was the case.

"You have a lovely room here, and an excellent view," Collin remarked as he gazed from the window.

"The room is perfunctory at best," Peggy returned. "I've become used to it."

Collin sat in a comfortable chair and methodically crossed his legs as he had previously done at their first meeting.

"You are a bit of a mystery," Peggy said as she took the chair opposite him.

"Oh, dear, I do hope so!" Collin exclaimed. "There should be a little bit of a mystery in everyone. If one knew absolutely everything about another person, there would be little to keep them interested. Perhaps lovers—I mean *true* lovers—know the most about each other, but even there secrets exist."

"I've no doubt there are many secrets about you, Collin."

"That's a rather brazen thing to say. It's my observation that you are quite magnificently emerging from your shell, Peggy."

Peggy thought a moment. "Why do you seem so very familiar to me?"

"Because we have met on a previous occasion," Collin replied. "Prior to that you saw me while you were standing here at your window."

"I didn't realize you had seen me that day," Peggy said and tried not to blush. "You said you were a visitor at the spa."

"I am."

"Have you ever been a patient?"

"No. I have come to take the waters from time to time."

"Ah, then you were here for the mineral baths rather than to visit a particular patient."

"I think it would be best if we would leave it at that for the present," Collin commented. "I've puzzled you, haven't I? Dear heart, that's all part of being a mystery. Rest assured that I am here for a specific reason. Although it appears I am a person with idle time on my hands, I am here with a precise mission."

"What did you say?"

"I'm here with a precise mission."

"Not that. You called me—?"

"Dear Peggy, I suppose. That is what I intended to say. I don't recall my every word." He smiled warmly and leaned forward. "I look at you with eyes of love—and see only beauty."

"You speak rather glibly of love," Peggy responded.

"Why shouldn't I? I was in love once—many times," Collin replied, making a flamboyant gesture.

"That is something Cousin Millijoy would say—as a matter of fact those were her very words," Peggy said as she looked deeply into Collin's mysteriously handsome face. "How peculiar."

"Millijoy? Ah, your cousin, you said, didn't you?" Collin repositioned himself, taking what Peggy considered to be an artistic pose. She could not determine whether he was posing *as* or *for* an artist. The thought amused her. Still she was abundantly impressed by him. Then a curious notion struck her, and she projected her hand toward him.

"Millijoy has the reputation of being the most outrageous of all the Phenwick Women," Peggy said.

"Ah, Millijoy Phenwick! The name is most familiar to me," Collin commented before he reached his hand forward to allow Peggy to touch it. "My circulation isn't always the best, which is fashionably desirable because I can wear gloves even in the hottest weather."

The touch of his fingers against hers caused Peggy to have a strange reaction. A moment later she retrieved her hand and stared at it. "I somehow have the feeling that you are part of a dream, Collin; and that I should probably be awakening at any minute."

Collin laughed. "What a thing to say!"

"Helga said it was not uncommon for persons undergoing the treatment here at the spa to have hallucinations."

Collin rose and stepped toward the window. "I wonder . . . how much of life and death are really a form of hallucination. That was a bit much suggesting that form might be hallucination. Yet, dear Peggy, you touched my hand."

"Why could Helga not see you when you sat with me the last time you were here?" Peggy asked.

"Perhaps she wasn't looking in the right place." Collin took a casual stance by the window.

"You said you looked at me with eyes of love. You hardly know me. How is that possible?"

"I have made a point of teaching myself to look at all people and all things with the eyes of love," Collin replied. "Love is an attitude which sees only good and beauty. It's quite extraordinary the results one gets when he perpetually sees with the eyes of love. Believe me, dear heart, I know."

Peggy stared at him again. "Did you ever take a train ride from San Francisco to New York?"

"I've been many places and I've done many things." As her curiosity began to trouble him, Collin went to where she was seated. Gently he put a hand to her shoulder, then he lightly caressed her hair with his other hand. "Peggy, you are loved, and you are beautiful."

Chapter Fifteen

The question that continuously returned to Peggy asked if she had been made love to by an illusion. Not a consummate act, but a lavish display of emotional as well as sensual stimulation. Never before had she had such an experience, not even during her relationship with Damien Brusco. Collin was a perfect gentleman, proper and aggressive only to a point, then he gently eased her into a less stimulated state, and left her with a parting kiss which held both promise and mystery.

"Why do you come to me like this?" Peggy asked several weeks later. "You arouse me, then softly let the emotion subside. But it doesn't really subside, because when you leave I constantly think of your visit and of you, Collin. When you're gone, I am left desiring fulfillment."

"My visits are a prelude to that which is destined to come your way, Peggy," Collin said softly. "I've come to let you have a taste of what being in love is."

"And I am in love with you."

"Are you, dear heart?" He kissed her cheek. "I would be wrong to question that. I can see love in your face, your radiant smile, the magical vibration in your eyes. There is no doubt in my mind that you are a person who is in love—and that very emotion of being in love is making you not only beautiful, but absolutely gorgeous."

"But you are not in love with me, is that the case?"

"That is *not* the case," Collin replied. "You have another five weeks to remain here at the sanitarium, then you will be expelled back into the outside world. It will be a world you have never known before." He stepped to the dresser. "There will be many handsome men who pursue you. Already you have become a stunning woman with a tremendous amount of appeal. Heads will turn and hearts will pulsate at a rapid rate whenever you are near."

"Why are you telling me this?" Peggy asked.

Collin held his hand toward her in an invitation to join him. She went to where he was standing. Their eyes met.

Peggy had a compulsion to lunge her face toward his, and she did.

"Collin, I want to know the completeness of you, to be made love to by you—all the way." She kissed him again.

Collin responded, but not with the force she would have liked to receive. There was the usual gentleness and encouragement in his touch, but he was reserved in making stimulating gestures. "Peggy, dear heart, you were right about me all along." Catching her attention, he gazed deeply into her eyes. "I am an illusion."

"You're *what*—?"

"An illusion. Not so much in your mind as I am a manifestation from the spirit side of life."

"You're not making sense, Collin. I know you. I see you. I feel the substance of you."

"The materialization—the manifestation."

"I don't understand."

"Nor did I expect that you would." He kissed her. "I came to you for one purpose, to let you experience the true emotion of falling in love. Now you must remember this feeling. Those men I spoke of, who will be in the outside world, mostly will look at you with one desire, and only one, in mind: their own selfish satisfaction. And you will be vulnerable to their persuasive ways because you have gone so long without physical and emotional satisfaction. They mean only to gratify themselves and at best give you a moment of physical release. I purposefully made you fall in love with me so you would know that sensation and be able to distinguish it from any other."

"This is incredible. I don't believe it."

Collin changed his position so that his back was directly to the mirror before he kissed her again. Even as their lips met, Peggy's confusion had begun to get the best of her, because she was convinced beyond a doubt that what she was experiencing was very much real. She permitted her hands to explore over him. He was solid flesh and definitely a desirable man. Then she reluctantly pulled her lips from his, stepped back slightly and gazed at him. All she saw was her own reflection in the mirror, her hands placed as if they were still around Collin.

"She is such a lovely lady, isn't she, Peggy?" Collin said as his voice seemed to be everywhere in the room at once. "Your attitude of love has transformed you. You're only a day or two away from your ideal weight. That has made a change in your body, but that wonderful attitude of love has made you beautiful."

"Collin?"

"Turn around."

She did and again saw him watching her from a few feet away from the mirror. "You're some sort of magician, and this is all a trick."

"An illusion, Peggy." He laughed. "And it's not done with mirrors."

"I don't believe this is happening."

"Don't you?" Collin glanced toward the door before a rap came from the other side of it. "You have a visitor."

Dumbfounded and thoroughly confused, Peggy all but crept toward the door. She glanced back before opening it.

Agnes Van Cleff was standing outside. "Miss Phenwick, do you have a moment?"

Peggy turned back to Collin and he nodded his head. "Yes, Mrs. Van Cleff, come in. I'd like you to meet—"

Collin cleared his throat and gently shook his head.

"Meet—?" Agnes asked as she stepped into the room and scanned about. "Is there someone with you?"

Peggy sighed. "Only an illusion."

"How's that?"

Peggy found her poise. "I'm having a jest, Mrs. Van Cleff. Won't you come in and visit awhile?"

"That's a very good idea, dear heart," Collin said. "I'll remain."

"You must be nearly ready to go home," Agnes commented after taking a seat.

"The last several pounds of weight have come off slowly," Peggy explained, "but I should have reached my goal by next week."

"Don't grow impatient and be like me, my dear," Agnes returned. "I have a pattern of losing what is desired, then go back to the world of opulent society, forget my resolutions and gain back what I had lost. This is my sixth stay with Dr. Werner. My husband suspects that I am having an affair with Dr. Werner, which is why I keep coming back. Dr. Werner is hardly that sort of man, but Frederick doesn't know that. Still the good doctor has assured my husband beyond any doubt that I have a problem with which he persistently must help me. It's men like Max Kramer who my husband should have concern about." She giggled.

"Max Kramer? Not Baron Max Kramer?"

"The same. Do you know him?" Agnes inquired.

"I met him in Vienna at a party given by my cousin Millijoy," Peggy said. "We were introduced. It didn't take me long to discover that he was one of a legion of impoverished nobility who will do anything—and I mean *anything*—to support their sagging financial condition. He was far too obvious in his approach."

"Max is as obvious as tulips in the springtime," Agnes replied, "but he is so terribly handsome and elegant. And he has such a sensational approach to intimate situations that I find it well worth overlooking his economic state. I tell Frederick that it is necessary for me to take special physical treatments, which are extremely expensive. Frederick is a dear. Besides, my husband has his intimate friends on the side. I don't believe either of us is concealing anything from the other. But we play the game."

"How can your marriage last like that?"

"It simply has," Agnes returned. "Besides, it costs Frederick far less to keep me married to him than it would to divorce me."

"But is there love?"

"There is an understanding, which I suspect is the closest thing to love," Agnes explained. "As to Max Kramer, I know for a fact that he is a man who admires fleshy women—but then, I daresay he fancies most women who can give him monetary assistance." Again she giggled.

"I hope I do not encounter such men as Baron Kramer when I get out of here," Peggy said, beginning to feel a bit uneasy with the conversation.

Agnes remained another fifteen minutes before she realized it was time for her to return to her room to receive her nightly medication which helped her to sleep.

"I'll be leaving next week," Agnes informed Peggy as she was about to depart. "We will visit again before then."

"She didn't see you," Peggy said as she closed the door behind Agnes Van Cleff and turned to regard Collin Williams.

"Just as the mirror did not catch my reflection, dear Peggy."

"Then you *are* a figment of my imagination."

"No. I actually do exist," Collin explained. "But I inhabit another dimension other than this which you know as earthly. I have been in the flesh several times, and I doubtessly will return to physical form as you know it—one of these days. Now I am on the spiritual plane, but I am very real; therefore, not a figment of your imagination."

"If that is the case, why have you appeared to me?"

"To help you, dear heart," Collin replied. "You are undergoing a tremendous change, the results of which will soon plunge you out into a world which is familiar to you as an observer, not a participant. You will feel very strange in it. You will find that you will be subjective to situations in which you were objective in the past. It could be so easy for a person like you to attempt to make up for the years of neglected passions and forsake ideals which are inherent within you."

"Why have you chosen the name Collin Williams?" Peggy asked after she gave consideration to his statement.

"It is a name of a wonderful person whom I greatly admired," he replied. "One who is very dear to me. Had I told you the name I last carried during an earthly existence, I might have frightened you. That would have been wrong, and it would have defeated my purpose for this visit. Yes, you first saw me on the train from San Francisco. I believe I told you then that you were destined to become one of the most outstanding Phenwick Women. By the transformation which you have accomplished, you have taken the initial step in achieving that position."

Peggy caught a glimpse of her reflection in the mirror. She stood tall and proud. "I will never forget you, Collin."

"I won't let you, Peggy." He stepped to her and embraced her. She responded with unbridled emotion and deep love. She did not comprehend exactly what had happened or why she felt as she did, she only knew that she had experienced love for the first time in her life, and that that love had caused her to evolve into a beautiful woman.

Peggy looked to the mirror again and saw only her reflection. Then, when she glanced back to where Collin had been standing, he was no longer visible to her. Still she felt his presence.

Shortly thereafter, while she was still standing in the same position, a knock was heard at the door. A moment later Helga entered with Eric Schmidt, the dress designer. He had brought four new gowns for her to wear.

"Are you feeling well, fraulein?" Helga asked as she observed Peggy's stunned expression.

"Yes, quite fine."

"Herr Schmidt has brought your new gowns."

"For a final fitting," Eric explained as he put three down and held the fourth up for Peggy to examine. "You will be a positive sensation in these."

Peggy was indifferent to the designer's enthusiasm, but she tried on each of the gowns and modeled them. Very few alterations were required.

After he had done all that was necessary, Eric Schmidt bowed and left the room.

"You will be an absolute sensation," Helga exclaimed as she turned to look at Peggy. "Is there anything I can do for you?"

"No, thank you. I'm quite all right," Peggy replied. "I have simply been through an overwhelming ordeal. I need to gather my thoughts and emotions."

"What is it, fraulein?"

"I'm afraid I can't explain it, Helga. How does one even justify an illusion, much less explain it?"

"An illusion?" Helga moved nearer to her. "Are you referring to Herr Collin Williams?"

"How did you—?"

"When you first told me of Herr Williams," Helga replied, "I inquired after him with various members of the staff, including Dr. Werner himself. No one had ever heard of such a person. Still I have watched you and your progress over these months, and I have reached the conclusion that some very strong spirit force must be guiding you. You've reacted and changed quite unlike other ladies who have been here. I knew from the beginning that you would emerge an attractive woman, but I didn't realize how beautiful you would actually become."

"Thank you, Helga."

"Oh, I almost forgot," Helga said as she went to the door. "A letter came for you today, which got misplaced. I picked it up when Herr Schmidt arrived. It is from Boston." She handed the letter to Peggy and waited as she examined it.

"From my cousin Donald," Peggy announced. She broke the seal and quickly scanned it while Helga watched her. "He has undergone his fourth and last operation. Since the other three were successful, the final one is expected to be perfect. I am so happy for him."

"You will be returning to Boston as soon as you leave here, won't you?" Helga asked.

"I think not right away," Peggy replied. "I've been thinking that I would like to go to Italy for a short time and perhaps Spain. I want to get used to my new self and the reaction I am bound to get before I go back to the United States."

"That may be wise," Helga said.

"It was your suggestion, don't you recall?"

Helga smiled broadly. She embraced Peggy, then went past the dresser on her way to the door. "Shall I get some water for this? Such a lovely thing. It will not last without water."

"I beg your pardon."

"I've never seen such a perfectly beautiful red rose," Helga commented, "and certainly never this time of the year." She picked up the flower and smelled it. "It couldn't have been raised in a hothouse to have such a powerful fragrance." Before receiving an answer, she put the rosebud in a crystal vase and added water. "I will see you bright and early in the morning. Good night, fraulein."

Peggy stared incredulously at the rosebud before she went to it. Then, on impulse, she put it in front of the mirror to see if it were reflected. It was. She smiled and said aloud: "You may be an illusion, Adam Truff, but your rosebud is not."

Chapter Sixteen

Peggy had kept up a regular correspondence with Donald Phenwick of Boston. The tone of their letters was basically always as they had been. Neither spoke much of the physical problems or the treatments they were taking to correct them. Peggy had written to Donald concerning her meeting and her developing feelings for Collin Williams. When she discovered the truth about her 'illusion,' she could not bring herself to explain the situation to Donald.

During the following two weeks after her last encounter with Collin Williams, Peggy had difficulty getting him from her mind. The entire situation struck her as being unbelievable; still she could not deny her senses and how he had appeared so very real to her. She was able to take the experience and identify with the emotions she had felt. It was simple for her to understand why so many of the Phenwick Women had allegedly been in love with Adam Truff.

The ground outside the sanitarium was covered with snow. Trees were heavily laden with white blankets which caused the limbs to droop down. Icicles hung like crystal cold fingers from the eaves, and frost distorted the views from the windows. Instead of taking the long walks she had taken in the summer and autumn, Peggy went through the halls of the large building which had once been a small summer mansion belonging to royalty. As she strolled through it, or walked at a brisk pace, she wondered if the Hapsburgs had played out their family dramas there. If so, were the echoes of their memory still lingering in the shadows? The thought both amused her and at the same time caused her to have a nervous reaction.

As she turned into one poorly lit corridor, a queer sensation came over Peggy. Was it a premonition? Or was it merely a creepy feeling generated to her from the old house itself? In either case, she accelerated her steps and hurried toward where it was brighter at the end of the hall.

Eyes were watching her. Peggy passed a suit of armor

and wondered if it was occupied. An even eerier sensation came over her. Why did she have such an edgy feeling? The startling sound of a man clearing his voice rumbled through the corridor. Peggy stopped in her tracks and looked about to see the source of the noise.

"Who is it?" Peggy asked in German. She had learned a few phrases from Helga.

"I have been watching you," the guttural baritone growled. "Fact is, I saw you earlier."

"Identify yourself."

A match was struck and put to a cigarette a short distance from where Peggy was standing. In the glow, she could behold the ruggedly handsome features of a blond man with a wide moustache, tall and imposing-looking. Softly blowing out the flame, he moved to where she was standing.

"I am Baron Maximilian Kramer," he said and clicked his heels together to punctuate his announcement.

"Baron Kramer?" Peggy questioned. She started to acknowledge her recognition of his name, but she hesitated. "Do you speak English?"

"I do," he replied in English.

"I speak very little German."

"Ah, you speak with an American accent," he said. "May I know your name?"

Not wishing to reveal her true identity, Peggy replied, "I'm Miss—that is—Miss Collins." The idea amused her. "Miss Wilma Collins."

"Wilma Collins? Ah, what a lovely name!"

She was having a game with him. "My friends often call me—uh—Billie Collins."

"Billie? But isn't Billie a man's name?"

"Not always." Peggy smiled and had a strong desire to

get to where the light was brighter. "Excuse me, I am exercising."

"A gorgeous lady such as you, with such a provocatively beautiful figure, exercising? Whatever for?" he asked.

"To keep the beautiful figure in shape, Baron."

"May I join you?"

"If you like. I will stop to take a cup of tea shortly," Peggy said. "If you care to, you may take tea with me." Her manner was somewhat flirtatious, and she reminded herself of Lanny.

Once they reached an area where the light was good, Max Kramer stopped and leaned, bracing himself against a table top. "You walk very fast, fraulein."

"It isn't exercise if you don't go at a brisk pace," Peggy replied. "The tea is just a short distance from here. Surely, you have the breath to go a little farther."

Peggy was clad in a snugly fitting, light blue woolen gown. It was one of Eric Schmidt's finest creation and it accentuated just the right parts of her newly discovered figure. Max Kramer even more admired what he saw and reacted with eager excitement.

Upon reaching the tearoom, which was not occupied, Peggy went to the door which led to the kitchen and asked that they might be served two cups of tea. Then she returned to where Baron Kramer was waiting at a small table. He held the chair for her.

"Thank you, Baron Kramer."

"You must call me Max, as my other friends do," he said as he sat opposite her.

"As your other *lady* friends do?" Peggy asked.

"As *all* of my friends do," he corrected. He looked impervious as he took a stoic pose. "Admittedly I have many lady friends."

"So I've been led to understand."

"Ah, then you've heard of me?"

"Agnes Van Cleff is a friend of mine. She has mentioned your name on several occasions." Peggy smiled.

"I find you extremely attractive, Miss Collins." He leaned forward as if he were presenting his face for a kiss. "That is, Billie."

Peggy suppressed an amused expression. "Thank you, Baron."

"Max. I like my intimate friends to call me Max."

"Intimate friends? I trust you're not presuming the wrong notion as far as I'm concerned, Baron."

"Max." He twisted his moustache and gave her a suggestive look. "You are indeed a creation of beauty."

"Your opinion is flattering, Max," she replied. Then she gave him a skeptical look. "However, I've been led to understand from Agnes Van Cleff that you prefer—uh—fleshy women."

"I only told that to Agnes because she is usually a fleshy woman. I like all women, for that matter; but I am particularly attracted to beautiful creatures as lovely as you are."

"Agnes tells me that you know a certain American lady by the name of Millijoy Phenwhick."

"Ah, Millijoy! What a lady!" Max thought a moment. "How did Agnes Van Cleff know about Frau Phenwick?"

"Perhaps she didn't," Peggy said. "I may have gained the information from another source. It isn't important. Then you know Mrs. Phenwick's granddaughter."

"I know Millijoy's son and daughter-in-law, her grandson and granddaughter-in-law and her elephantine cousin from San Francisco."

"Elephantine? Is that any way to speak of a lady?" Peggy asked.

"Well, when a woman is that large, what else does one call her?"

"But Agnes told me that you found Mrs. Phenwick's cousin attractive," Peggy persisted, trying to remain objective and casual in her conversation.

"The Phenwicks are a remarkably wealthy people. A man in my position would be foolish not to attempt a liaison with the only available member of the family. Her name is Peggy Phenwick. But why are we speaking of her?"

"Agnes gave me the impression that you had practically proposed marriage to this Miss Phenwick."

"Agnes Van Cleff couldn't have known that."

"She could have if Miss Phenwick had told her."

"Ah, that is a possibility."

The tea things arrived. Peggy gave a cautious glance to the serving girl. It worked. The server said nothing. Max's eyes followed the girl as she returned to the kitchen.

Peggy smiled sweetly and gazed suggestively into Max's eyes. "I think you're an unprincipled scoundrel, Baron Kramer."

"I beg your pardon?"

"Lemon or cream?"

"Lemon." Max blinked. "Why did you call me a scoundrel?"

"I actually called you an unprincipled scoundrel."

"At what provocation?"

"For what you said about Miss Phenwick."

"I spoke only the truth."

Peggy looked at him with a raised eyebrow. "Baron Kramer, I have a confession to make to you. I personally know Peggy Phenwick."

"You do?" Max tried not to look alarmed. "Then it was from Miss Phenwick that you heard of me? Please do not repeat to her that I called her elephantine. I had no idea you were even acquainted—I mean to say—"

Peggy stood and took a pose as Frau Mueller had explained that fashion models took that was considered most provocative and sophisticated. "Do you think I really have a lovely figure, Max?"

"Enchantingly so." He rose and started toward her.

"That's close enough," Peggy said. "Do you know the sort of place this sanitarium is?"

"Yes, it is where fat people come to shed—" He stopped short.

"I misled you, Max. My name is not really Wilma Collins. And I've been a patient here for nearly six months. Look at my eyes, my face, my features. Aren't they familiar to you, a great deal less bloated than when last you saw them, but familiar?"

"No! It can't be!" Max had turned a bright red.

"But it is, Max. Now I must ask you to excuse me. After what you disclosed to me, I don't believe I wish to remain in your presence. Excuse me."

"But Fraulein Phenwick, it would be different now. You have changed," Max exclaimed as she strode majestically toward the door.

Turning halfway around, Peggy smiled cynically at him. "But you have not changed, Max. And you have revealed your motives. Good day." Grandly, with a triumphant air, she left the room. She had made her first contact with the past and felt elated to think that it had been so easy for her to retaliate. She tried not to think of it as 'getting even,' but that was the reaction she had—and it felt good.

Peggy said goodbye to Helga Krankenschwester on the twenty-fourth of January. It might have been a tearful parting if each had not prepared and braced herself for the inevitable. Helga embraced Peggy and held her for a full minute before she was able to speak.

"I will miss you, Fraulein Phenwick. Dr. Werner instructed us in the beginning not to allow ourselves to become attached to the patients. I find that difficult to do. Forgive me."

"And I knew better than to become attached to you, Helga," Peggy confessed, "but I did." She kissed the round-faced woman on the cheek. "I will correspond with you. I promise."

"The one promise I wish you to make to me," Helga said, "is that you never *have* to return here again as a patient. You have been through hell. Be kind to yourself and never put yourself in the position where you must come back—not as a patient."

"I will do my best to keep such a promise, Helga." She kissed her again and abruptly left before tears came.

Dr. Kristofer Werner greeted Peggy with open arms a short while later. "Ah, Fraulein Phenwick! You have made it! You entered a marathon, and you have won!"

"Have I won, doctor? Or has the fight only just begun?"

"The fight, as you call it," Werner said, "will continue for the rest of your life. You may live the life of a normal woman except for your intake of food. You will always have to be remarkably careful about that. You have learned how to eat what is proper for you. Furthermore,

Frau Mueller assures me that you have become accomplished in poise and grace, and all the other subjects she has taught you. You are in for an altogether new experience in life. Enjoy it and make the most of it. And make the most of the glamorous, attractive and exciting woman that you are."

"I intend to do that."

"A word of warning," Werner interjected, "do not attempt to make up for all that you have missed in the past. The past is over and gone. Live for each day and discover the joy and beauty that you will find. I will give you another word of advice. The sooner you find the right man, fall in love with him and marry, the happier you will be. Too often woman like you try to catch up on all which they have missed, only to find themselves emotionally torn apart by such reckless activity."

"That thought scares me, Dr. Werner," Peggy said. "I know I have missed much in my life, and I constantly have to fight the idea that I will want many men to compensate for what I have lacked. But I do want to be loved. I only pray I have the good sense to attract the right man."

"You will. You will." Dr. Werner extended his hand to her to shake. She took it; then, at his touch, she pushed herself forward to embrace him. She hugged tightly and kissed him on the cheek.

"Thank you, Dr. Werner. Thank you for bringing me back to life. I know I was dead and entombed. Now I've been resurrected. Forgive me for calling you all of those vile names in the beginning."

"What vile names?" Dr. Werner laughed. "You Americans who speak no German are vulnerable to Helga's little pranks. The words you shrieked at me were quite the opposite of vile or profane. But, because Helga Krankenschwester was your attendant, I well got the drift of what you meant." He laughed again, kissed her on the cheek and released her. "Now you must go, fraulein. I have other fat people to trim down. Since you no longer fit that category, you're no longer welcome here—as a patient. Auf wiedersehen."

"Good bye, Dr. Werner."

A sleigh was packed with her luggage and waiting to take her to the railroad station when Peggy walked out the door she had entered six months before. She was definitely a changed woman.

Chapter Seventeen

Peggy took a hotel room across the street from the railroad station in Vienna, since she planned to be there only a short time. Because she had discarded many of the things she had with her when she had entered the sanitarium six months before, her luggage was relatively light and consisted of only a few personal things, and the new wardrobe that Eric Schmidt had designed and created for her.

After settling into the hotel room where on a whim she had registered as Wilma Collins, Peggy arranged to be driven to the office of Dr. Augustus Ornby.

"Miss Collins, this is highly irregular," Augustus said as he interviewed Peggy in his private office. "You are most fortunate that the weather is so unpleasant, or I would not have had a cancellation."

"That was a chance I had to take. I'll only be in Vienna a short while," Peggy said. "In which case, I will immediately come to the point. I am looking for a Mrs. Millijoy Phenwick."

"Millijoy? Why, she returned to the United States in late September," Augustus replied. "Unfortunately her health has taken a turn for the worse. There is a great deal of deterioration in her body, which will make her vulnerable to one illness after another throughout the rest of her days. But Millijoy has lived a full life. I suspect she will will herself to an early death rather than live out her days as an incapacitated invalid."

"*Will* herself to death?"

"That is quite possible with a person who has the determined mind which Millijoy possesses," Augustus stated. "Quite frankly, I never expect to see her again—and I'm certain she felt the same about me before she left."

"Did her granddaughter return to Boston with her?" Peggy asked.

"Lanny did, yes." Augustus leaned back in the chair and observed Peggy with folded hands and pointed index fingers at his chin. One eye squinted nearly closed as he studied the young lady. "There is something extraordinarily familiar about you, Miss Collins, but I can't precisely place my finger on what it is."

"What if I told you I was related to the Phenwick family?" Peggy asked as she tried to contain her amusement.

"Ah, that would explain!" He sat forward. "I can see now that you have a remarkable resemblance to the late

Nancy Phenwick. Yes, that must be the reason you appear familiar to me."

Peggy rose and moved in a direction opposite to which Augustus was sitting. She knew he was appraising her beautifully proportioned figure. When she had given him sufficient time to notice the back side, she slowly turned around, as Frau Mueller had instructed her, so that he could get a full view of first her profile, then her front. "There was another Phenwick traveling with Millijoy and Lanny, wasn't there?"

"Yes, a cousin from San Francisco, who has gone off to a san—i—tar—" The word stuck in Augustus' throat. He slowly got to his feet, his lower jaw dangling in astonishment. *"Peggy?"*

"Did you think I was so beyond hope that the treatment wouldn't work?" she asked as she repositioned herself, aware of the light coming in through the window.

"I have known that Kristofer Werner has performed miracles in the past," Augustus stated, "but I have never seen such dramatic results of his ability. Why did you tell me your name was Wilma Collins?"

"First, I wanted to see if you would recognize me, and you didn't. It wouldn't have been such an interesting game if you had known my name," Peggy said playfully. "Secondly, I've decided to go by the name of Wilma Collins for a while. It was a name suggested to me by a very close and dear friend. Besides, I'm not certain I wish to think of myself as Peggy Phenwick for a while. After all, the Peggy Phenwick that everyone knew was quite a different person than I am."

"You have a very good point there." Augustus stood closer to where Peggy was positioned. "Who was the friend that suggested the name?"

"Have you ever heard of Adam Truff?"

"Certainly. He was practically a Phenwick," Augustus said. "But Adam has been dead for some time now. Ah, he must have visited you in San Francisco."

"No." She laughed, but she felt like she wanted to cry. "Suffice it to say that I associate the name with Adam Truff. I'll be leaving for Rome tomorrow, now that I know cousins Millijoy and Lanny are no longer here."

"To Rome?"

"It should be considerably warmer than Vienna," Peggy replied. "And I want to have a bit of a holiday before I return to America. After all, I would hardly call my stay at the sanitarium a vacation. Not hardly. Besides, I want to get used to my new body and the reactions others have to it before I go back."

"That is wise," Augustus said. "I received a letter from my brother Joseph the other day, and he told me that Donald Phenwick's operations had been most successful." He watched for her reaction, since Millijoy had told him of Donald's feelings for Peggy. He was disappointed that she did not show more enthusiasm in her attitude.

"I am pleased to hear that," Peggy said, almost indifferently. "Donald had a tremendous ordeal ahead of him when we last saw each other. I have received letters from him."

"I thought you might be more overjoyed to hear the news."

"I am happy for Donald." She observed her appearance in a wall mirror. "I'll not take up any more of your time, Aug." She kissed him on the cheek, shook his hand and quietly, but grandly, left the office.

Augustus stood at the door and watched her leave, then he went to the window to see her move out into the street and hail a cab. What he witnessed was such a surprise that he decided to cancel his other appointments for the day and go to his club.

Statuesque and aware of the attention she attracted, Peggy took a private compartment on the train to Rome. She was aware that she was ogled the entire time she was in the railway station. Even the porters fell all over themselves to get the opportunity to assist with her luggage. Eyes followed her as she moved to her assigned compartment.

When the rotund conductor entered the compartment to collect her ticket, he stood gazing at her as one might scrutinize a celebrity. His liquid face began to perspire all the more as he permitted his thoughts to run rampant with impossible speculation. "Kictit, please."

"I beg your pardon?"

The conductor mopped his brow. "Oh, forgive me, madam. "Tickport and passit, please."

"Do you not speak English?"

"That was the best I could do under the circumstances."

Peggy smiled and handed the mān her passport and ticket.

"These will be returns to you in the morning," he stammered and backed from the compartment.

It was an overnight ride to Rome. The train pulled into the station shortly before noon the next day. There was a new conductor aboard, and although he was abundantly impressed with Peggy's appearance, he was less clumsy than his predecessor in her presence. He arranged to have a porter take care of her baggage.

As Peggy was leaving the train platform, she noticed a

group of school children standing a distance ahead of her. Her first impulse was to attempt to avoid them and the remarks children had cruelly made to her in the past. There was no escape. When she did get close to them and realized that they were in their early teens, three of the pubescent boys turned their attention toward her and gazed with what appeared to her as salacious stares. The whispered remarks they made among themselves were far from the abusive statements which had been hurled at her in former days.

Aware that she was attracting attention everywhere that she went, Peggy began to feel very conspicuous. She wondered if average girls received such acknowledgment and interest.

Peggy checked into the elegant Hotel Roma under the name of Wilma Collins and went to her room for a short period of relaxation.

Later that afternoon, Peggy went to the hotel dining room to take a late lunch. Every male hotel employee who was interested in women eyed her and obviously made a point of being noticed in hopes that she might find one of them attractive and desirable. She only caught a glimpse of them with peripheral vision. Then she tried to contain her reaction of amusement.

Men seated by themselves in the dining room as well as several who were with ladies stopped as she passed their tables. Once she was seated, several made attempts to gain her attention. She ate very little and lingered over coffee.

Why had she come to Rome? she questioned herself. It was a whim, and she thought it would be warmer than it was. She decided simply to be a tourist for a day or two, then travel on to Spain.

As Peggy returned to the hotel lobby and was again made aware of the attention directed toward her, her first impulse was to return to her room. She quickly thought better of that and found a comfortable seat from which she could observe the passersby.

"Ah, Miss Collins!" a voice announced as it came near to where Peggy was seated. Expecting it to be one of the hotel officials, she was surprised to look up and see a familiar face: The short man with black hair and a well-trimmed moustache gazed at her with flashing eyes. It was Damien Brusco. "I would know you anywhere, Miss Collins. I believe we met at a party several years ago. I travel about so much of the time that the precise incident escapes my mind. Allow me." He clicked his heels together and bowed as he handed her his card.

"Didn't we meet in New York, or was it Savannah, Mr. Brusco?" Peggy asked as she decided to play along with his game temporarily, and at the same time, have a little game of her own.

Surprised to think that she had actually recognized him, Damien was momentarily caught off guard. "I doubt that it could have been either of those places you mentioned, since I've never been to Savannah, and my visits to New York have been extremely limited. Do you mind if I take a seat with you?"

Peggy motioned to the chair beside her. She waited until he adjusted himself. "Oh, yes, I recall, you're a gigolo, aren't you?"

"Did you ever indulge in my services?" Brusco asked with wide eyes.

"Don't you recall? You were the one who spotted me."

"Well, in all modesty, there have been so many," Brusco stated. "One can't remember every one."

"How did you know my name, then?" she asked.

"I confess I overheard it when you checked in," he replied.

"Then you don't remember me from the past. Not even from San Francisco?"

"San Francisco?" Damien sat forward. "I have spent much time in San Francisco—before—well, let us say I made a mistake or two and a wealthy man of extreme influence had me removed from that city."

"Did you kill someone?"

"No such thing!" he stated. "I merely performed an indiscretion and got caught at it. Perhaps you have heard of the Phenwicks of San Francisco."

"The name is familiar, however—"

"A very wealthy family. I am basically a very flexible person," Damien explained, "and I like women of all shapes and sizes. But you see, now don't laugh, the Phenwicks had this enormously large daughter whom they wanted me to marry. I could have done that—and again I ask you not to laugh—but I would have had to have a variety of women on the side to compensate for such a situation."

"I'm *not* laughing, Mr. Brusco," Peggy said through her teeth. It was then that she hit upon a plan. "You were saying?"

"Well, the gigantic lady in question," Brusco continued, "caught me in an upstairs bedroom with one of the maids. I honestly thought she was too big to be able to climb that many steps. But, miraculously, she did. Such a stupid person she was. She must have been terribly naive to believe that any normal man would be attracted to her—unless he was paid to pretend to be."

"You make this lady sound quite a monster."

"That, dear Miss Collins, is an understatement."

"Why are you telling me all this, Mr. Brusco?"

"I don't know." He smoothed his moustache with the back of his index finger. "I really don't know. I simply began talking, and all of a sudden it just started coming out. Are you offended by what I have said?"

"Goodness, no, why should I be? I find your tale almost as amusing as you do, Mr. Brusco." She took a nonchalant pose.

"Are you occupied this evening?" Damien asked.

"As a matter of fact, I am not. I've just arrived in Rome and I don't know my way around," Peggy said. "I was preparing to ask the desk clerk if he could recommend some sort of service—tour guide service."

"Ah! I know Rome like I know the back of my hand," Damien replied eagerly. "I would be delighted to show you around. But there is one thing—"

"Yes? Your price?

"How perceptive of you, Miss Collins."

"You set the amount."

"The amount depends on the services you desire rendered."

"Whatever the maximum amount is," Peggy said, maintaining an aloof pose, "that is what I will require, Mr. Brusco. Will you pick me up here at eight?"

"Most definitely."

Taking that as his reason to leave, Damien got to his feet, clicked his heels, bowed and darted away from where Peggy was seated.

Peggy watched him leave. She had four-and-a-half hours to devise a plan, and she intended that it should be appropriate.

"Revenge is sweet, dear Peggy, but be careful, it could backfire on you."

From where had the voice come? Then Peggy decided it was simply a thought that had come to mind. Well, she would put such thoughts aside until she had sufficiently dealt with Damien Brusco.

Chapter Eighteen

The inexpensive cologne had a spicy fragrance which created a slightly offensive aura about the cocky person of Damien Brusco. Wax made his moustache glisten. A touch of rouge had been added to his cheeks to accentuate whatever youthful qualities he had left. His bristling, eager attitude was somewhat amusing, because his enthusiasm was unbridled and overdone. He obviously thought of himself as a Lothario with considerable magnetism.

The dark trousers he wore had a distinct shininess to them. Still, compared to most of the Italian men Peggy had seen in Rome, Damien was as well dressed as the next one, and better than most. His step, which was almost like a dance, was confident, and he walked proud, a man assured of himself. Yet there was a comical attitude about his confidence.

Entering the hotel lobby as if he were striding onto a theatrical stage, Damien pranced up to the main desk to have himself announced to Miss Wilma Collins. The clerk merely pointed to a group of high-back chairs in a remote corner. The little man adjusted the brim of his hat and set it at a rakish, yet somewhat artistic, angle as he neared where Peggy was seated. Doffing his hat grandly, clicking his heals noisily and bowing with a flourish, he presented the lady a large smile which was full of implications and perhaps an insinuation or two.

"Ah, Miss Collins! Damien Brusco, at your service!" Another click of the heels and another bow. "You're ravishingly beautiful tonight. The subtle light at night always seems to bring out a certain lovely, mystical quality about a person, don't you think?"

"In your case, Mr. Brusco, I would say the quality is more mysterious than mystical." Peggy was wearing the most elegant of the creations made by Eric Schmidt. It was golden yellow brocade and soft lemon-yellow taffeta. The bodice was low cut, and the mutton-chop sleeves were bellowy. White gloves covered her forearms nearly to where the large sleeves of the gown puffed out. A lustrous chain of pearls hung about her neck and were knotted at the base of her cleavage with an additional loop hanging nearly four inches below. A three-strand of pearls bracelet adorned each of her wrists. Her hair had been fashioned in a bouffant design with two long, wide finger-curls cascading down the right side of her neck. Three egret plumes were artistically positioned at the back of her head in place of a hat. Although her waist was slim, she wore a corset to give her even more of a wasp-waist appearance. The support also made her sit very erect, which augmented her sophisticated beauty and attitude. She had started to wear the cameo brooch which Donald Phenwick had given her on their first meeting; but, because of the nature of the plans she had for the evening, she thought better of that and wore a buffed gold lapel watch on the left side of her bosom. She eyed the watch before she glanced up at Damien. "Ah, Mr. Brusco, you are precisely on time."

"I make a habit of being punctual," Brusco replied. "I detest being made to wait, so I know how it must annoy my clients."

"Your clients?" She presented her gloved hand to be kissed as he bowed again, after clicking his heels.

"Ladies who patronize my profession," he replied with flourish.

"And, therefore, you think of me as merely another client, is that the case, Mr. Brusco?"

He shook his head, then smiled sheepishly and shrugged. "I would like to think of you in another way. You are an extraordinarily beautiful lady. And I would judge from your dress and regal appearance that you are either a member of royalty, or you have mingled with such people most of your life."

Peggy smiled without making comment. She remembered the long hours she had spent getting instructions from Frau Mueller, who herself had been raised in the Hapsburg court.

"What is your pleasure for the evening?" Damien asked, his eyebrows bouncing up and down to punctuate his question. "I am completely at your disposal."

"I have made reservations at Mario's," Peggy replied, "where we will dine. They have entertainment. You do care for opera, don't you, Mr. Brusco?"

"I'm Italian, aren't I?" Damien motioned to the chair next to her and sat after she nodded in approval. "Mario's is extremely expensive, and they cater to wealthy people and nobility."

"So I was told." Peggy fingered the pearls. "I have ordered a loge so that if we find the performance loses our interest, we can close the heavy velvet curtains and converse in private."

Damien's eyes twinkled with insinuation. "You seem to have thought of everything."

Peggy's eyes narrowed as she looked at him. "I believe I have, Mr. Brusco." Then she smiled sweetly. "Shall we go?"

Peggy ordered a small green salad without dressing, a bowl of clear broth, and delicately seasoned shrimp, which were broiled and served in a nest of lettuce.

"You do not have much of an appetite, do you, Miss Collins?" Damien observed after they had ordered and he had asked for an elaborate seven course meal of pasta and exotic Italian cuisine.

"I have learned not to live to eat," Peggy returned, "instead, I eat to live. However, I do not think of you as a glutton simply because you have an enormous appetite."

"My profession being what it is, I confess I do not always have the opportunity to eat well," Brusco commented. "That being ithe case, I take advantage of whatever situation presents itself."

"Don't you fear becoming stout?"

"All the more of me to love," Damien replied. "I have found that there are women who admire fleshy men."

"And I suppose that is true the other way around, isn't it?"

"Oh, yes. I understand there are men who relish having affairs with plump ladies."

"Yourself included, Mr. Brusco?" Peggy asked as she attempted to control vitriolic implications in her voice.

"I accommodate whatever sort of clients I may have," he said with an air of one who takes pride in his work.

"Oh, yes, I recall your speaking of that heavyset girl in—Chicago, was it?" Peggy baited him.

"Heavyset—? Oh, no, not Chicago—San Francisco." He cringed. "The Phenwick lady."

A properly uniformed and mannered waiter brought wine, which Peggy declined.

"Do you abstain from spirits as well?" Damien asked as he poured into his glass.

"I drink only mineral water," Peggy replied.

"I like the light-headed giddiness that wine causes me to have," Brusco returned. "It makes me all the more amorous."

Peggy glanced from the man with the eager stare and pretended to examine the decor of the loge. The area was about twelve feet by twelve feet. Deep red paper covered the walls. Brass holders supported flickering gaslights.

Beyond the opening which overlooked the rather large stage, Peggy observed the other patrons, who were seated at tables down below. She could also see other loges on the opposite side of the enormous hall. A large-chested woman was singing a soprano aria on stage to the accompaniment of a piano, violin, trumpet and drum. A mixed quartet stood a short distance behind her to sing the chorus parts. The audience loved the soloist and called her back for an encore.

As Damien attacked his antipasto, more food than Peggy had eaten in the past three days, she turned her attention back to the stage before she swept her eyes about the audience and across the way to the other loges.

A handsome couple entered the box opposite to where they were seated. Recognizing something familiar about the pair, Peggy reached for her lorgnette opera glasses. Upon raising them, she saw that the lady opposite was gazing in their direction through her opera glasses. How embarrassing! She quickly turned her head and focused her attention in another direction. Then, when she had inconspicuously scanned as much as she could see, she casually let her head turn back so that she could view the occupants of the opposite box. A cold chill ran over her, mixed with a prickly sensation of excitement.

"Is something wrong, Miss Collins?" Damien asked, food stuffed in each of his cheeks.

"No, not at all. I like to see a man with a hearty appetite."

"Food excites me," Damien admitted, "and garlic rouses me to passion." He took her gloved hand and kissed the back of it.

"Have you ever been in love, Mr. Brusco?"

"Love! Love!" he said somewhat contemptuously. "Love is a woman's game. I love what I am doing—love my profession. I cannot see the reason a person should devote himself to only one woman. There are so many available and so many more desiring of my services."

"Modest, aren't you?"

"I try not to be."

"I can tell."

A while later Peggy permitted her attention to drift to the box opposite to where they were seated. The attractive young lady rose, permitted her escort, who was standing, to kiss the back of her hand, then regally left the compartment.

"Excuse me, Mr. Brusco," Peggy said. "Do continue with your dinner while I take a brief, but necessary, recess."

As he stood up, Damien wiped his hands on the napkin which was tucked in his collar and covered his shirt-waist.

When he started to put greasy lips to her white gloves, Peggy pulled away, smiled demurely and retreated from the box.

Passing the headwaiter, she nodded a cue and grandly made her way to the ladies' lounge. The outer room was elaborately furnished with brightly upholstered overstuffed furniture. Several ladies were present, some of whom were smoking. They glanced up at Peggy with looks of envy and admiration. She tried to avoid looking directly at them, but she knew they were appraising her beauty.

Peggy was standing before an enormous gilded framed mirror observing the reflection of loveliness to which she still had not become fully adjusted. Her eyes met those of the handsome lady who had been seated in the box opposite to where she had been. Peggy watched the other's mirrored eyes squint as if she had recognized something familiar about Peggy but could not place what it was. Peggy turned to face her with a warm, yet curious, smile.

"Hello."

"You are an American, then?" the other questioned.

"You could tell that by my merely saying 'hello'?"

"My husband and I are here on holiday," she said. "I had observed you sitting in the box opposite us and I said to Mr. Stocker that I thought there was something remarkably familiar about you, and he concluded that you were probably an American."

"Your husband was correct, Mrs. Stocker," Peggy returned. "I did get the name correct, didn't I?"

"Yes." She shook her head slightly. "The more I look at you—and you must forgive me for staring—the more familiar you seem to me. Even your voice sounds like a voice I should know."

"Do you know it, Mrs. Stocker?"

"I'm uncertain."

"I go by the name of Wilma Collins," Peggy said.

"I don't know the name."

"I shouldn't think that you would."

"Am I annoying you? I don't mean to do so. It's just that I have this uncanny sensation when I look at you. I'm almost certain that I must know you. Perhaps we have met merely in passing, or I've only seen you somewhere. Excuse me, I am Mrs. William Stocker from San Francisco, California."

"The Stockers are a very well-to-do family in San Francisco, aren't they?"

"Yes, quite. William—that is, Mr. Stocker—insisted that his parents join us on this trip. Fortunately we were able to escape them tonight to have a little intimate time by ourselves. I love my in-laws dearly, but you must know how it is."

"I've never been married."

"I didn't mean that." She cocked her head and stared again at Peggy. "I'm the former Miss Phenwick of San Francisco."

"I know the Phenwick name."

"Ah, then we have met. We're staying at the Hotel Roma. I wonder, Miss Collins, if you would care to call on me there."

"That's a coincidence, I'm also staying at the Hotel Roma," Peggy said. "When I was in San Francisco last, there was a Miss Phenwick, I recall, who was—well, shall I be kind?—plump."

"My sister Peggy. Surely, if you were in San Francisco, that is where we met each other. I doubt that you could have known my sister—she had few friends. Quite frankly, she has always been an embarrassment to us, that is, her family. We do love Peggy, but she is simply a—well, a—"

"Freak?"

"I couldn't have said that about my own sister, but now that you've suggested it, I must admit you are correct."

"And you honestly do love the—uh—freak?" Peggy tried to control her emotion.

"She *is* my sister."

"Even though she is a butterball?"

"Butterball? How curious! That's what my brother used to call Peggy."

Peggy struck a somewhat aloof pose and turned profile. "I'm detaining you from your husband, Mrs. Stocker; and my gentleman friend is waiting. Perhaps we can meet tomorrow for tea."

"Yes, by all means." Her eyes ran over Peggy's face again. "I'm certain I should know you." She extended her hand and Peggy shook it. "Until tomorrow." She turned to leave.

If they had not shaken hands, Peggy's reaction might have been different. But the touch contact caused her to lose her composure. "Lola . . ."

Lola froze in her tracks and slowly turned around as gooseflesh bubbled all over her. "How—how did you know my name—?"

"Lola, don't you know me?" Peggy asked, a pathetic tone in her voice.

Lola stepped back to where Peggy was standing. Incredulously she scanned the face before her. "Can it possibly be—?"

"Yes, it's me, the butterball—but I've melted a little."

"Peggy? Oh, my God! Peggy?"

Peggy nodded her head as tears began to streak down her face. Lola immediately went to her and embraced her; she, too, was teary-eyed.

Chapter Nineteen

Shortly after Peggy had left the loge, and Damien Brusco was busily eating as if he were making up for lost time, the door opened and two scantily attired young ladies appeared. They wore tiny skirts over flesh-colored tights. Their only other accessories were paper flowers, which were sewn onto various parts of the tights in a suggestive manner. Speaking Italian, they announced that they had come to be of assistance, and introduced themselves as Gilda and Violetta.

Overwhelmed by the sight of such beauty, it was all Damien could do to continue eating. He ogled first one and then the other as they released the velvet draperies and pulled them closed. Violetta lit the candles on the table, while Gilda removed Damien's napkin and suggestively tied another around his neck.

"Is this the customary part of the service?" he asked.

"We always try to make the customers happy," Gilda replied as she pushed herself against him.

"I am not dining alone."

"But you seem to be dining alone, signor." Violetta got on the other side of him and gently brushed against him.

"My client—that is, my lady friend—should be back in any moment.

"Violetta will stand at the door and give warning when she returns," Gilda said.

"But I must save myself, my strength and energy for the lady," Damien protested.

"How silly! A man as powerful as you could no doubt take on a harem of ladies," Violetta teased.

"Of course, I could, but not all in one night," Damien replied. Gilda was stroking him in such a suggestive way that he could not help but respond.

"It would be best if you stood on the outside, Violetta," Damien said. "That way you can see before she gets here. Rap lightly on the door and do your best to detain her from entering."

"It will be better if I have Giuseppe watch for us," Violetta stated. "Gilda and I work together. It's called a sister act."

"Mama mia!"

Violetta stepped from the box long enough to allegedly make arrangements with Giuseppe before she returned to join Damien and Gilda, who had become very much entwined in each other.

Lola begged Peggy to join William and her, but Peggy insisted that she could not. They would meet early the next day.

When Peggy went toward the box and the congenial Giuseppe, who seemingly was standing guard, they merely exchanged glances. Giuseppe nodded and Peggy smiled. Then she made her way downstairs.

One hour later, there was a rap on the door to the loge. A mad scramble took place inside.

"Who is it? Miss Collins?" Damien asked.

"No, it is the headwaiter," was the reply. "I have brought you the check."

"The check?" Damien was rapidly adjusting his clothing. "But the check is for the lady."

"The lady has gone."

Damien jerked the door open. "What do you mean she has gone?"

"She has gone, that is all. There is no meaning other than that," the headwaiter replied. He projected a bill on a silver salver.

Inching past Damien, Gilda and Violetta scampered from the compartment, only briefly glancing at the waiter.

"I do not understand," Damien said. "What happened to Miss Collins?"

The waiter forced Damien back into the loge. "The lady arrived nearly an hour ago. I intercepted her and informed her that you were occupied with Violetta and Gilda. Being a lady of discretion, she merely thanked me and said she would not remain."

"Impossible!" Damien was flustered.

The waiter held up the bill so that Damien could see the figures on it.

"Santa Maria! I don't have that kind of money," Damien exclaimed. "I have no more than three lire in my pocket. The lady was to have paid for everything."

"That may have been the case before she learned that you were being entertained by Violetta and Gilda."

"Those hussies invaded me! It was their idea! Did you tell Miss Collins that?" Damien was red-faced and shaking.

"I said nothing other than that you were occupied with the girls," the waiter said. "Now, then, can you pay this bill or not?"

"I cannot."

"Then I will have to call the police, signor. You have committed a criminal act. Fraud—misrepresentation—infidelity."

"Please, please, get a hold of Miss Wilma Collins at the Hotel Roma," Damien begged as two burly men came to remove him from the loge. "She will understand and get me out. After all, she secured my services. Do you hear me? Contact the lady I was with at the Hotel Roma. She will get me out. Miss Wilma Collins."

"Miss Wilma Collins?" the headwaiter said. "The lady you were with wasn't Miss Wilma Collins."

"What? But of course she was." Damien suddenly looked scared. "If she wasn't Miss Wilma Collins, who was she?"

"Why, Miss Peggy Phenwick, Signor Brusco," the waiter replied. "Miss Peggy Phenwick of San Francisco!"

Damien swore in amazement. "Impossible! Miss Peggy Phenwick of San Francisco is a huge woman, much more than an armful."

The headwaiter looked at him coldly, somewhat cynically. "Not anymore she isn't, Signor Brusco."

Damien Brusco swore again before the two men roughhoused him down the stairs and outside to where the police were just arriving.

When the van pulled away from the restaurant with Damien screaming at the top of his lungs, Peggy stepped from the small room near the entrance. She reached into her bag and pulled out the agreed-upon price for the headwaiter's services, as well as to pay for the check.

"May I ask you a question, miss?" the headwaiter said after he had pocketed the money. "Where is the real Miss Peggy Phenwick?"

"*I am* the real Peggy Phenwick."

"But Signor Brusco said that she was huge."

"She used to be, but she has changed," Peggy said. "You've been paid well. Once you have seen to it that Damien Brusco is prosecuted to the letter of the law, and he is forced to serve an adequate sentence in jail, I will give you the balance of what we agreed upon for your efforts."

"You are a most shrewd and calculating lady," the waiter observed. "Could what Signor Brusco did to you in the past have been so terrible that you have taken such drastic measures?"

"When one plays ruthlessly with another's emotions and unfairly leads that person to believe in the other's sincerity," Peggy replied, "I can justify any means of retaliation. I have had many years to witness and feel the injustices around me, not to be a little vindictive—shrewd and calculating, as you said.

"Do you delight in taking vengeance?" he asked.

Peggy thought a moment. "I don't know. But for the moment, repaying Damien Brusco for the hell he put me through gives me a sense of satisfaction. Good night."

As Peggy rode back to the hotel, she considered what she had said to the headwaiter. *Vengeance* seemed a hard and unscrupulous word; yet she could not deny that she had long nurtured feelings of neglect and desire for retribution from a world that did not understand the agony through which she had gone.

Examining her appearance in a large mirror in the hotel lobby, Peggy was pleased with what she saw. The six-month ordeal through which she had gone at Dr. Werner's sanitarium was well worth it. The overall transformation was far beyond what she had anticipated when she first went to the spa. She took great satisfaction and pride in what she had accomplished. Even her own sister had not physically recognized her. There must have been something about her, however, which had caused Lola to feel as if she had known her. If not physical, then something spiritual, her personality which shone through whatever exterior she revealed.

Glancing at the reflection of the clock above the lobby desk, Peggy saw that it was ten o'clock. She was keyed up and filled with excitement. Certain she would never be able to sleep for at least another hour or two, she was about to take a chair and watch the people coming and going. That which gave her the most satisfaction was the expressions she observed on the faces of men when they passed her, looks of stimulated interest and, as often as not, prurient desire. Yet she thought back about her experience with Collin Williams and of the great desire she had had to know the fulfillment of love with him. That proved to be an illusion. Still she honestly believed she knew what the true emotion of love was because of the situation.

Before she turned to go to a nearby chair, Peggy noticed two different men making abrupt halts and staring at her. Since they were positioned at different parts of the large room, neither knew of the other's interest. They both started toward her at the same time. Before they got to where she was, they saw each other and seemed to perceive that they both had the same intention. Each shrugged and pretended that they were headed elsewhere.

Again she examined her reflection to observe the two men going away from her in opposite directions. Before she could remove her attention from the glass, she beheld the entrance of Mr. and Mrs. H. Caswell Stocker.

Amanda Stocker waited near a potted palm and pretended to be scrutinizing a handsome bouquet of yellow roses as her husband went to the front desk. Her eyes swept about the room until they reached the place Peggy was standing. Since Amanda's eyesight was not the best, she mistook the stunning young lady for Lola and went toward her.

"Is William not with you?" Amanda asked as she approached Peggy. "I was under the impression that you two intended to stay out into the wee hours of the morning."

"I beg your pardon," Peggy said coldly, as if she had been approached by a stranger.

Amanda reached to find a pair of eyeglasses, which she never wore in public. Donning them, she gasped when she realized the lady was not her daughter-in-law. "Oh, dear! I beg *your* pardon. I thought you were someone else."

"I am someone else, but probably not the someone else you imagined me to be."

"That's a curious remark," Amanda returned, somewhat fascinated by Peggy's attitude.

"I'm known for my curious remarks, Mrs. Stocker."

Amanda was in the process of removing her eyeglasses before her name was mentioned. Upon hearing it, she quickly put them back into place and gawked curiously into the pretty face before her. "Do I know you?"

"You apparently thought you knew me when you came over toward me," Peggy replied.

"Then I thought you were my daughter-in-law, Lola Stocker." Amanda squinted and pushed her face forward. "How do you know my name?"

"You're Mrs. H. Caswell Stocker of San Francisco, aren't you?"

"I am."

"I was present at your son's wedding."

"*You*—you were?" Amanda looked perplexed. "I don't recall seeing you."

"Oh, I was very much in evidence," Peggy replied.

"You must be a Phenwick. No wonder you look remarkably like Lola."

"I am a Phenwick."

"One of those relatives who came from a distance," Amanda suggested. "Not the wife of John Adam or Luke, are you? No, of course not, they weren't born Phenwicks."

"I was one of the bridesmaids," Peggy said softly.

Amanda took another appraising look at Peggy. "Why, that's impossible. I know all of the bridesmaids. And certainly I would have never approved of having such a radiantly lovely lady like you in the wedding party, who would attract attention from the bride. That sort of thing isn't done. Unless, of course, that stunning individual happens to be a sister or perhaps a close cousin to the bride."

"You did your best to keep me hidden and as inconspicuous as possible," Peggy replied. "That was like trying to hide a lion among a group of house cats."

Amanda gasped and clutched her breast. "You're not—?"

At that moment, Caswell Stocker strode to where his wife was standing. "Are you ready, my dear?"

"But you couldn't be," exclaimed Amanda.

"But I am," Caswell rejoined. "Whatever is ailing you, Amanda?"

"Look at this young lady, Caswell. Do you know her?"

"I would certainly like to," Caswell replied before he thought. "Should I?"

"This is Lola's sister," Amanda said, then asked, "aren't you?"

"I am."

"I thought Lola only had one sister," Caswell remarked, opening his mouth wide enough that it would easily fit his foot. "The one who made our mansion look like a doll's house."

Amanda nudged her husband. "You must forgive Caswell, he doesn't always say the acceptable thing."

Peggy gazed directly into Caswell's eyes. "I am Peggy Phenwick, Mr. Stocker. Perhaps the next time I visit your doll's house, you'll take a better look at the mansion."

"However—" Again Amanda gasped. "Oh, dear, I've never seen such a remarkable change in anyone. I'm both shocked and amazed. You must join us tomorrow. We have tickets to the opera, and I'm certain we can pick up another for you. William and Lola will be with us."

"I think not, Mrs. Stocker," Peggy replied sedately. "I really have no desire to be seen with you in a social situation. You may be the elite of Nob Hill, but I am still the Peggy Phenwick that I always was. True, there is less of me now, but I still have my pride and feelings. And I still remember the unkind things you said about me. Thank you, anyway, but I will be busy tomorrow night." She made a slight nod, and with the regal grace she had learned from Frau Mueller, Peggy walked away from the Stockers.

"That was rude, wasn't it, my dear?" Caswell commented.

"Rude, perhaps, but I deserved every word she said to me," Amanda commented. "Come along, it's time that we retired."

Chapter Twenty

Peggy took a ship the next day from Italy to the eastern coast of Spain. Disembarking at Barcelona, she checked into a first-class hotel and took a suite of rooms overlooking the Mediterranean, which had become silver in the afternoon sunlight. The day had been warm, but the breeze was cool and delightfully refreshing. Gray clouds were moving west over the sea, and the bellboy had informed her that rain was expected by late that night.

Relaxing on the terrace, watching gulls elegantly soar over the beach and water beyond, Peggy sat back and gathered her thoughts. She liked the new her and the positive, favorable attention which she attracted. Although she had only had a short visit with Lola, the two sisters found that they really had a tremendous respect and admiration for each other. Lola was unable to get over her shock at seeing the transformation in Peggy; and Peggy made her promise not to tell a soul in San Francisco about the alteration—she wanted it to be her surprise. Reluctantly Lola, William and the senior Stockers agreed to keep Peggy's secret.

Suddenly Peggy felt alone in a strange place. Her life had been plagued with loneliness for over twenty-five years. She rationalized that she had become used to it; in some ways she had. But she also knew that she was a human being who basically needed the companionship and love of other human beings. As she pondered the events that had transpired since she left Dr. Werner's, she thought of the reaction she had had to men who had found her attractive. In many cases, she had to admit, she had felt their interest both stimulating and provocative.

There were times in the past when Peggy was relentlessly obsessed with curiosity and interest in men. For long periods she would sit in the solarium at her home on Nob Hill and watch people as they passed by on the street, especially the men. She even caught herself ogling the male servants, and occasionally she had been almost blatantly flirtatious with them. Now that she had changed, she liked the attention which men paid her. She enjoyed seeing their expressions of stimulated reaction. And she remembered how she had watched Lola and Lanny in the past as men had similarly reacted to them. That was normal human nature. She concluded that if individuals were not attracted to one another, it could be a very desolate and lonely world. She had known the loneliness, now it was time to reverse that aspect of her life. But, remembering Collin's words, she knew she had to be careful and not try to make up for lost time. Yet there were strong urges in her that made her want to fling herself out into the world and have as many experiences as she possibly could because of what she had lacked.

That evening Peggy dressed in a soft blue gown trimmed with white organdy. While not as flamboyant as her yellow dress, the blue one was extremely attractive and revealing of the figure she had newly trimmed into a work of beauty. She wore a broad-brimmed picture hat with large, blue cabbage-roses on it and a white chiffon band about the crown, which hung down her back. Her white gloves were augmented by the presence of sapphire-studded bracelets. She wore a mounted sapphire on a white ribbon about her neck as a choker, and the cameo brooch given her by Donald Phenwick at the apex of her cleavage. Stunning, elegant and obviously a lady of fashion, she left her room and eventually descended the grand stairway to the magnificently splendid hotel lobby.

Eyes turned as Peggy appeared at the top of the stairway. For a moment she responded with that old feeling of being stared at by people who looked on her as a freak. Then she remembered, and taking command of the situation, she stepped down each level as if she possessed the greatest confidence in the world. Action below halted as speculated interest about her buzzed through the lobby. Surely, she must be a member of nobility, or an extremely wealthy lady of society, or even the daughter of American opulence and position.

As she reached the floor level, Peggy tried to avoid the dozen or more pairs of eyes that were fastened on her. Perhaps it was the gown which attracted such attention; but Peggy realized beyond a doubt, although the dress was eye-catching, that it was her own beauty that had garnered the interest.

Suddenly she felt the touch of a hand at her elbow. She turned but saw no one there. The experience unnerved her, and she nearly lost her composure for a moment.

"Have no fear, dear heart, it's only I."

"Collin?"

"I thought it best for me not to materialize. You've stunned the throng sufficiently without my doing my little bits of magic to amaze them. I've simply made my

*presence known to let you know that I was standing by
with whatever assistance you require.*

"Collin?"

"I beg your pardon, señorita?" a handsome man in his
thirties asked. He was tall with long, attractive features,
sleepy, seductive eyes and dark blond hair. Dressed in
fashionable evening attire, he presented a picture of the
ideal gentleman. "My name is not Collin. Permit me to
introduce myself. I am Jorge Catalon. I am not Basque,
but I am part Castilian and part French. Are you unes-
corted?"

"I appear to be, don't I?"

"Ah, but you must be expecting someone by the name
of Collin," he said in English seasoned with a slight Spanish accent.

"No. I know no one in Barcelona," she returned. "It is
just that your voice reminded me of someone."

"An American?"

"That is perceptive of you."

"May I know your name?" he asked with an intense
look in his eyes.

"I am Wilma—" She stopped and studied his sincere
expression. "No, I am Miss Peggy Phenwick, originally of
San Francisco, California. I'm traveling alone and I'm
only in Barcelona for a short time."

"Alone? Alas, I know what loneliness is."

"You? How can that be?"

Jorge laughed. "My dear Miss Phenwick, even the most
attractive people in the world—and I say this in all modesty—can be very lonely. It is my observation that those
who are common and have ordinary appearances are
much happier than those who are possessed with extraordinary handsomeness."

"Or those possessed with ugliness," Peggy inserted.

"I suppose that must be the case," Jorge replied. "Never in my life have I beheld such a beautiful woman as you. Have you, too, known loneliness?"

Peggy lowered her head. She was aware that they were being watched by several curious pairs of eyes. "Yes, I have—but for another reason than you have known loneliness, Señor Catalon."

"I, too, am alone in Barcelona," Jorge said with a sigh. "May I offer you a bit of libation."

"I will take a cup of tea with you, Señor Catalon, or perhaps a cup of coffee."

"And have you plans for dinner?"

"None as yet."

Jorge offered his arm and Peggy took it. She liked the sensation that physical contact with the man produced. Like that, she was increasingly aware of the attention that was directed toward them—and she very much liked the feeling.

The austere waiter showed the lovely couple to a table on the covered veranda, where they had an excellent view of the sea and the beach. Night had fallen, still, people could be seen walking along the shore, silhouettes which were darker than the backdrop behind them. Stars twinkled above, but the approaching clouds were beginning to take them from sight. In the far distance, occasional bursts of lightning brightened the clouds. When everything was extremely quiet, the faint cannon-blasts of thunder could be heard rumbling. A sweet, mysterious fragrance was on the night air. The periodic twittering of night birds added a touch of mystery to the setting.

"Are you certain you will be warm enough out here?"

Jorge asked as he gazed across the candle flame into Peggy's eyes.

"Plenty warm. The breeze has an almost sultry quality to it," Peggy remarked.

Jorge lifted the candle to a cigarette, then set it to the side so that he did not have to look over it to see her face. "You fascinate me, Señorita Phenwick."

"How so, Señor Catalon?"

"I have been acquainted with many ravishingly beautiful women in my time," he replied. "But never have I encountered any with such exotic beauty as you possess."

"That is a compliment. Thank you."

"I suppose, likewise, you have met regiments of attractive men, haven't you? How could you not with such exquisite loveliness?" Jorge commented. "I have known other American women of various European extractions, but, for the most part, they resembled their coarse and peasantlike ancestors. You, on the other hand, are remarkably fragile and as delicate as a Dresden figurine."

"Such flattery, Señor Catalon!" Peggy laughed as she remembered Lanny laughing when she had been paid a similar compliment.

"Have you ever been married?"

"No . . . never." Peggy shot him a curious glance. "Why do you ask?"

Before Jorge could reply, the waiter came and took their order. As usual, Peggy ordered very simple food and mineral water.

"You eat like a canary," Jorge commented after the waiter departed. "Do you fear gaining weight?"

"I haven't much of an appetite," she replied, hoping to avoid any further discussion about that.

"Ah, then you must be in love," Jorge pronounced. "I

understand that being in such an emotional state of love takes one's appetite away."

"I cannot say that I am in love—nor have I ever been in love except with an illusion."

"I beg your pardon?" Jorge leaned forward. "An illusion?"

"Don't we all fall for an illusion of love at one time or another? The absolute ideal of love would have to be an illusion, wouldn't it?"

"Perhaps you are right," Jorge replied.

"Have you been married, Señor Catalon?"

"Si, once."

Peggy thought a moment as she observed a distant look come into his eyes. "And are you still married, señor?"

His eyes met hers. "No, señorita, I am not. I married young, only to discover that once the innocent blush left my wife's face she became adventurous and flirtatious. I admit I was deeply hurt—especially when she left me for another man. Oh, she would have gladly remained married to me and accepted my financial support as long as I allowed her to have her little assignations on the side. I could not tolerate that. We separated."

"And divorced?"

"We are Catholic," he said. "Divorce is not permitted."

"Then, how long have you been separated?"

"Nearly eight years—eight years in June. And I must add that it has been a long and lonely time for me." Jorge had been looking away. He suddenly turned his full attention back to Peggy and smiled warmly.

"Have you never fallen in love again since then?"

"I may have verged on falling in love a time or two after my separation," he replied. "But how could it be real? I can never ask a lady to marry me."

"That isn't right," Peggy complained. "You're a marvelously handsome, obviously virile man. Being without love must be very difficult for you."

"Can it be any more difficult for me than for you, señorita?"

"I believe that it might be," Peggy replied. "After all, you have been in love and you've been married."

"And you've been neither?"

"I didn't say that—only that I hadn't been married."

"And only in love with an illusion." Jorge smiled. "You speak like a romantic woman, one who idealizes love. How can it be that you've never been in love? Naturally, you are young and beautiful; but you are not so young that you could have avoided the inevitable emotion of such a romantic person. Would you wish me to believe that you had recently escaped from a convent?"

Peggy thought a moment. "A convent of sorts, yes—a self-induced imprisonment. I can tell you no more than that."

The dinner arrived. The conversation turned to light and somewhat frivolous matters. Peggy did her best to keep the topics away from anything serious; still she had developed an interested curiosity about the man and she wanted to know more about him and his background. Conversely, Jorge wished to become acquainted with the real person Peggy was.

Although the lightning was getting nearer and the drumming of the thunder louder, Jorge invited Peggy to take a short stroll after dinner. By then the wind had increased, and Peggy had to use a scarf to secure her hat in place.

Stopping in a shadowed and secluded place, Jorge took Peggy's hand. They had been walking in silence.

"Señorita Phenwick, I would very much like to make love to you."

"I must say you are very forward about your wishes," Peggy countered.

"I feel we have a mutual attraction to each other," Jorge stated. "Is that not true?"

"I will have to consider that question," she replied. "As you yourself observed earlier, I am very much of a romantic. That being the case, you surely must realize that I would not submit to lovemaking at such a short acquaintance." She was aching to throw herself into his arms as trembles of excitement shivered through her.

"I did not mean—" Jorge apologized, quickly changing his tactics. "Surely, I've given the wrong impression. I wish to kiss you and take you in my arms, señorita. I will eagerly extend my stay in Barcelona that we may become greater acquainted."

"I thought you—that is—" Peggy felt as if she were blushing. Why couldn't she keep her entire body from shaking? "You wish to kiss me?" The words barely came out. She tried to remember the time of her illusion with Collin Williams. Had that been entirely in her imagination, a daydream that had taken on some kind of real proportions, a fantasy at best?"

"May I?" Jorge asked.

Peggy sensed that she was swaying, tilting backward, then falling forward into his arms. A bolt of lightning struck a short distance out over the sea as he took her in his arms and pressed his lips to hers. She had no strength to resist. Jorge was not an illusion, but very real flesh and passion.

Chapter Twenty-one

The fourth bolt of lightning struck much closer than the one previous to it. Peggy felt as if it had ignited her entire person with an electric reaction. Every part of her was alive in response to Jorge's aggressive passion. A fire seemed to be kindled in her innermost parts, the flames of which were blazing higher and higher with greater intensity, as if they intended to consume her. The roar of thunder that followed appeared to vibrate in her solar plexus and send quivering, ever-increasing rings of excitement through her.

The fifth crack of lightning hit very near, struck a tree limb and caused it to crash to the ground. A drop of rain on her hand splashed Peggy back to a sense of awareness.

"We'll be drenched!" she whispered.

"With passion?"

"No, with rain."

"Passion and rain," Jorge corrected. "Do you wish to return?"

"We must."

"Because of the rain?"

Peggy hesitated. "Because it would be best if we did."

"Do you not find me stimulating?"

"Extremely stimulating, Señor Catalon."

The form of a man neared where they were standing. "You'd better get back into the hotel. We're in for a storm."

"He is right," Peggy said. She pulled herself from Jorge's hold and reached for his hand.

"He?"

Another streak of lightning seemed to splash where the silhouette of the man was standing. But it did not illuminate his face.

"There is no one there."

"In that case, we must get back." She jerked him forward. Tiny drops of rain had begun to fall.

By the time they reached the shelter of the veranda, Peggy felt as if the starch had gone from her dress, and she sensed that she was as limp as the garment.

Jorge attempted to take her again in a passionate embrace, but she resisted.

"No, Señor Catalon, we must desist this," she stated. "I am wet. If I change out of my gown, I can have it tended to at once."

"Do you let rain stand in the way of romance?" he asked.

"Is it the rain? Or is it propriety?" The outer part of her picture hat had become set and drooped about her face.

"Propriety?" Jorge gently caressed her hand. "You kiss like a woman who has been starved for love."

"That well may be, Señor Catalon," Peggy managed to say, "but I am not without principles."

"Does that mean you are offended by what I have done?"

"Not in the least," she said. "I am flattered that you have shown me such affection. If you knew the truth about me, you would comprehend why I am reacting now as I must."

"The truth? Ah, then you *have* been in a convent?"

"No. No, not that."

"Are you saying that I have no need to extend my stay in Barcelona?" Jorge asked softly.

"That, of course, is up to you," Peggy returned. "I will be here for at least two weeks. I think I would be most happy if you were in Barcelona for that same period of time. Now you must excuse me."

Jorge caught her in his arms again and kissed her as he had done before. She weakened and fell against him, supple, pliable and emotional in his hands.

"Señor Catalon . . . please . . . don't . . ."

Jorge covered her lips again with his. "I want you, Señorita Phenwick. I am beyond control."

As lightning again brightened the night, Peggy caught a glimpse of the man standing nearby. She sensed it was the same who had previously interrupted them. Gently, but forcibly, she pushed herself away from Jorge's embrace.

"You must let me go now. I will gladly see you tomorrow—if you have not been too disappointed by tonight," Peggy said.

"Disappointed? Si. Discouraged? Far from it. Too much too soon diminishes the mystique," Jorge replied. "Being left wanting only motivates me toward greater aggressiveness. But it also makes one reevaluate the desire."

"Reevaluate the desire?" Peggy questioned. "I don't understand."

"Where does illicit desire end and love begin?" he questioned.

"What are you saying?"

"If you were to submit to me now, it would merely be the passion of the moment," Jorge said. "But, if you leave me wanting, unsatisfied physically, yet with a strong emotional reaction, I am liable to have deeper desires for you.

You are a wise woman. And I thought you were a bit naive to the ways of romantic relationships."

"You thought I was a pushover?"

"Forgive me for underestimating you, señorita." He held her hand. "If you are not disappointed with me, I should very much like to call on you tomorrow."

Peggy thought a moment. A blue artificial rose had obstructed the vision of her left eye. "I would very much like to see you tomorrow, Señor Catalon."

Jorge kissed her hand. "May I see you to your room?"

"It would be best if we parted here," Peggy replied.

"We will meet tomorrow, Señorita Phenwick. I'll put a call through to your room by noon," Jorge stated. "And thank you for a lovely evening. *Muchas gracias.*"

"And thank you, Señor Catalon."

Peggy hurried through the lobby, catching only a brief glimpse of herself in the large mirror in the lobby. People were watching her. Fortunately the hat was the only part of her outfit that was wilted by the rain.

No more had she removed her gown and hung it where it would get plenty of air to dry, and she had placed the hat where it's shape might be restored as the water evaporated from it, than she went to examine her face in the mirror. What a lovely expression she beheld despite the effect of the rain. Her cotton underthings were dry.

"It's a good thing I happened to be around, isn't it?" a voice said from a large chair.

"What? Who is it?" But before she turned to see, she instinctively knew who it was. "Collin?"

"Dear heart, you were going at it most passionately out there," Collin replied. "Didn't I warn you about such eventualities?"

"I couldn't help myself," Peggy said. "I couldn't help but respond as I did."

"How do you feel now?"

"What kind of question is that?" Peggy asked.

"Do you have a desire to run back to find your elegant Spanish gent? He may merely be an opportunist," Collin commented. "Chances are, he is. Suppose you had submitted to him and discovered that he had checked out tomorrow. How would you have felt about that?"

"I would be disappointed," Peggy replied. "But I don't see how I could be any more disappointed than I am now."

"Disappointed in the man?"

"No, not at all. Disappointed in not discovering the fullness of a relationship with him," Peggy said. "Collin, I am nearly twenty-six years old. There are girls at sixteen who are married and have children. Ten years or more of my life have been wasted."

"Only ten?" Collin mused.

"Why are you here? Why did you interfere? Don't tell me you have such powers that you were able to bring the lightning!"

Collin laughed. "I did not affect the lightning in one way or another."

"Nor did the lightning affect you!" Peggy charged.

"As to interfering, Peggy, I was merely trying to keep you from getting hurt. Get to know Señor Catalon. Then, if you find he is sincere, that he is loving and affectionate, I would be the last one in the world to impede the fulfillment of what you desire. But be rational and fully understand the situation before you lose your heart to an impossible situation."

"Are intimate relationships such holy things?" Peggy questioned.

"They are if they affect your emotions, mental reactions, yes, and your sanity," Collin said. "Frankly, I don't believe you're ready to have an affair right now. I doubt if you could cope with it. At least give yourself time to get to know Señor Catalon. And if you must have a relationship with him, be aware that that is all that it is. He cannot marry you, he told you that himself."

"He could renounce being a Catholic."

"Could he? I wonder. His religion has been ingrained in him. Were he to divorce, he could be plagued with guilt—and that would only bring ultimate unhappiness to you."

"How?"

"He could blame you for causing him to leave his church," Collin warned. "I do not say it is right for him to have such attitudes, but it is something that you must be aware of." He paused. "Do you think you are in love with him?"

"I don't know! How can I know? What is love, anyway?" Peggy fired. "Do you know? I know who you are—or at least who you were: Adam Truff. And I also know that Adam Truff never married—and for that matter never fell in love with any*one*.

"Didn't he?"

"How can *you* possibly know what being in love is?"

Collin sat quietly for a moment. "I know, Peggy, believe me, I know. Love manifests itself in many ways, not always in conventionally acceptable ways—but it is still love. Simply know beyond the slightest doubt that Adam Truff experienced being deeply in love." He rose and moved to where she was standing. "I could tell you many tales. I won't. They're unimportant to you." He went to the open window. "When your eyes see no other person but that one special person, even when you're in a crowded room, that is what love is. When your thoughts are constantly held on that person, even when you have a million other things on your mind, you have touched upon love. When you desire the highest good for that person at all times and he holds you equally in esteem, you have discovered the truth of being in love. Most of all, Peggy, love is total giving and total receiving, sharing in every aspect of that which each of you is, not only physically, but in all ways—then, when you have that attitude toward another person, you will be in love." He turned back to her. "Your emotions—yes, and your body—ache for Jorge Catalon at this moment. He represents what you dearly desire. But people are not always scrupulous: They play with other people's emotions for their own satisfaction. I don't say for you not to know the fullness of an affair with Señor Catalon—I would be the last person to moralize about such a situation—but I do advise you to use reason and get to know the man well before you permit a relationship that will only be based on animal passion and desire."

Peggy was staring at him. "Collin, it's different with me because I was as I was."

"That is a poor excuse, Peggy. Submit once to base desire and you'll do it again and again—and never find that for which you are seeking."

"And what do you suppose it is I am seeking?"

"True love. Belonging to one person and he to you, and knowing the entire magnitude of what true love really is." Collin stepped to her. "Peggy, that which you are seeking is right now seeking you. Know what you want in a man, establish your ideals of love, and don't compromise for anything less."

"You're too idealistic, Collin."

"Am I? I think not. I can see backward and forward in time. And I can tell you that right now, although you're unaware of it, you are deeply loved. Furthermore, love is coming to you. Keep that in mind."

"Who is in love with me? You? You're only an illusion!"

Collin chuckled. "I can only tell you that you are loved. You will have to discover for yourself who that person is who loves you. An illusion or not, I wouldn't bring these thoughts to you if you did not want them or need them."

"Are you my conscience?"

"If that is what you wish me to be."

Peggy turned toward the mirror. A thought struck her when she did not see Collin's reflection. And when she turned back, the illusion had vanished.

For the next two hours Peggy pondered Collin's words. The entire experience was mystifying. Argue as she might against what he had said, she could only conclude that what he said was right.

Still she could not put thoughts of Jorge Catalon from her mind. His touch remained a burning sensation against her flesh. Why was it so important to save herself for just one man? And, if so, where was he? Why hadn't he materialized in her life before this?

Peggy had prepared herself for bed. She couldn't erase the memory of Jorge's touch, of his emotions and passions. Fantasies about the man played in her imagination and that only aroused her all the more.

Whether she was in love with the man or not, Peggy

decided that she was going to experience as much of him as she could. Would she get hurt? She might. Would she feel guilt? Again, that was a possibility. Yet, for her own peace of mind, she believed she had to discover what any relationship with a man would be.

And supposing Jorge Catalon were to fall in love with her and asked her to live with him, would she dare become involved in such a situation? She wished Lanny or Katherine were there that she might speak with them and get their good advice—or even Millijoy. What did Adam Truff know about such things?

As she was about to go to sleep to the lulling rhythm of the falling rain, Peggy thought she heard a voice.

"An entity lives many lifetimes in the bodies of both genders, and experiences the emotions, reactions, trials and tribulations of each. That is what the life experience is all about: to learn and emerge a well-balanced entity. I do know what love is—and I've been hurt by it many times."

Peggy opened her eyes. "Leave me alone, Collin. Let me sort this out for myself."

A faint sound of laughter rumbled through the room, then all was quiet.

Chapter Twenty-two

Like a musical work which begins with a slow melodic theme and ultimately crescendoes into an impassioned, romantic melody, the events of the next three days in Peggy Phenwick's life developed. Jorge Catalon was a persistent suitor, a gentleman and a considerate human being. He instinctively knew that Peggy had a mysterious past. He couldn't begin to guess the nightmares through which she had gone nor the inner struggle and conflict she had known. She was a beautiful creature, in his eyes, all that he desired in a woman. Yet she was complex. She reacted to his stimulation as other women had—and more so. He concluded that she was affection-starved and, at the same time inexperienced in the ways of romance. The very awareness of that perplexed him. It all made her seem so extremely paradoxical and puzzling.

By the end of the third day in the company of the handsome Castilian, Peggy's resistance was completely worn down. She eagerly embraced him and kissed with such hungry desire that both knew there was only one thing that could possibly satisfy the intensity of emotional and physical craving.

The following morning when she awakened beside Jorge Catalon, Peggy considered what had happened. She glanced at the man, studied him as he breathed heavily in sleep and remembered as the events of the night before replayed in her mind. She had been fulfilled as a woman, the mysterious door had been unlocked and opened to her, and she knew beyond a doubt that her life had been sadly lacking and incomplete before then.

After pulling the covers back and gazing at Jorge with contemplative interest for nearly fifteen minutes, Peggy awakened him with a kiss, and the adventure continued to heights greater than she had even realized the night before.

The affair with Jorge Catalon progressed for seven days. Peggy was insatiable, and her handsome lover was capable of meeting all her needs. Never before had either of them had such an experience.

"I cannot believe that such a beautiful woman as you," Jorge said on the morning of the eighth day, "can have lived a life of celibacy, yet be so ravenous for love and affection."

"I'm afraid if I were to tell you why I did, you would never believe me," Peggy replied. "Or perhaps you might be repulsed by what I had been."

"Stretch marks tell me you were not always as slender as you are now, my lovely," Jorge commented. "Yet you are an angel of remarkable beauty. Have you fallen in love with me?"

"I believe that I have."

"And I believe that I have fallen in love with you," Jorge returned. He smiled, but his expression slipped into a frown and he suddenly looked worried. Standing before the mirror, he examined his attire. His appearance was perfection.

"Do you have something to do today?" Peggy asked as she watched him.

"Only a little errand, my sweet," Jorge replied. He kissed her softly and gently caressed her. When she pressed heavily against him and kissed him with the ravenous hunger that he had come to know from her, he returned her passion for a moment before he tenderly tried to make it subside. "Peggy—dearest Peggy—we have fallen in love—but I wonder if it is as it should be."

"Why do you say that? Is something disturbing you?"

He kissed her again. "Nothing important at the moment. Now I must go. We will meet this afternoon. The sun is shining brightly, it is a lovely day."

After Jorge was gone, a strange apprehensive feeling

came over Peggy. Something was very definitely wrong. She stared at her reflection in the mirror as more and more a negative premonition came over her. What was it?

Later when she descended the hotel stairs, Peggy felt as if she must run, that a tremendous urgency was pulling her from the place. She walked rapidly toward the center of the city. What was driving her? What was compelling her?

Several blocks from the hotel, Peggy was startled by the loud ringing of church bells. Gazing up, she saw the tall, tile-covered spire with the stately cross atop it. A sudden charging sensation struck her chest, but it seemed to come from within and up from the innermost depths of her. Hypnotized by the din of the bells and the compelling majesty of the steeple of Moorish design, she ran until she reached the church entrance. Fortunately, she thought, she was wearing a hat.

As she entered the somewhat musty-and-incense-smelling church, Peggy hesitated. She had never been in Catholic surroundings before. The awe and grandeur of the place practically overwhelmed her. As she went into the sanctuary, her eyes adjusted to the dim atmosphere, and she marveled at the statuary of saints and the candle-lit altars. Stained glass caught the sun's reflection, and she seemed to feel the colors as they radiated on her.

Quietly she sat at the back of the church and watched devoted parishioners as they came to pray. Why had she come there? And why was she lingering? This was not her church. She did not understand the religion, much less the procedures or any of the significance of any of the symbols.

Nearly ready to escape from the place, Peggy's attention was drawn to the clicking sound of the door to a confessional booth as it opened a tiny bit. Almost immediately it was pulled closed. Curious.

A few minutes later, the door to the other side of the booth opened and a middle-aged padre pushed his way out. The man was plump, bald and humble. His round face beamed a sanctimonious expression as his eyes became accustomed to the brighter light. After first looking at Peggy, he smiled and crossed to where she was seated.

"Señorita," the kindly appearing priest said with a heavy accent, "I am Padre Juan Pedro. I would like to have a word with you."

"With me?" Peggy looked bewildered.

"There is a small chamber beside the main altar, señorita. We will go there where we will not be disturbed."

"I am—I am not of your parish, Padre, nor of your faith."

"I am well aware of that, my child. Come this way, please."

The whispered shuffling of Juan Pedro's sandals caused several veiled ladies to glance up as he passed. Peggy followed him, even more perplexed than when he had first spoken to her. The singular thing that occurred to her was that he spoke to her in English instead of Spanish when he first greeted her.

The tiny room had thick, stuccoed walls and heavy rustic doors. The furnishings were modest, wooden and not particularly comfortable. Peggy sat where she was directed and stared curiously at the holy man.

"What do you want of me, Padre? Why have you brought me here?"

"You are an American, are you not?"

"I am."

A dreamy expression came to the priest's face. "Ah, I have always wanted to go to America—to California. Padre Junípero Serra was one of my favorite people. I have read many tales about him."

"I was born and raised in California," Peggy volunteered. "I am not a Catholic."

"Si, I realize that. I saw you from the confessional booth, and you did not go through the necessary ritual of one who is of our faith."

"Now that that's cleared, what is it you wish to speak to me about?" Peggy asked, trying to quell her impatience.

"We of the Catholic faith have very definite attitudes toward sin, señorita," Juan Pedro stated.

"Sin?"

"That which is right and wrong," he explained. "For one thing, we do not believe in divorce, for when a man and woman are married in the eyes of God, it is a lifelong covenant—a contract of fidelity. Therefore, it is expected that such persons are only to indulge in intimate relationships with their marriage partners—no one else. Furthermore, once a person is married into the church, he or she—although they be separated from their spouse—is guilty of committing an abominable sin if he cleaves unto another who is not his spouse."

"Why are you telling me this?" Peggy questioned.

"I believe you know, señorita."

"Jorge?"

"Señor Catalon has been to see me every day for the past three days."

Peggy's jaw dropped, and she registered an expression of shock. "But he has been with me the larger part of the last three days."

"I am well aware of that fact, señorita. Señorita Phenwick, isn't it?"

"Yes."

"I must tell you about Señor Catalon. As a boy he was devoutly religious. After his confirmation, he had strong inclinations toward the priesthood and he was earnestly encouraged to go in that direction," Juan Pedro related. "He did spend nearly a year in a monastery before he realized that the urgings of the flesh were too great for him. He left the monastery to marry. The marriage was not ideal, and there is question that he was ever in love with his wife. Still he formed a marriage contract. They lived together only a relatively short time before they separated. It was hoped that Señor Catalon would return to monastic life. But he had had a taste of intimate passion and could not rid himself of the desires of the flesh. He tried a reconciliation with his wife—but that was impossible for him to do."

"If it was impossible, why wasn't he permitted a divorce?"

"Divorce simply is not recognized by the church," Juan Pedro stated. "Although Señor Catalon had affairs with other women—and there were many—he could not forget his strong religious background. He enjoyed the physical part of such relationships, but the spiritual and mental anguish caused by them, drove him to a state of despair. Guilt is a terrible thing."

"Then why has he been made to feel guilty?" Peggy asked.

"Because that is the law of the church."

"Is it the law of the church that Señor Catalon will be forced to feel guilty the rest of his life?" Peggy snapped.

"He has confessed his sins and has been forgiven,"

Juan Pedro said. "I told him what our Savior told the sinner: 'Go and sin no more.' Señorita—although this may be painful for you—Señor Catalon has taken my advice."

"What do you mean?" Peggy snapped, a fearful surge of emotion bursting up from deep within.

Juan Pedro took an envelope from the folds of his cassock and handed it to her. "This is from Señor Catalon."

Peggy took the letter with trembling hands, ripped it open and hurriedly read it.

"Please understand that Señor Catalon is basically a devoutly religious man," the priest said. "The truth is, he feels that he has fallen in love with you. He is a man torn by guilt."

Tears came to Peggy's eyes as she read the words that told her she would never again see Jorge Catalon. "*You* have torn him apart with guilt, Padre Juan Pedro! You made him feel that he was sinning!"

"Not I, the church."

"*You* are the church! Well, I'm going to go to him and tell him that you are wrong! That I love him as much as he loves me! And if that is sin in the eyes of God, I don't think very much of Him." She started to leave.

"He has left Barcelona, señorita. I will pray for you."

"You detained me so he could get away! That's what you've done!" Peggy screamed. She jerked the large door open. "I believe God will forgive both Jorge and me long before he forgives you, Padre! Love, no matter how it is expressed, is the most beautiful, most wonderful thing in the world!" She stormed from the room, ran around to the sanctuary and up the aisle to the door. She did not look back to see Padre Juan Pedro standing contritely beside the statue of the Virgin Maria. When Peggy was gone, the priest fell to his knees and wept.

Peggy arrived back at the hotel within ten minutes after she left the church. Going to the desk, she was informed that indeed Señor Jorge Catalon had checked out fifteen minutes before and that he had not left a forwarding address. The only information she received was that he had left in an automobile, which he drove himself.

Bursting into tears before she reached her room, Peggy flew to the closet, flung all of her wardrobe onto the bed and telephoned to the desk to have someone sent up to help her pack.

While the packing was being done and the bewildered bellboy listened to her sniffling and sudden outbreaks of rage, Peggy managed to control herself long enough to ascertain when she could get the next train to Lisbon.

Dressed in her least exotic attire, Peggy took care of the hotel bill and informed the clerk that she was destined for Portugal and ultimately back to the United States. The heavy veil she wore did not disguise the fact that she was in tears.

"Is there nothing I can do for the señorita?" the clerk asked.

"Nothing. There is only one person—no, nothing."

During the train ride to Lisbon, Peggy sat in solitude, staring out the window, but not really seeing anything. The image of Jorge Catalon danced through her mind as she relived the precious moments she had spent with him. The excitement, the thrills, the heights of exotic delight before the explosion of pain, which could only be described as beautiful, were fully remembered. And the memory caused her to weep all the more.

"I warned you," the voice said as if it were thundering through the compartment. *"You simply had to learn the difficult way, didn't you?"*

"Please leave me alone, Collin! Please!"

"*I can't really do that, you know. I've too much concern for your ultimate good and happiness. Now, more than ever, I am convinced you are to be one of the greatest Phenwick Women of all time.*"

"I don't want to hear such a thing!"

"*A place is being vacated for you.*"

"What a queer thing to say! What do you mean by it?"

"*You think you are frantically running away from; but, dear heart, you are actually urgently running toward. Believe, and it will help the pain.*"

The pain, Peggy thought, and it hurt her all the more.

Still, by the time the train pulled into the Lisbon station, a peculiar sense of peace had descended over Peggy. When the conductor came to assist with her luggage, she smiled at him. It was a smile, she thought, that one smiles when awakening from a pleasant dream. Was Jorge Catalon only a dream? No, he was not an illusion, and she knew precisely what she wanted.

Chapter Twenty-three

In the long run, Peggy came to believe that it was fortuitous that the sea voyage from Lisbon to New York took what seemed to be an eternity. She continuously had thoughts of Jorge Catalon and the traumatic confrontation she had had with Padre Juan Pedro. Once she was able to circumvent her rampant emotional reactions, and become as objective about the situation as she possibly could, she realized that Jorge was really a very disturbed individual who would probably spend the rest of his life attempting to find himself. He was too easily under the thumb of the church, and as long as that existed, he would never be free to receive from life that which he wanted most.

It had been an experience, Peggy kept telling herself, one from which she intended to grow. Although she had the opportunity to meet several different men during the sea journey, she avoided such encounters, aware that such persons were at best looking only for a shipboard romance. Furthermore, she vowed to herself that she would make every possible effort to find the right man for herself, fall in love with him and not submit to any intimate relationships until she was married. She had overcome one major obstacle in her life by shedding the poundage that she had, she was certain she could accomplish anything she set her mind to.

There were days aboard the ship when Peggy wished that Helga Krankenschwester was with her to bolster her with the courage that she had given during those tedious days of change at the sanitarium. But Helga was of another world; and Peggy intended to become mistress of her own environment.

Upon arriving in New York, Peggy made plans to travel by rail to Boston. While in Manhattan, she acquired a more extensive wardrobe and made several purchases of fine jewelry. Europe and the past were well behind her, and she would not permit sentimental memories to linger in her consciousness from the past.

During her three-day stay in Manhattan, Peggy attended a performance in which Augusta Phenwick II was the starring player. Although she had never met her distant cousin, Peggy made a point of going backstage afterward.

Augusta II was kind and cordial, but since Peggy was virtually a stranger to her, they had little in common other than to discuss relatives.

When Peggy reached Boston, she checked into a hotel near the railway station. She needed time to get herself together and decide precisely what she would do. During the ocean voyage, she had considered going directly to San Francisco from New York, but she dearly wished to see Lanny, Katherine and Millijoy again.

Gowned in a yellow dress, which was a bit ostentatious for day wear, yet gave lift to her spirits, she hired a cab to take her to Triumph House. In her mind, she imagined the reaction of Millijoy and the others to her transformation. Her fingers played nervously with the cameo brooch which Donald Phenwick had given her. After leaving Triumph House, she intended to call at Edward House to see Ruth and Donald.

Stoically handsome, although aging, Victor Samson opened the door to Peggy. His eyes were red and swollen, and his cheeks were rosy and shiny, which indicated that he had been under severe emotional stress.

"I've come to call on Mrs. Millijoy Phenwick," Peggy announced.

"Mrs. Phenwick is—Mrs. Phenwick is seeing only members of the family," Samson replied.

"I am Miss Phenwick."

Samson peered into Peggy's face. "Apparently you're not a Miss Phenwick whom I've met before. I've always taken pride in recognizing the Phenwick ladies."

"We've met before, Samson. You simply don't remember me." Peggy took an elegant pose and smiled sweetly.

Uncertain, yet in an agitated emotional state, Samson

merely observed and left Peggy waiting in the round entrance hallway. As she gazed up at the gigantic crystal chandelier with the prisms reflecting light from she knew not where, a curious sensation came over Peggy. Something was wrong. A pall hung heavily over Triumph House, and she suspected it had to do with sadness. She recalled Collin's saying something about a place being vacated among the Phenwick Women, a situation she was destined to fill. "Oh, no!"

Samson did not return to fetch Peggy, instead Lanny moved down the stairs toward her with a regal grace. She smiled, yet tilted her head slightly in an attempt to identify the startlingly beautiful woman standing below.

"You are Miss Phenwick?" Lanny asked.

Peggy's expression was emotional. She ran toward Lanny and embraced her. "Oh, Lanny, is it Cousin Millijoy? Is she—?"

"My God! Can it possibly be Peggy?" Lanny incredulously questioned.

"It's me."

Lanny kissed her and hugged her tightly. "Who would have ever believed that I would have been able to wrap my arms around you? Oh, Peggy, Peggy, for goodness' sake! I'm stunned."

"You didn't tell me about your grandmother," Peggy said after she had returned Lanny's affection.

"She has had her things packed, her affairs in order," Lanny explained, "and she has been waiting at the station for the train called transition—change. Those were her words. Yet she has been lingering as if she were waiting for one last person to come and say 'bon voyage' to her. I suspect that person has arrived."

"Me?"

"Come upstairs with me," Lanny instructed. "For the past three days she has mentioned your name on several occasions. It's as if she has been asking for you."

"Why me?"

"I suspect because you were her last challenge," Lanny replied. "When she sees you, the new you, she doubtlessly will consider you her last triumph."

That morning a beautician had come to Triumph House to arrange Millijoy's hair. Although she looked tired and weary as her head lay propped against the large white pillow, a shadow of her old magnificent beauty lingered in her face. Still she appeared fragile and a bit pathetic. Her eyes had a gray film over them and, although she directed her gaze, she sensed the presence of those around her more than she actually saw them.

Tommy and Evelyn Phenwick were standing near the bed; Dr. Joseph Ornby was on the other side of it. Katherine and Philip were near the window overlooking the terrace, and John Phenwick was seated at the desk. Most of those in attendance glanced up at Peggy as if she were a stranger in their midst.

Millijoy had closed her eyes. Her head moved restlessly from side to side, as if she were experiencing discomfort. "Joseph, why must it take so long?" Her eyes opened, and she tried to focus on her old friend, who was both her doctor and distant cousin by marriage. She smiled and turned her head to the other side. "Tommy, Evelyn—I hate to detain you from all you have to do. You needn't have come all this way just to say goodbye. I'll be around—somewhere."

"Mother," Tommy said as he put his hand to hers. "Mother, I would never have been the success that I've been without you. My career has really been a part of your career."

Evelyn put her hand atop Tommy's, but she could not speak.

"When I have sold property," Millijoy remarked, "I have not liked to see it vacated until the new tenant arrived. Whatever can be keeping her?"

"Who, Mother?"

"My replacement." Millijoy chuckled hoarsely. Her attention turned to a large bouquet of red roses on the nearby table. "Adam sent those, you know. However he manages to do that sort of thing, I'll never understand—but perhaps I will soon." She could vaguely see Lanny standing in the doorway and only a silhouette of Peggy beside her. "Lanny? Is that you?"

"Yes, it's me."

"We should really have a train schedule, you know," Millijoy stated as she beckoned the dark-skinned girl nearer to her. Her face suddenly brightened. "Ah, you brought her with you!"

Katherine turned to Peggy; perceptively she knew who she was and to what Millijoy had been alluding. "Go to her, Peggy. She has been waiting for you."

Joseph Ornby rose and tried to cover his expression of astonishment. "Can it actually be Peggy Phenwick?"

"It is, Joseph," Millijoy said. "I knew she would be successful. She is destined to be the grandest Phenwick Woman of all. Adam has told me so."

"No, not the grandest," Peggy corrected. "Second only to the grandest, who, of course, is you, Cousin Millijoy."

"That is kind of you to say, Peggy," Millijoy replied. "But of all the accomplishments I have made, I have never achieved any to surpass the monumental transformation which you have made." She made an all-en-compassing sweep of her head to indicate to the others. "May I speak privately with Peggy for a moment?"

Tommy and Evelyn hesitated before stepping toward the terrace. Katherine took Philip's hand and led him to where John was seated. Joseph Ornby checked his watch before he motioned with his head for Lanny to join him, and they went to the far side of the room.

Peggy glanced up at the large painting of Adam Truff before her eyes drifted back to Millijoy.

Millijoy followed Peggy's gaze. She smiled as she viewed Adam's likeness. "Is the name Collin Williams familiar to you?"

"Collin?" Peggy looked startled.

"I can see that it is. You needn't look so alarmed. There are two sides to every coin. I happen to be on the same side that you are now; shortly, I will be on the reverse side—but, in any case, it is still the same coin—merely another point of view."

"I don't quite comprehend the meaning of your words," Peggy returned.

"You must think about it, then." Millijoy held her hand toward Peggy. "I am very proud of what you have accomplished. Obstacles are put into person's lives to be overcome. And you have overcome. When it comes to the final analysis of what success is, I would judge that it is overcoming, for nothing has the value that accomplishment has. You have achieved, and with achievement you are certain to go on to greater triumphs. Somehow or other, from the other side I will imbue you with encouragement. You will be the Phenwick Woman that I could never have been. I came into this life with the stigma of mixed blood. You don't have that problem, therefore you will become fully accepted. A matriarch steps down, vacates her throne for the new and younger queen. I wear a very large crown, so you will have to strive hard to keep it from wobbling and falling from place."

"Why have you chosen me?" Peggy asked.

Millijoy glanced again at the picture of Adam Truff. "Sometimes there are other forces who make such decisions." She looked to the other side of the bed, and a large smile came to her face. "Ah, you must have tiptoed in."

Peggy turned her attention to follow Millijoy's eyes. She saw the likeness of the one she had come to know as Collin Williams. He smiled warmly at Peggy, then reached his hand to Millijoy.

"I love the roses, Adam," Millijoy said softly. "but then I always have enjoyed them. You have impeccable taste. Take a rosebud, Peggy, and it will help you fulfill your destiny."

"Collin—is she—?" Peggy asked.

"She is going with me now," he replied. "Her course, this time around, has been completed. We're going to a graduation ceremony." He smiled warmly. "Don't take a rosebud from Millijoy's bouquet, but go out into the garden where you will find a magnificent blossom. That is the one meant for you."

"Millijoy?" Peggy questioned. A smile was frozen on the woman's face, an expression of contentment and fulfillment. Suddenly feeling awkward, she turned back to where Lanny and Joseph Ornby were standing.

Joseph interpreted her look and quickly stepped to the bed. Lanny was immediately behind him. The others in the room were startled by the sudden movement, and all stepped closer to the bed.

Upon examining Millijoy, Joseph shook his head. His eyes met the eyes of those who were watching him. Again he shook his head.

Evelyn burst into tears; and tears streamed down Lanny's face. Tommy's eyes had become misty, as had John's and Philip's. Katherine contained her emotions and stood impervious in her husband's embrace.

Peggy stared at the bed and the lifeless form for several minutes, then she majestically moved toward the large bouquet of red roses. Her fingers outlined one of the rosebuds. She could not cry. Where was the sorrow? She had witnessed the beauty of the transformation that had taken place with Millijoy. How she had been able to perceive that she could not explain. Was it, too, an illusion? She was almost certain that it was not.

Taking her attention from the roses, Peggy stared up at the large portrait of Adam Truff. She couldn't help but smile.

Lanny locked her arm in Peggy's after the others had drifted out of the room. "We have much to catch up on, haven't we?"

"I wonder if you will be able to believe what I have to tell you," Peggy said. "I actually wonder if I believe it all. No, I must, I do. We'll discuss it at another time."

Peggy passed Samson as she descended the steps. The stoic butler had obviously received word of the passing of his old friend and employer. He avoided the young lady's glance and hurried up the stairs.

As Peggy reached the ground floor of the round entrance hall, a curious thought struck her. It was late March, far too early for roses to be in bloom. Those upstairs had been raised in a hothouse; yet Collin had told her to find a rose in the garden. She went through the music room and through the French doors which led to where the roses were growing.

Chapter Twenty-four

The salt-scented sea air had a chill to it. Patches of blue appeared among the gray clouds. At first Peggy considered going back into the house and getting a wrap. Then a peculiar warmth came over her. She stood still on the terrace and scanned the ocean and a tiny dot, which must have been a ship on the horizon. Her thoughts went to Millijoy, and she felt as if she should weep; but that was impossible.

What a long journey she had taken, she thought. What tremendous dramatic changes had taken place in her life. Yet, despite all that had transpired, a sense of loneliness came over her.

As she walked to the terrace rail, Peggy gazed at the dormant rosebushes, thorny sticks, many of them wrapped at the base to protect from the icy winds of winter. Technically it was spring, but the temperature had not risen appreciably. Still, as she looked, she could discern tiny sprouts of leaves along the thorny boughs.

The rose garden stretched from the terrace rail to the low wall that ran along the cliff with a narrow margin beyond it. Stepping stones were strategically placed between the rosebushes. When she had attempted to navigate her way through the plants the last time she had been at Triumph House, her width had caused her dress to become snagged on the thorns. On a whim, she decided to stroll in among them.

Near the outer wall by the cliffs, Peggy saw a single red rosebud rising from a bush. She made her way to it. Surely, that was the one which Collin had indicated she would find. Excitedly, she plucked the nearly perfectly formed blossom, the fragrance of which was almost over-powering as she held it to her nose. It was thornless, and she was able to press it to the side of her face.

For nearly five minutes she examined the rosebud until a singular sensation began to come over her. What was it? Was someone watching her? She pivoted around and stared at the house. Despite its beauty, there was some-thing frightening about the imposing structure.

The French door from the music room opened, and a tall man came out, walking erect with a quiet poise. At first Peggy thought it was Tommy Phenwick, grieving for his mother. But, as she drew closer, she could discern that it was not Tommy. He was clad in fashionable attire, shades of brown with a light beige muffler about his neck.

Curiously Peggy followed the stepping stones back to the terrace. He was a Phenwick, there was no doubt of that. In many ways he reminded her of Donald Phenwick, except that he did not have a patch over his eye, nor was he walking with a limp.

"I was too late. I just learned about Millijoy," he said as Peggy neared where he was standing. When he glanced over at her, she noticed that only one of his eyes moved. Only upon extremely close scrutiny would she have been able to tell that the other was glass. "Oh, I beg your par-don. I thought you were—well, probably Katherine. I am Donald Phenwick."

A gush of excitement went through Peggy at seeing the transformation in her distant cousin. Whimsically she decided to have a game with him. "Some persons know me as Wilma Collins," she said, not telling an untruth.

"Wilma Collins?" Donald repeated. "That's singular. While I was in the hospital undergoing surgery, I was made aware of the name of William Collins. It's similar, isn't it?"

"Quite," Peggy replied, after she considered the matter. "Were you visited by this William Collins?"

Donald laughed awkwardly. "I was—in a way—but he was an illusion."

"An illusion? Why, whatever do you mean?"

"A figment of my imagination, it would seem. He claimed to be a spiritual entity who manifested himself to me. You see, I underwent quite an ordeal, during which time my mind played all sorts of tricks on me. Dr. Joseph Ornby told me that such was not uncommon under the circumstances."

"Were your operations successful?" Peggy asked.

"Yes. Imagine all these years of being a cripple and suddenly being able to walk erect and without a cane," Donald said. "I even got me a glass eye to improve my appearance."

"Are you married?"

"No. But now that I've made such a radical change, I pray it will not be long before—well, I've been accused of living in a dreamworld."

"Are you in love, then?" Peggy asked, curiously admiring the appearance of her distant cousin.

"I believe I am."

"Oh." She sounded disappointed.

"At least I thought I was until I met you, Miss Collins," Donald added.

Peggy frowned. Yet as she studied the look in his eyes, she was reminded of the intense expression Jorge Catalon had in his when he would gaze longingly at her. "You don't know me, Mr. Phenwick."

"I feel as if I do," he replied. "I feel as if I should, if I don't. I sense something so very familiar and, at the same time, mysterious, about you. I confess I am intrigued."

Peggy turned away from him. "But you said you believed that you are in love with someone else."

"I wonder. Is there a point where pity turns to love?"

"Pity? Pity for the woman, or pity for yourself?" she questioned.

"Perhaps a little of each," Donald returned. "True, I did pity my lame condition. I did not feel myself worthy of a normal woman's love."

"Then, I take it, the woman of your romantic interest would not necessarily be thought of as a normal person," Peggy said.

"Only in that she is extremely overweight."

His words struck with remarkable accuracy at her heart. She trembled.

"It's getting cold out here," Donald said. "Why don't we go inside to the music room where it will protect us from the chill winds?"

"That sounds an excellent suggestion."

Once inside they stood near each other gazing out of the window. Peggy ran her hand over the rosebud and put it to her nose. This time the scent was close to overpowering. She glanced at Donald.

"I perceive that you fancied that you were in love with

the lady of your interest because you felt sorry for her, is that not the case?" Peggy asked.

"I did feel sorry for her," Donald agreed. "But I found she had a remarkable mind; and when I looked beyond appearances, I actually discovered a beautiful person."

"Now that you've changed your own physical condition," Peggy suggested, "you realize that you are perfectly appealing to so-called normal women, therefore you are having second thoughts about your butterball friend."

"Butterball?" Donald exclaimed. "That is unkind—but it is a word used by her brother to describe her."

"And could you imagine yourself making love to that butterball?" Peggy persisted.

"I have fantasized about that. Really, when one knows the true depth of character of a person, and realizes that that person can be loving and responsive, I believe that the act of love would not be difficult."

Peggy thought a moment before she looked directly into his eyes. "And then you met me?"

"Are you leading me on?" Donald asked.

"I might be."

"Why?"

"Because I can see you have a stimulated interest in me."

"I have. I'll readily admit that. And that confuses me."

"Why should you be confused, Mr. Phenwick?"

Donald looked away from her. "I was told that I would meet a woman such as you—attractive, beautiful, lovely in every way—and that I would fall in love with her. I denied that such a thing was possible because I was certain I was so deeply in love with Peggy."

"Peggy? Is that her name?"

"Yes."

"And where is this Peggy now?"

"Somewhere in Germany, I believe. She went there in an attempt to lose part of her weight," Donald explained. "I suspect she has not been too successful at it, or she would have written to me about her progress. I know how I would have felt if my operations had been unsuccessful. I really should go to Germany and visit her now that I'm able. Another month and ocean travel will be pleasant."

"What if she's no longer there? For that matter, what if the lady you knew and corresponded with no longer exists?"

"But she *does* exist. I'm certain of that."

"As she *was?*"

Donald had braced himself against the piano. Despite the success of his operations, he occasionally felt pain in his legs. "That I cannot answer."

Peggy moved to the other side of the room. "Is yours a one-sided love?"

"I beg your pardon."

"Does your plump lady friend love you?"

"We've never spoken of it. We were always just good friends. However, it always seemed that I had a stronger feeling of romantic love for her than she had for me."

"Romantic love?" Peggy mused. "I sense a tinge of envy."

"Envy?"

"Envy mixed with annoyance," Peggy added. "Envy that you should have such strong feelings of love, and annoyance that the object of your affection is so unaware of your feelings. I want to respond with a contemptuous attitude toward her."

"I am to blame, because I never permitted her to know how I truly felt."

Peggy smiled. "And now you've met me."

"Didn't you say that before?"

"I probably uttered something similar to that." Peggy stepped back toward where he was standing. "It would seem to me, if you truly did love this Peggy—was that what you called her?—and that that love was provoked by the inner personal qualities you found in her, you would surely know her anywhere, under any circumstance."

"I'm certain I would."

"Yet you know nothing of me, and you find yourself attracted to me?"

"It is a physical attraction, I cannot deny that," Donald replied. "I do sense an inner depth in you. I can't explain why, but I feel as if I have known you for a long while. William Collins said it would be like that."

Peggy moved even closer and put her hand to her breast. "Donald, do you recognize this cameo brooch?"

He examined the ornament. "I am reminded of the cameo which I gave Peggy when I first met her in San Francisco."

"There is an excellent reason for that." She put her hand to his and experienced a thrill of excitement. "It *is* the same cameo you gave Peggy. I took the name of Wilma Collins because the illusion which I encountered told me his name was Collin Williams, but he sometimes reversed it. I can't believe that I am jealous of your feelings of love for the old me, when I know you are physically attracted to the new. Why did you keep your true feelings such a secret from me?"

"Peggy?" Donald gasped. He stood back to get a better look as his initial shook subsided. Then he rushed forward and took her in his arms. "It's unbelievable! Oh, Peggy, Peggy, can it possibly be?"

Peggy felt remarkably warm and comfortable in his embrace. *"And then you met me."*

He laughed.

She did not wait for him to make the first move. Instead, she reached up, caught hold of his chin and guided it down to hers. Their lips touched.

"Oh, Peggy, *you* did it! You actually did it!" Donald exclaimed as he lifted his lips from hers. Then he went back for another kiss as he held her as tightly to him as he dared.

"We were two lonely pathetic souls when we first met, weren't we, Donald?" Peggy observed. "The misfit compromising for the misfit."

"We each had challenges and we met them," he replied. "Why didn't you identify yourself when we first met out in the garden?"

"I would have. I might have if I hadn't seen that you were attracted to another lady, not the Peggy Phenwick you had once known," she said. "For a moment I felt a tinge of jealousy. It was then I realized that all this time I have had deep feelings of love for you. Imagine, being jealous of myself!" She laughed.

"I knew I was in love with you when we first started to correspond years ago," Donald said after he had kissed her again. "But I felt inadequate to you because of my physical condition."

"And I was looking everywhere but in the right place for my Prince Charming," Peggy returned. "What fools we must have been!"

"Not fools. Blind people are not foolish, they merely

are unable to see," Donald observed. "We were both blinded by our self-pity."

"I have had experiences with other men—men who approached me only as a physical creature—an animal," Peggy confessed a short while later as she stood in his embrace. "Those were learning episodes in what must have been a retarded way of life due to lack of opportunity to become educated earlier. Still I should have known that you loved me, really loved me, because you were the only one who took time to know the real me, my thoughts, my frustrations, my desires, all that was buried beneath my former facade. The physical is part of the whole, but far from the complete whole."

"You are beautiful, Peggy," Donald whispered. "Yet, in reality, you always were beautiful to me."

The handsome young couple remained for nearly an hour in the music room becoming reacquainted and discovering all the reasons why they were destined for each other. Not only were they physically stimulated, they discovered that they were mentally and emotionally compatible. And something spiritual happened between them.

"Is it wrong of us to experience such happiness in each other?" Donald asked.

"Why should it be wrong?"

"I mean at a time like this," Donald added. "Millijoy's death."

"I believe that Cousin Millijoy had a tremendous amount to do with our falling in love," Peggy replied. "Now I recall things she said to me. She forever mentioned you while we were together in Vienna or traveling over the Atlantic."

"And I confessed my love for you to her," Donald admitted.

"She had seen the change in you," Peggy commented. "Then she saw the miracle that had taken place in me. She realized she could leave her body in peace. But I do not believe she is gone. I sense that she is very much near to us at this moment." She looked at the rosebud which was still as fresh as when she had plucked it. "And Adam—"

Donald placed another kiss on her lips, and it was exciting beyond any kiss Peggy had previously known.

"Katherine said I was destined to become a Phenwick Woman."

"You were born a Phenwick, Peggy," Donald said softly. "And when you marry me—"

"I will be a Phenwick Woman all the way." She kissed him. "If that was a proposal, I accept."

"It was, dearest Peggy, it most certainly was."

Chapter Twenty-five

It was a bright October day, one of those special days in autumn when the skies over San Francisco are a remarkably clear cerulean, washed clean and cloudless. Hayden Phenwick's stylishly long hair, golden from the summer sun, whipped around his head like an aura as he climbed the hill. Two nights ago he had carried on a curiously puzzling conversation with his sister Lola. She seemed to be harboring an enormous mystery, which she was bent upon keeping a secret. He had mentioned Lola's singular attitude to his mother, and Lottie Phenwick was equally as puzzled as Hayden was.

Hayden had made a special point of calling on his brother-in-law William Stocker, who refused to shed any light on the situation. Finally, Hayden called that afternoon at his father's office. Paul obviously was uninformed. Whatever Lola's secret was, it had caused a great curiosity among her immediate family members.

As Hayden reached the crest of the hill where the Phenwick house was located, he paused to take a panoramic view of as much of the city as he could see. As he did, his attention was drawn to a motor car that was having enormous difficulty navigating the hill. He was about to turn into the walk and go through the gates, when he observed his cousin Donald Phenwick seated in the back seat with an elegantly beautiful young lady beside him.

"Cousin Donald!" Hayden exclaimed as he ran to the car, and opened the door even before the vehicle had reached a full stop.

"Hello, Hayden."

"You've changed. Oh, you're not wearing the patch over your eye," Hayden commented.

"Furthermore, I'm happier than you've ever known me to be, Hayden," Donald replied. "This is my wife. We were married just prior to leaving Boston. And, in fact, we're planning a second ceremony here in San Francisco. This is my wife, Mrs. Phenwick. Darling, my cousin, Hayden Phenwick."

Hayden looked closely at the lovely, elegantly gowned lady who stepped from the automobile. "I know you from somewhere—I'm certain I do."

Peggy could no longer contain her emotion. She threw

herself into Hayden's bewildered embrace and held to him with a trembling reaction.

"I'll say this for your wife, Donald, she *is* friendly," Hayden remarked.

"Hayden . . . it's me . . . Butterball," Peggy managed to say before she burst into tears.

"Butterball? That's what I used to call . . . Good Lord! This gorgeous creature can't possibly be my— Peggy? Is it really you, Peg?" Unable to contain his reaction, Hayden wept with his sister. "I didn't know you, Peggy!" He hugged her tightly.

"I thought Lola might have told you about me."

"So this is what she's been acting so mysterious about," Hayden exclaimed, brushing tears from his eyes and cheeks. "This calls for a celebration!"

"We stopped in Denver to see Luke and Joyce," Donald inserted when the brother and sister became quiet and simply gazed at each other in amazement. "Lola and William have been contacted. They're planning a little party for this evening."

"Don't surprise Mother and Dad in front of others," Hayden warned. "Mother hasn't been in the best of health, and a big shock might upset her."

"I'm afraid she'll be shocked whenever she sees me," Peggy returned.

"In that case, we'll go right in and confront her," Hayden stated. "I'll break the ice for you, and you can do the rest."

To their surprise, as the three young people entered the house, Lottie Phenwick was in the entrance hallway arranging chrysanthemums. The light was dim and she appeared to be arranging the flowers more by touch than by sight. "Oh, Hayden," she said without looking up, "this is unexpected." Her hands moved over the blossoms.

"Why haven't you put on the lights?" Hayden asked.

"Well, my goodness! It's Peggy!" Lottie exclaimed. "Peggy, why didn't you let us know you were coming home?"

"You're not looking at Peggy, Mother," Hayden remarked. "How did you know she was here?"

"I'm perceptive," Lottie replied. She laughed, turned around and held her arms up to embrace her daughter.

Before Peggy could step to her mother, Hayden ran his hand through the air before Lottie's face.

"What was that?" Lottie asked.

"How long has this been going on?" Hayden questioned. "You're practically blind."

"Oh, dear! I was hoping no one would notice," Lottie said somewhat pathetically. "I can see out of the extreme sides of my eyes. It's been coming for some time. I've trained myself to see largely with my hands. And my sense of perception has developed remarkably. You mustn't tell your father."

"Mother! Oh, Mother!" Peggy exclaimed as she ran to Lottie's arms.

Lottie hugged her daughter. "Peggy, Peggy! I only sensed you were here." She was suddenly quiet as her hands ran over her daughter's back, arms and waist. "Peggy? I know it's you—instinctively I know that—but there's so little of you." Her fingers found the outline of Peggy's face. "Oh, and you've become so beautiful, too. Your father will be very pleased."

Indeed, Paul Phenwick was both pleased and proud of Peggy's accomplishment, as were John Adam and Carol and other family members and friends. Peggy felt as if she had left San Francisco a coward and returned in triumph. She had accomplished what few people were able to do, a complete transformation.

Three weeks later a second wedding ceremony was planned for Peggy and Donald Phenwick, one which could be witnessed by the Phenwicks of San Francisco as the Phenwicks of Boston had attended the first. Perhaps the second ceremony was only symbolic, but it pleased Lottie, especially, to have a large society wedding for her other daughter, the one she thought would never have such an experience. Amanda Stocker assisted in the arrangements as if the marriage was into her family. The only concession she found difficult to make was that Peggy insisted on having red roses instead of the traditional white for the service.

"Who would have ever believed it?" Paul Phenwick declared as he met Caswell Stocker after the families and guests had gone to the reception.

"When we saw Peggy in Rome, both Amanda and I were dumbfounded," Caswell returned. "And for Amanda to be left speechless, that is an occasion."

Paul put his arms about Peggy and held her. "If only you had been like this while you were growing up, things would have been so different."

"Would they have been?" Peggy asked. "Although the first twenty-five years of my life were perfect hell, I am truly glad that I had the opportunity of changing myself."

"Why do you say that?" Paul stroked her shoulder.

"Because I have learned that meeting challenges head on, and overcoming them," Peggy replied, "brings about one of the greatest senses of accomplishment that one can have. And, I suspect, the bigger the obstacle, the more the effort that is put into surmounting it, and, therefore, the greater the actual achievement."

"I have found in business," Paul stated, "that one act of accomplishment seems to open the doors to more and better accomplishment. I learned that long ago. Yet I have known persons who have never made any significant accomplishments in their entire lives, simply because they didn't start out with small projects first."

"Do you think my project was small, Daddy?" Peggy asked with a teasing smile.

"Not in the least," Paul admitted. "Still, I daresay, once you had made up your mind, you required a significant amount of help to get where you did."

"I even needed help to make up my mind." Peggy thought of Millijoy.

The time Donald and Peggy stayed in San Francisco was like one big party after the next. It seemed that entire city knew about Peggy and her problem—she was the Phenwick that was never invited to any social event. Suddenly she was the person most in demand and she quickly gained a reputation as being a celebrity of sorts.

"We'll return to Boston," Donald announced when Hayden wondered if he and Peggy would be looking to live in San Francisco.

"All the more excuse for me to visit Boston and the origins of my ancestors," Hayden remarked.

"Your sisters-in-law, Joyce and Carol, are Phenwick Women," Donald explained, "and perhaps they are influential in their own territory, but it was Cousin Millijoy's belief as well as the opinion of others that Peggy is to be one of the most predominate Phenwick Women of her era. Once we return to Boston, she will preside as mistress of Edward House. We'll refurbish the old monstrosity and become a part of the gala social set. I had never been previously inclined to that sort of thing. But I, too, have changed. I want to show Boston society that I can dance, and that I have the most beautiful of all the Phenwick Women for my wife."

"Peggy is attractive," Hayden commented. "But the most beautiful? I simply don't know about that, Donald."

"I do. Although it's a cliché, beauty very definitely is in the eye of the beholder. And, dear Hayden, if you could see your sister through my one good eye, you would be absolutely astonished with what you beheld."

Hayden laughed.

Word reached San Francisco that Ruth Phenwick had taken a turn for the worse. Donald and Peggy cut their visit short. Hayden rode as far as Denver with them, where he wanted to visit his brother Luke and Joyce.

"You're left the only unmarried member of our immediate family," Peggy said to Hayden as the train moved through the Utah mountains. "Do you suppose you will ever marry?"

"I think not," Hayden replied. "I enjoy my freedom too much to be bound to any *one* person."

"I rationalized that at one time," Donald interjected. "Then I realized that I was only enjoying a part of what complete happiness is. Now I wonder how I ever managed to live alone as long as I did."

"It's different with me," Hayden returned. "I have my own distinct life-style. Would you care to take a little stroll with me, Donald?"

"I will, if Peggy will excuse us."

"Certainly, darling." Peggy said and held her cheek for her husband to kiss. "You'll not be long, will you?"

"Not long." Donald put his hand to Hayden's shoulder, and the two left the compartment.

Peggy sat in contemplative silence. She recalled the last time she had taken the train from San Francisco to Boston. How very long ago that seemed to be. Yet practically every detail of the journey was vivid in her mind. The one thing she noticed remarkably different was that this time she did not avoid looking at her reflection in the window.

"Well, dear heart, you've done it, haven't you?" The voice came to her from the seat opposite to where she was seated before she saw the likeness of the man.

"Collin? What are you doing here?"

"Just having a last look in on my prize patient."

"Your patient?"

"Without me, dear heart, you might not have made it through the ordeal with flying colors," he boasted.

"But you're not—"

"Real? Aren't I? Simply because I'm in spirit doesn't mean that I'm not exceptionally real." He laughed. *"Dear heart, you will find, before you discard that now-elegant flesh, that every coin has two sides."*

"You've said that before."

"If I have, doesn't that prove I'm real? Surely, you couldn't have imagined all that I've told you." There was a moment of silence before the voice came again, and the likeness of the man began to slowly disappear. *"Love yourself, Peggy, as you are for what you are; and love your husband enough to want to keep him happy. The greatest gift in the world is love, and you have received it with a huge red ribbon around it. Be happy and enjoy."*

Peggy smiled. She didn't comprehend all that had happened to her; and certainly not the interference of Collin Williams.

Donald was alone when he returned, explaining that Hayden had struck up an acquaintanceship and would be detained for a while.

Peggy went to her husband, despite the jerking movement of the train. They embraced as the happy lovers that they were.

"Did you know Adam Truff?" Peggy asked.

"Quite well."

"Was he really as bizarre as they say he was?"

"Dearest Peggy, if I were to begin to tell you about Adam, I fear you would accuse me of telling falsehoods." He kissed her.

The rumble of laughter that ran through the compartment was largely lost in the monotonous sound of the wheels.